Acknowledgements

You simply don't do this sort of thing alone, and I highly doubt I'd have had the courage to do it without the support of so many great people. One does not simply walk into Mordor, at least without the right fellowship.

And perhaps it's just as much a fool's errand as any quest in a story, writing. It's audacious, brash, a little presumptuous, arrogant even. I appreciate my companions along the way including you the reader. You've taken the time to read my book and all I can do is put my ideas out there and hope people find them worthwhile.

I'd like to thank my friends and pro bono proof readers; Laura Davidson, Lexi DeJonge, and Tina Bartolini. If I pull a 'Rowling' on this I owe you all a coffee, at least.

A special gratitude to all my beta-readers and, none more surprised than me, fans. Lacey McKaig, Kristen Beecroft, Ardith Gubbles, Larissa Brittan, and Alastair Connolly. Your encouragement has helped me, slowly, have faith that I'm not a talentless hack.

Thank you to Eloise Kimble who recognized my gifts so many years ago and sparked an undying ember that refused to be extinguished.

Thanks to John Robert Colombo for his sage guidance in helping me navigate the strange, alien wilds of publishing.

Thank you to my literary heroes; Stephen King, Michael Crichton, Douglas Adams, and J.K. Rowling.

Thank you to my spirit guide Alan Watts.

Thank you to Amber Lucier and Bob Barwick, you know what you did.

Finally, thank you to my wife Jaclyn for all her unconditional love and support. You don't always understand why I need to do things but thank you for understanding *that* I need to do them. I love you.

PROLOGUE:
GETTING SOME AIR...

T immin couldn't sleep. Actuality, fairies don't sleep, but on that night she was restless. There was a disturbance in the air, and she found the best remedy for that was a night fly through the woods; stretch her wings a little.

In fairy terms 'the air' is the lifeforce of everything around them, the fabric of reality. However, there is something lost in translation from Fairy to spoken word.

The forest seemed to glisten as much with its own illumination as it did with aid from above. Fireflies buzzed around in fluid constellations; it excited Timmin to fly straight through them and try to catch one. They scattered like bursts of fireworks, only to regroup elsewhere. It was all in good fun, and it was always catch and release.

She streaked through the woods like a florescent-gold shooting star and left a trail of fairy dust in her wake, a by-product of her lifeforce.

Fairies are born of pure magic, pure energy. They never celebrate birthdays except for their first one because after that their lives are no longer affected by time. They are born with a certain measure of energy, some more gifted than others. But it's up to them how they use their power and it's that usage that determines their lifespan.

The oldest and, sometimes, wisest choose a life of quiet contemplation. They're the philosophers, spiritual leaders, historians and, quite frankly, the ones who are just incredibly lazy. They expend very little energy and live simple, incomprehensibly long lives.

At the other end of the spectrum are the warriors, artists and even the ones who just love to show off. They are ruled by their passions and would rather burn out than fade away. Instead of birthdays, fairies celebrate life, they celebrate love, they celebrate friendship.

Timmin herself was quite gifted, magically speaking; a prodigy by fairy standards. On more than one occasion she was dismissed from school for being a disruption, assuming she bothered to show up at all. Her teachers lectured her about her wasted potential, but the truth was she wasn't very stimulated in school, she wasn't challenged. In many ways she was even ahead of her instructors. She debated dropping out completely; she just wanted to live. There had to be more than lectures of static dogma.

She had a mischievous streak a mile long (quite a distance for a fairy), but also an incredibly loving heart. She lived for the present moment and she didn't dwell on the future.

For the time being, was a beautiful night, a perfect night.

Perhaps she would drop in on Red and see-

A twig snapped somewhere off in the distance. Timmin paused, mid-flight, and hovered. The breeze had died, and all was still. She drifted forward unconsciously as she listened.

She pushed on, somewhat slower.

Maybe she would visit the castle and formally meet the new prince-

A louder crack split the silence. The wing beats of a dozen or so birds fled to the sky and as many deer and small animals made tracks away from the immediate area.

Timmin came to a dead stop; her wing beats slowed, and her glow diminished.

She wasn't alone, she knew it, she felt it. She could see shadows, she could hear whispers; whispers and growls. Some things were on the move all around her.

The first howl stopped her heart; a chorus of howls echoed in response. Timmin landed on an old stump and, as light as she was, fell to her knees. She didn't dare move, not so much as a twitch. She dowsed her own light, but it was an absurd gesture, they had seen her, they just didn't seem that interested. She didn't look up, but in the corners of her eyes she saw them pass by.

'They couldn't be back,' she thought, 'HE couldn't be back'

The only thing in the direction they were headed was the castle; the king had to be warned.

Her wings ignited as she leapt into the air. A crushing pressure wrapped around her whole body, she couldn't move. Timmin looked down, she was enwrapped by the long boney fingers of a furry hand, (or was it a paw?)

'What soft fur' she thought.

She was brought in for closer inspection by the hand's owner. Two piercing, grey eyes looked back at her. Timmin couldn't decide if it was curiosity or hunger.

'What pretty eyes.'

She could feel the hand's pulse, gradually it came in sync with her heartbeat. The world around her faded away and awareness was forced inward; into her mind.

The violation was intolerable. It wasn't as though she were hiding any dark secrets. Fairies, as a general rule, are quite open and honest with their minds, it's how they talk. That was entirely beside the point. This was intrusive, a little presumptuous and quite rude. There was an etiquette to these things.

'Show me everything.', the intruder's voice whispered in her head.

He flipped through the pages of her life's diary. He saw her birth and her loving parents. He saw an enchanted hollow of the oldest trees where they made their happy, harmonious home. He saw a supportive community who rallied around one another. There were conversations with a cousin, Tinkerbell, and her plan to run away with some boy she met. There were parties and celebrations at the drop of a hat. Timmin could feel the intruder was perplexed at what he saw; and curiously, a little sad.

He attempted to withdraw his hand but Timmin wouldn't let him. She had been more than tolerant. If he wanted to share, then they were going to share.

She pushed back; at first it was like running through a knee-deep bog, but she persisted and marched right into his subconscious.

He struggled to let go.

'What's your hurry?' She insisted.

She saw scattered images, it was hard to make sense of it at first. She saw a furry infant, his big grey eyes looked innocently out at the world; he had yet to cut his fangs. She saw a loving mother and a questioning, suspicious father.

"Oh, my sweet little William." His mother rocked him and sang to him.

His father refused to accept the abomination. He worked all day and when he wasn't working, he was drinking. He never hit women, but his anger had to go someplace; what else did you do with a dog?

She saw William run from a gang of boys that taunted him mercilessly.

"Here doggy!" They'd call after him, "come on boy!".
Sometimes they threw sticks. "Fetch boy! Fetch!" Other times they threw rocks.

She saw angry villagers pound on his family's door. Livestock had vanished, and they demanded his head. His father let them in. His mother tried to bar their way, but she was knocked aside. William ran to his room and escaped through the window. He fled to the woods, looking back only once.

She saw The Big Bad, she saw the war. She saw what they had planned for tonight.

William jerked his paw away from Timmin and cradled it as if he had burned it on a stove. A moment passed frozen in each other's gaze.

She entertained the notion of escaping; she could have, easily, but didn't. William reached out and picked up Timmin, gently this time. She didn't resist.

3

A low solitary howl pierced the night and brought William's attention back on task. He had to go. He placed her into the pocket of his long dark overcoat. They would talk later. There were much larger matters to attend to.

Tonight, was their night. Tonight, their king would get his crown.

CHAPTER 1:

KNOCK, KNOCK...

At the edge of the forest, in the middle of a huge clearing stood Camelot, the castle and court of King Arthur. The forest, the clearing and the castle bathed in the pale blue majesty of a full moon, with only the brightest stars able to compete for their place in the sky.

Jared and John typically held watch most nights, outside the main gate on the draw bridge. The steady rhythm of crickets timed the slow passage of their evening.

"So, there I was. trapped at the edge of a cliff," John barely kept his balance on top of an old wine cask. "twenty-four drooling, snarling wolves were crawling towards me, their fiery, yellow eyes piercing deep into my very soul."

John had always been a hand talker but when he told a story it was a wondrous, and at times dangerous, ballet of gestures. His speech was slurred, and he had almost fallen into the moat twice; alcohol may have been a factor.

Jared felt partly responsible, he brought the wine. He stifled his laughter as best he could; it was hard to breathe and his whole body ached as his glee tried to force its way out through his chest. The tale got better every time John told it and Jared couldn't resist ribbing on the ever-evolving narrative.

"I thought it was only twelve wolves." Jared said

John's voice trailed off and his arms slowly dropped to their sides. Jared folded fast, he couldn't do it to John. He knew his friend hadn't really seen very much action during the war; he had only enlisted towards the end. He wasn't even on the front lines.

"You know what?" Jared said, "I was thinking of that story you told the other night. My apologies, please continue."

John's face lit up again. "Where was I?"

"The cliff.".

"The cliff! So, there I was. Surrounded on all sides by, damn near, thirty wolves..."

"Surrounded on all sides..." Jared said.

"All Sides."

"...on a cliff...", Jared thought his glee may have cracked a rib on that one.

"I raised my mighty axe and charged" John stepped off his makeshift stage on to nothing, he fell straight down in a seated position on the barrel. His outstretched arms, mid story, had aided in steadying him. He teetered backwards towards the moat, his legs kicked out for counterbalance. He laid a top the barrel in a ridiculous spread eagle.

"You charged the wolves with the burning ferocity of a dragon and sent them running for the hills." Jared finally released a fervent laugh, "I could have used you in my garrison." He righted his companion on the barrel.

John clutched him by the forearms and looked him, very nearly, dead in the eyes, beaming.

"Do you mean it?"

"You bet, old friend." Jared answered. He was lying, of course, a compassionate lie. John would have been cut down like wheat and partially eaten.
But there was also a grain of truth in it; the difference between John and him was eight years of war. Given enough time, and luck, John might have been just as battle hardened. Jared was glad the war was over before that could happen; he liked his friend the way he was.

The colour drained from John's face and he tightened his grip on Jared's arms. Jared guided his friend to the edge of the moat and held him from falling forward. An impressive amount of vomit later John stopped heaving and spat the taste from his mouth. Jared gave him an encouraging pat on the back and lead him back to the barrel.

He handed John the water skin.

"Drink this. You saved the kingdom once again." Jared laughed and downed the rest of John's wine, it was a shame to waste it. It was from Jared's family farm; a batch of the "good stuff", aged in a whiskey cask.

Before the war he was to take over for his father; he had inherited the farmstead as a wedding present. Not long after, Jared and his wife Anna had their first child; a daughter, Rose.

Life was idyllic, for a time.

Then livestock started to go missing– the odd chicken at first, then a calf. His neighbors complained about the same thing too; but these things happened, it was part and parcel of being a farmer. At first, no one was particularly worried; they organized casual hunting parties to deal with whatever animal was loose in the area. Most of them started at the local pub and sometimes they even managed to go hunting.

But the problem persisted and escalated. Local legend spread of a wolf-man who prowled the night. The tales were dismissed until the strange wolf child was born in a nearby village. The child's mother was rumored to be in league with the forces of darkness. The woman's husband drank his days away at the pub and his stories got the farmers riled up; it was he who led an angry mob to his own doorstep and stepped aside to let them in. Jared wouldn't be a part of that, it was unconscionable. The child managed to escape; the mother disappeared. The reluctant father was torn apart in his sleep two nights later.

The attacks increased as well as the numbers reported in the sightings. There were roving gangs of wolves, they were organized, they had a leader. Entire herds of livestock were slaughtered, entire villages raided. King Arthur got involved. His knights and eager volunteers enlisted to deal with the threat.

Jared was concerned, of course; he helped his neighbors where he could, but he saw no need to get involved beyond that. He had a family and a farm to look after. The problems of a kingdom were too big for him.

He could still hear their screams. He could still feel the tightness in his chest and the terrible ache in his stomach as he sprinted from his field back to the house under the light of the harvest moon. He could still feel the burn of his hands and wrists as he tripped and fell in the dirt; and how hard it was to grip his pitch fork with bleeding hands as he kicked in his front door. He remembered dropping to his knees in a puddle of Anna's blood and the warm wet sensation as it soaked into his pants. He couldn't recall how long he sat there, but it was daylight when he finally noticed one of his farm hands was beside him, shaking him and trying to get him to respond.

Rose was never found. Jared buried Anna beneath her favorite tree in the western field; where they would sit on a low hanging branch and watch the sun set behind the mountains.
Jared enlisted shortly thereafter.

The war lasted eight years, but for Jared it would never be long enough. His life had been replaced by an obsession. He could never kill enough wolves, and if he died spitting his last breath at them so be it. But their number only increased. The battle seemed futile.

And then suddenly, one day, for no apparent reason, it was over. The Wolves were just gone.

Jared returned to his farm but not the house, he built a small cabin suitable for one. He burned the old farmstead to the ground and spread the ashes on his vineyard. He picked up around Anna's grave and placed a marker for Rose. The work seemed to help him reclaim his life, at least a little. He volunteered at the castle on guard duty. Some nights he just couldn't stare at the walls. That's where he met John.

After the third water skin John could finish sentences and maintain eye contact, both good signs.

"You might not feel like it now," Jared said, " but you'll feel a lot better if you got some food into you." He spun around behind the barrel to his bag. He was sure he packed a fresh loaf and some cheese.

"Jared..." John's voice was barely audible.

"Hmm?" Jared replied; he fished through the bag, positive he packed a knife.

"Jared." John was off the barrel and backed up against the main gate.

Jared followed his friend's petrified stare to the end of the drawbridge and the dark cloaked figure who had, somehow, arrived without a sound.

Jared stood, he was an imposing figure at his full height, but the stranger might have been taller.

"Greetings." Jared said. "Can we help you with something?"

The stranger said nothing.

Jared's hand came to rest gently, instinctively, on the hilt of his sword.

"Are you lost... friend?", he believed in being cordial until that time had passed.

The shadow tilted its head slightly, but its posture was otherwise unmoved. A gentle breeze rippled its cloak.

John fidgeted for his sword, he had leaned it against the gate; it was dreadfully heavy, and he had never once needed the thing. The blade rattled as he attempted to draw it from his scabbard.

Jared put his hand on John's shoulder, his trembling eased somewhat. Jared walked forward, his hand stayed with John a few seconds longer.

"Please, state your business or I'm going to have to ask you to leave."

The shadow chuckled.

Jared drew his weapon. John could barely hold his sword above his waist, his arms quivered.   Jared felt the weapon posed more danger to John than anyone else.

"Are you a friend or foe?" Jared demanded.

"Neither," said the shadow, he removed his hood. "I'm family." He flashed a jagged yellow toothy smile.

"Wolfric!" Jared hissed.

"Wolfric?" John stammered to get the words out. "The B-Big Bad." The colour drained away from his face.

"You have me at a disadvantage, sir." Wolfric said.

Jared wasted no time closing the distance between them, his sword eager to cut the mangy son of a bitch in half.

Wolfric's amiable grin seemed to widen the closer Jared got. He parried the strike with little effort. He twisted Jared's sword from his grip and kicked the backs of his legs as he passed. He spun Jared around on his knees and held him with the blade at his throat.

John was ghost white and whimpering with a puddle of urine at his feet. All notions of bravery were abandoned with his sword on the ground. He clung to the main gate, barely standing.

"John," Jared's voice strained against the pressure of the sword.

Wolfric eased the pressure on Jared's throat.

"Yes," Wolfric teased, "talk to your friend, he seems frightened."

"John, Look at me." Jared said. His voice was calm and collected.

John shook his head and cried,

"Big Bad," he wheezed, "Big Bad" he repeated. He slid down the gate to the ground next to his sword.

"It's a lot to process," Wolfric said, "I get that. It's okay John, you just wait there." He giggled, "We'll be with you in a sec."

He dug his claws into Jared's scalp.

"You know," he said, "your pasty, hairless faces all look the same to me, but I never forget a scent."

Jared felt a chill and the world around him fell away. Wolfric pushed his mind under, drowning him in his own memories. Jared flashed on Anna and everything froze.

"Oh, that's right!" Wolfric said, "Wow, small world."

Jared felt the sword tighten against his jugular. Wolfric leaned in close to Jared's ear.

"Rose say's 'hi'."

Jared raged against Wolfric's grip. Wolfric kicked Jared in the back and pulled the blade clean through his neck; his head bounced twice before it rolled to a stop at John's feet.

"Big Bad.... Big Bad" John mouthed. The power of speech had left him.

Wolfric tossed Jared's body into the mote; he strolled casually towards John.

Other shadows emerged from the woods. John's breathless screams were further muted by the proceeding howls.

Wolfric loomed over John, but he wasn't looking at him. His eyes were focused on a spot just above him; he smiled as if greeting someone.

John felt cold hands on either side of his head followed by a sharp twist, followed by a snap, followed by nothing.

CHAPTER 2:

FAMILY REUNION...

It was his majesty, King Arthur's turn to get up and attempt to lull Prince Eric back to sleep. Eric was only a year old, but Arthur definitely saw Gwen's beautiful eyes and his strong chin; almost definitely. He couldn't get over how big Eric's eyes were, but he supposed his son would grow into them. Arthur rocked him back and forth in the chair by their bedroom window. The last comforting embers of a fire still glowed in the hearth and the two of them were bathed in the glow of the moon.

Gwenevere still lay in bed; he could watch her sleep forever. Her dark hair fell around her shoulders and cascaded over the pillow; that face, punctuated by the sweetest lips in the world; the gentle rise and fall of her perfect breasts. Not only did he still love her after all these years, he was still in love with her. The fact that love could produce something so magical as a child astounded Arthur. And he knew something about magic.

The announcement that she was pregnant came just after the war had ended. It was as though his son had ushered in an era of peace. How could he not feel a swell of pride? His son, the prince, a herald of peace.

"I saw a light on." Merlin appeared just inside the closed bedroom door. "Is everything alright?"

"Fine," Arthur said. "A treasonous prince is keeping his king awake. Come on in"

Merlin was suddenly beside Arthur, his hand gently on Eric's head. As accustomed as Arthur was to Merlin's sudden appearances it never failed to give him a start.

"I really hate when you do that." Arthur said.

"I didn't want to wake the queen or the prince." Merlin said.

"You're up late."

"Or very early." Merlin looked out the window to the castle grounds. "Just out for some air."

"You're a terrible liar." Arthur said. "What the matter?"

Merlin left the window and walked to the fireplace, he stoked the fire a little with a slight hand gesture and warmed his hands.

"Old habit I suppose." He said.

"It's been two years." Arthur said, "He's gone."

"I've had centuries of experience." Merlin ran his hand along the blade of Excalibur, carefully preserved above the fire place. "Evil like that is seldom so easily dissuaded. Besides, I know him, I raised him."

"You can't keep blaming yourself." Arthur placed his free hand on Merlin's shoulder, this time it was Merlin who jumped slightly. He wasn't even remotely aware Arthur was standing next to him.

Merlin paced across the room in no particular direction.

"Oh please, interfering in human events is what I'm best at. It was like Lancelot all over again except worse."

"Who?" asked Arthur.

"Nothing," Merlin said. "What I mean is, I took pity on him and persuaded you to take him in. I schooled him. I never let myself see what he was."

"You always taught me that compassion was the best way. That we can't fully love without being open to both good and bad equally." Arthur was again beside his old friend without warning. He put his free arm around Merlin. "You couldn't have known what would happen."

"There was a time I would have." Merlin said.

"There are those of us trying to sleep through the night." Gwen's head was propped up on one hand and her tired eyes regarded both of them bluntly. Even when she was vexed, she managed to be beautiful; it was that fire Arthur found most attractive.

"Sorry." Arthur said and Merlin in unison.

"We were," Arthur looked for the words in Merlin's face and vice versa.

"We were discussing important matters of state." Merlin finally managed.

"Un-huh..." Gwen grumbled flatly.

Actually, she had been up as long as Arthur; she loved to watch him with the baby when he wasn't looking. When he got up and walked towards Eric's crib she would always arrange her hair in a flattering display and wipe the drool off her mouth. She exaggerated her chest movement while 'sleeping' just enough to make Arthur come back to bed that much sooner. With the arrival of the wizard she chose to speak up. She was never completely at ease around Merlin.

"You both need your sleep," Merlin said, "Perhaps I should take Eric-"

"No!" Snapped Gwen. The atmosphere of the room as well as the fire seemed to bow to the queen's voice; even Eric stopped fussing.

Gwen locked eyes with Merlin. Arthur was at a loss to explain the awkward tension as he looked back and forth between his wife and his friend.

"Well," Merlin began, tentatively, "I think I'll let you three..."

The wizard was interrupted by a horn from outside, it was the night watch's alarm. Arthur had almost forgotten what that sound meant. It took a few extra moments for his mind to register the implications.

Arthur and Merlin went to the window. Outside two guards on the battlements pointed and shouted to something outside the walls. A guard blew the horn once more before he was dragged over the side. Another ran along the wall shouting for battle stations before he too was picked off. Down below men scrambled from the barracks, half dressed and suiting up along the way.

Gwen joined the two of them by the window. Arthur handed Eric to her and went straight to the wall. His armor had a fine layer of dust, but Excalibur never dulled. He had hoped he would never have to feel the weight of either again.

A dreadful pounding shook the castle walls, even their bedroom. Arthur geared his armor on faster.

An entire garrison stood ready by the castle gate. A strong breeze came through the crack between the doors; it creaked and bent as if under some tremendous pressure.   A team brought timbers forward to brace them; before they could position them, the doors exploded off their hinges and scattered the knights into the yard.

As the dust settled, they discovered the terrified, urine-soaked, and lifeless body of John. He was pinned to the door through his chest by Jared's sword with a note, inked in blood, that read 'Knock, Knock'.

An army of steel-clad werewolves poured into the courtyard, others came over the walls; they immediately set upon the knights.

Wolfric walked, very nearly strutted, in among the madness. He made eye contact with Merlin up in the window immediately; he smiled and waved.

Arthur was almost fully armored.

"What do you hope to accomplish?" Merlin said. "You must order an evacuation."

Arthur placed a hand on Merlin's shoulder.

"We both know it's too late for that." He said. "I'm going out there to finish this."

"This is suicide." Merlin said.

"Take Gwen, and Eric and anyone else you find along the way and get them out of here."

Arthur caressed Eric's chubby cheeks and stroked his hair. He kissed Gwen deeply on the lips.

"I love you." He said.

She held him tightly, reluctant to let go.

"I love you too." Gwen said. "I'll see you in a little while."

He kissed them both once more before he turned to leave.

Merlin clung tightly to Arthur's wrist before he left.

"I'm sorry" Merlin said.

Arthur put his helmet on and ran through the door. He stopped just outside and called down the hallway.

"You two men," he ordered, "Guard this room with your life."

Arthur glanced one more time at his family and closed the door behind him.

$$\triangle \ \triangle \ \triangle$$

The wolves were much more agile than the castle guards and there seemed to be no end to them. Wolfric stood and drank it in. He dispatched the occasional hero who wanted to dance but there was, really, only one name on his card. Only one that could give him the fight he wanted.

Finally, there he was, along the top of the wall, Arthur.

"Isn't he glorious?" Wolfric said to a lifeless knight in his clutches. "Like some golden god from myth or legend."

Arthur charged down the stairs to the courtyard; He came to stand on the opposite side of the battle from Wolfric. The commotion seemed to part between them. Wolfric had chills; there was nothing but that moment, and he was very nearly moved to tears if that were possible. Merlin always told him that all true power lay in the present moment, he never really understood the old man's ramblings till just then.

'Merlin!' In the excitement he had nearly forgotten why he had come. *'Soon, old man, soon.'*

"You." Arthur said.

"Me." Wolfric replied.

Under his fur there were goosebumps. Arthur's commanding voice filled with self-righteous indignation. If he never became a king, Wolfric was positive Arthur would have been the mayor of some insufferably forthright community at the very least.

"What do you want here?" Arthur demanded.

"We never talk anymore." Wolfric said. "You're just all work."

He threw the dead knight over his shoulder into a small pack of wolves behind him. A bloody feeding frenzy ensued.

"To be honest this is not a social call," Wolfric said, "I have some business to conclude with you, that smoldering queen of yours, the wizard, oh and I'll be taking my son."

"What are you yammering about?" Arthur said.

"You still don't know." Wolfric gently bit his fist, he was positively euphoric.

$$\triangle \; \triangle \; \triangle$$

From the sound, it did not seem to be going well for the guards outside the door. With a gesture, Merlin braced it with timbers and sealed it shut from the inside. Merlin twisted a candle stick on the wall; the fireplace opened on one side to reveal a dimly lit stairwell that headed down.

"Come, my lady." He said. "I must get you both to safety."

Merlin headed down the secret passage. Part of the way down he looked back over his shoulder. He had taken for granted the Queen was in tow. She was not; she stood there in silent contempt of him.

"Your highness," Merlin said, "Your husband charged me with the safety of his wife and his son."

For a moment, all was silent outside in the hall, the silence was soon replaced by a steady pounding that beckoned entrance.

"We both know Eric is not Arthur's son." Gwen said.

"I beg your pardon." He said.

The pounding continued at the door, one of the timbers cracked.

"A woman knows her husband's touch." She said. "The night he came to me he was off in battle somewhere, yet somehow he came to me."

She slowly descended the steps toward him.

"It looked like him," she said, "it sounded like him. But it wasn't him, he felt differently. At the time, I was so happy to just be with him, but as time passed something about that evening didn't seem right. You did something, didn't you?"

"I really think we had better..."

"What did you do?!" demanded Gwen.

"Merlin!" Wolfric's voice called from outside the bedroom window. "Merlin, we agreed."

Gwen's glare persisted.

"People were dying." Merlin said. He puffed up to a slightly more distinguished stature. "I don't have to defend myself to you, you don't understand the larger picture." For a moment, he almost convinced himself.

"Please, explain it to me." Gwen said.

"He wasn't going to stop."

"You made this choice for us? And you trusted him?"

"I can still fix this."

"You've always been soft when it came to Wolfric; more like blind."

Gwen kissed Eric on the cheek and squeezed him tightly. She rocked him back and forth for a moment and then handed him to Merlin.

"Go," she said, "Protect your child." She climbed the stairs back up to the bedroom.

"My lady." Merlin said.

"Why Arthur looked up to you is beyond me."

She twisted the candle stick; the door closed on them.

Merlin's heart sank, he looked down at the child in his arms. Despite the commotion Eric seemed strangely calm. Merlin continued down the stairway.

△ △ △

Arthur charged Wolfric and brought his blade down hard. Wolfric caught Excalibur in both hands. The two stopped dead against each other's strength.

"I can't tell you how much I've been looking forward to this Arthur." Wolfric said. "it's like sparring practice all over again." He shoved Arthur away.

"You were always rubbish in a fight." Arthur said.

They circled one another. Most of the pack had finished with the palace guards and had grouped around the two kings to watch the show. They cheered, growled and howled in excitement.

"Believe it or not, I looked up to you." Wolfric said, "like a brother. I tried so hard to earn your respect, everyone's respect. But no one could see anything but the monster."

"You became a monster all on your own."

Arthur thrust his sword. Wolfric leapt and rolled but Arthur was hot on his heels and didn't give him much time. He smashed his shield down on top of Wolfric and pinned him to the ground. Arthur flipped Excalibur in his hand to stab the blade down Wolfric's throat.

"I'm already bored with this." Wolfric said. "Gale!"

A stumpy, barrel-chested wolf emerged from the crowd and inhaled slowly. The backdraft stayed Arthur's hand and pulled Excalibur from his grip. Gale held his breath and ducked as the sword spun passed his head. He blew back at Arthur, the wind carried him across the yard and slammed him against a wall.

Gwen ran to his side. She helped him to his feet.

"What are you still doing here?" Arthur said.

"I couldn't leave your side, my love." She said.

"Where is Eri..." He looked into her eyes. Her big yellow eyes. He grabbed her shoulders and pushed her to arm's length.

"It's the eyes," she said, "isn't it?" Her breath was absolutely foul. "I can never get the eyes right." She giggled manically, and her entire form changed; Arthur beheld a slender hairless wolf with muted features.

"Shifter," Wolfric said, "That's enough."

"Goodbye my love" Shifter said in Gwen's voice. He coiled his whole body, snake life, around Arthur before he took his place at Wolfric's side.

William emerged from the door atop the wall with five other werewolves in tow. He carried an unconscious Gwen over his shoulder.

"Where is the wizard and the boy?" Wolfric said.

William seemed somewhat distracted and only glanced at Wolfric in response. He was deep in thought; well, he was deep in her thoughts. Her eyes were rolled back into her head.

Arthur charged at William who only gazed back casually. Another squall from Gale threw Arthur back against the wall, harder this time.

William's attention gradually came back to reality. He lay Gwen on the ground and contemplated the stillness of her face for a moment. He walked over to Wolfric and assumed the position. They placed hands on each other's temples and stood with their foreheads together.

Wolfric gently pushed into his mind. Just the highlights. He gave William the ability because of his inquisitive nature. He was also completely mute and therefore he could trust William to keep a secret when needed. Of course, Wolfric could do it himself but too much time in other people's minds took away from his own perspective.

He saw the sad exchange between Merlin and Gwenevere, he chuckled. He saw the secret passage close, and since she knew were it led to, now so did he. Unfortunately, she knew nothing beyond that.

Just over William's shoulder, Wolfric saw Arthur crawl, more drag, his broken body toward Gwen.

"You always had spirit, Art." Wolfric said.

He sauntered over to Arthur and stepped on his back.; he pushed Arthur's chest into the dirt.

"However, time is somewhat a factor here. Well not here but where I need to get back to. I won't bore you with the details."

Arthur reached out for Gwen, he couldn't tell if she were alive or dead.

Wolfric rolled Arthur over, straddled him and pinned his shoulders to the ground.

"If you were a washed-up necromancer, running from me like a pathetic coward, where would you take the baby his best friend thought was his but was, in fact, mine?"

Wolfric pushed into Arthur's mind. Arthur sincerely didn't know.

"Wow," Wolfric said, "Merlin really never trusted you either, did he? What a piece of work."

Arthur struggled in futility.

"I'll tell you something though." Wolfric said, "That Gwen. They call me an animal, I still got the scars on my back."

Arthur spat blood into his face. Wolfric lapped it up with his tongue.

"All in good time Art," he said." You know, if she's still alive I promise I'll keep her warm for you."

He looked one last time into Arthur's eyes; a thousand memories raced through his mind, all of them he could finally put to rest and forget.

"Goodbye Arthur," he said. "I'm going to miss you, really."

He sunk his teeth into the king's throat and broke his neck.

Wolfric got to his feet, wiped his mouth on his sleeve and howled. The pack joined him in song. A ravenous horde of werewolves descended on the body.

"There's only two people alive Merlin would trust with his secrets." Wolfric strolled over to Gwen's body.

"Gale!" he barked.

Gale ran to his side. "Yes, my alpha."

"Pay a visit to the pig." Wolfric said. "Tell your brother to find the girl."

"Yes, my alpha."

He cradled Gwen in his arms and stroked her hair.

"Don't worry, darling." he kissed her palm and nuzzled her cheek with his face. "I will bring our son home." He sunk his teeth into Gwen's perfect neck.

CHAPTER 3:

OVER THE RIVER AND THROUGH THE WOODS...

t was nearly a day's hike from the market in the closest town to her grandmother's cottage; Red could walk it blindfolded. She had made the trek nearly once a week since she was nine to bring the old woman her groceries; the basket of goodies her grandmother used to call it. After the incident, Red learned the hard way to stay on the trail and not to talk to strangers; the same lesson had also taught her to carry a big stick, a quarterstaff.

Her given name was Emily, though she never went by that. Red started more as a nickname given her fondness for the colour; specifically, a red hood and cape her grandmother had given her for her birthday, she was never without it. As she grew she added to it, repaired it as needed, even embroidered ornate designs into it; all in red.

"Hello, my Little Red Riding Hood" her grandmother would say as she answered the door, and the name stuck.

It was a truly versatile piece of clothing, she wondered why everyone didn't have one. It kept her warm; she could string it up between two trees and make a hammock out of it; she could enjoy a picnic on it, there seemed to be endless uses for it.

By late afternoon she had arrived at the front door, it was slightly ajar.

A cheerful voice greeted her as she entered.

"Is that you dear?", the voice almost sang.

"Yes". Replied Red.

"Well come in dear and let me see you my precious child."

"Of course," Red put the basket on the table and gripped her staff more tightly.

"Ill be right there." She glanced up at her grandmother's portrait above the hearth.

She entered the bedroom to find a somewhat sweet, somewhat old, vaguely feminine version of her grandmothers' portrait, complete with bonnet and housecoat, snug as you please in her grandmother's bed.

"How are you feeling?" Red asked.

"Oh, just fine dear," the old woman flashed a grotesque yellow grin, "come sit by me, child."

Red smiled and sat next to her on the bed. She placed her hand on the sweet old gal's furry hand (It was really more of a paw).

"You know grandma" Red said, "I never noticed what big, beautiful eyes you have."

"Why thank you, she said, all the better to see you with."

Red squeezed the paw a little more firmly.

"And granny, what big hands you have." Red squeezed it harder still.

Granny glanced down at their hands, her smile faded a little.

"All the better to hold you with, my precious, precious child." she said.

Red dug her nails in hard.

"Wow, my dear, said Granny you have one hell of a grip."

""Oh, I'm sorry, grandmother." Red got in close and stared into those massive yellow eyes, she traced every whiskered contour of the old woman's face.

It really wasn't that bad of a likeness; If her grandmother had been an insane bush woman who didn't take care of herself, and if she hadn't been dead for 15 years, Red might have almost been fooled.

"Grandmother?" Red said.

"Yes dear?"

Red's nails had started to draw blood.

"What a big hole you'll make."

"I'm sorry my dea-"

Red twisted the old woman's arm and sent her crashing through the bedroom window into the back yard.

The old lady hollered from outside, "Dammit! You crazy bitch!"

Red marched out back to continue the family visit.

Shifter usually liked to practice specific forms before he tried to fool people, practice made perfect. Regrettably, time had been a factor and there wasn't a single mirror in the whole cottage.

"You're not Wolfric," Red said, "but I'm willing to bet he sent you."

Shifter laughed as he picked himself up off the ground.

"Right down to business." He said in an old lady voice. "You don't call, you don't write, it breaks my heart."

"What do you want here?", she demanded.

"Were looking for the Wizard." He changed to a grotesque caricature of Merlin." You haven't seen him, have you."

"I would have thought the castle would be the obvious choice." Red said, "Why come to me?"

"Well, about that." Shifter said.

He elongated into a giant cobra and lashed at Red. She slipped his strike and brought her staff down on his spine with a solid crunch. Shifter hollered, retracted into his old self, and snarled at Red. He grew into a massive ogre, uprooted a well-established tree and swung it at her. She bounded out of its path.

He slammed the trunk down on top of her, but she evaded him once again. The roots stuck in the ground. Red leapt onto the tree. She charged along the trunk, dug the staff into a secure notch, and kicked Shifter in the face. He fell backwards to the ground; he spat out some teeth and blood.

Truth be told, he loved to roughhouse. Since he could be anything, then every inch of him was basically a cluster of nerve endings and pure potentiality. And with that kind of sensitivity his whole body was one big erogenous zone. Depending on his mood he could derive pleasure from anyone, anything. And right then and there, with his unabashedly low self-esteem taking a good beating, he was in ecstasy.

A tentacle sprung from the ground beneath Red and wrapped around her arms and legs. Shifter rose to his feet and kept rising. The tentacles had grown from his tail; He swept Red off her feet and brought the two of them closer together. He squeezed the staff out of her hand.

Shifter sang as he slowly moved in. Red wasn't familiar with the tune.

"You sure are lookin' good. You're everything that a big bad wolf could want."

He howled; he loved being him, the possibilities were endless.

"All the better to see you, feel you, taste you my dear."

A sharp, excruciating pain intruded on his bliss.

"One moment, sweetie." Shifter said.

The pain was nearly euphoric, but he wondered if, perhaps, they should have decided on a safe word.

He turned his head completely around to his back to see an axe firmly embedded between his shoulders. His pleasure quickly gave way to shock; he dropped to his knees and his grip on Red loosened. She wrestled herself free and grabbed her staff.

Shifter pulled the axe from his back, which may have hurt more than the initial strike.

"Et tu...whoever?" He giggled.

He searched the tree line for signs of where it might have come from. An arrow pierced his back, and then two more in quick succession.

"You're late." Red said.

A shadow emerged from the woods. It was a huntsman; it was Red's huntsman boyfriend, Braum.

"I'm sorry," Braum said, "I heard the commotion, so I thought it was best to approach down wind." He walked passed the heap that was Shifter and straight into Red's arms; they kissed.

"Are you alright?" he asked.

"I had everything under control." She said.

"I sensed that, but I decided to intervene all the same."

It wasn't a conscious choice to start a relationship with a huntsman; she was perfectly comfortable in her single life. Her father had been a huntsman, but he died during the war; and huntsman had rescued her from her from Wolfric; unfortunately, not in time to save her grandmother.

When the wolves came for her a second time it was a soldier, Jared if she remembered his name correctly, who rescued her; that time they had gotten her mother.

She was brought to the castle to live and became a ward of the kingdom. She was raised and schooled along with other orphans of the war. Merlin had taken it upon himself to see to their schooling.

On her days off she would watch the knights train and became fascinated with the art of combat. After much persistence, Merlin finally agreed to ask the King if she might be trained. The King agreed.

It wasn't a conscious choice to fall for a huntsman, but it wasn't a complete surprise to her either.

She met Braum in the woods on her way home. She had inherited her grandmother's cottage and took possession when she was old enough. She allowed the kings hunting parties unrestricted access to the surrounding forest, also hers.

She passed by Braum for months without so much as a hello; though every day he would greet her with a smile and a cordial bow.

And so, they stayed out of each other's way; that is until the following winter. Braum had been caught off guard by a freak snow squall and came knocking on the door of Reds cottage for shelter. She took him in, they talked all night.

Shifter pulled the arrows out of his back. By this point he was dull to the pain.

"I'm just glad you're okay." Braum said. He kissed her once again.

Red found it sweet Braum still worried about her, though she could probably best him easily one on one.

Shifter dragged himself across the ground. He tried to change but it was difficult. A wound was a wound and even though he healed faster than most, he couldn't make violent trauma just go away. He felt his shoulders being grabbed and before he knew it he was pinned up against a tree. Red bound him with a rope.

"What does Wolfric want with Merlin?", she demanded.

Shifter snickered and spit up blood. Braum pushed a thumb into one of Shifters wounds. He cried out as much in agony as ecstasy. He summoned up all the strength he had; he knew what he was about to do was really going to hurt. With a hideous roar, he elongated out of the ropes and grew a mighty pair of wings. Red and Braum were thrown back as Shifter awkwardly took to the skies. Braum shot a volley of arrows; they hit their mark, but they didn't stop him.

"We've got to go to the castle." Red said, "Well need Jacob."

$$\triangle \; \triangle \; \triangle$$

All things considered, Gale thought he had the easier job. Wolfric had briefed him and his brother on what to expect. The girl sounded like a handful. But a pig? He wasn't famished, but he could eat.

It took him most of the morning, but the brick house was exactly where the alpha said it would be. He marched up the front steps and pounded on the door.

"Hey, little pig.", he said. "I know you're in there, let me in."

"Not by the hair on my chinny-chin-chin." A voice replied from the other side of the door, Gale noted the mocking tone. He hated tones. Why did people have to use tones? And it was a pretty messed up response. Wolfric's world got progressively weirder and weirder to him; he desperately wanted to go home.

"Then," Gale said, "I'm gonna huff, and I'm gonna puff and I'll..."

The door opened, just a crack.

'That was easy.', he thought.

Gale hesitantly reached for the door handle and slowly pushed in. His eyes strained to adjust to the darkness. He stepped on the 'Welcome' mat. There was a mechanical click followed by, what sounded like, the grinding of gear wheels.

"What the hell?' Gale said.

A massive wooden mallet dropped from the ceiling and pounded Gale square in the chest; he rolled backward down the steps and landed, unceremoniously face down in the dirt.

Gale cradled his rib cage and gasped for breath as he stumbled to his feet.

"What, the actual, fuck!" He shouted. All he could see was red; he almost wanted to cry.

He was briefly reminded of that Christmas movie with the kid and the boobytrapped house; and how they should have just locked the little prick inside and torched the place. That was it, 'pork chop' was dead. This little piggy was going to cry 'wee-wee-wee' while being crushed by his home.

Gale put his best foot forward, widened his stance and planted himself firmly into the ground. He liked to start off slow, it allowed him to build lung capacity but also the head rush was kind of a trip.

He inhaled and then exhaled. Then in again deeper and then out again deeper still. The trees around him fluttered with each successive change in the local air pressure. Then a final and impossibly deep inhalation. His chest expanded to a freakish capacity. The front door to the house slammed shut as if in anticipation. Gale let go.

The entire structure creaked under the strain of the wind, but it stood firm on its foundation. Gale's breath was tapped; his head swam, and he loved it.

The wind reversed direction, even harder this time as he inspired once again.

He exhaled; small to medium sized trees uprooted behind him and launched at the house. They pummeled the side of the brick. The window glass imploded but metallic shutters fell into place. Gale contracted his core to a pressure that could have formed diamonds. The sound was deafening. Funnel clouds touched down in the immediate vicinity.

It was entirely possible he would hyperventilate, but he rooted his feet deeper and drew in one last time.

He thought he might black out; he was sure he saw a shutter open and a chubby hand release something that looked like a balloon. The object sailed directly into Gale's mouth and ruptured. He coughed and choked.

"What the hell?" His voice was several octaves higher and squeakier than normal.

The door opened and Jacob, the pig, stepped outside. He wore a strange apparatus on his back. A hose ran from the backpack to a large bellows he held in both hands. A small candle flame flickered on the end of the bellows. He wore his heavy blacksmithing apron and a pair of dark goggles.

"I'm sorry," Jacob said, "you knocked?"

"You should have stayed inside pig," Gale screeched, "I'm going to send you through your house, through your back wall and through the forest behind your back wall."

He set his feet firmly.

"You know the funny thing about that gas," Jacob said, "beyond your voice?"

Gale inhaled for one final bluster.

"It's flammable," Jacob said.

He compressed the bellows, a torrent of flame shot from the end towards Gale.

Gale felt hot pain shoot down his throat. An explosion ripped his insides and an inferno belched from his mouth.

Before everything went black, he had the distinct sensation of leaving the ground and sailing over the trees.

Jacob descended the steps and pulled the goggles up. He smiled; he loved a beautifully executed plan. That one was for his brothers.

Jacob was the middle child from the same litter of three. But as inseparable as they were, and despite the fact they shared a birthday, they couldn't have been more different. When they went out into the world to build their own lives they did so as neighbors.

Eli was the runt of the litter, the baby by five minutes. He was earthy and laid back, he insisted on building a house of straw, a hut really. The other two just stared at him as he described his vision. But at the end of the day they always had each other's back and they pitched in; literally, pitchforks were involved. The straw was packed tightly, and it did keep the rain out. Jacob suggested they dig into the ground for extra warmth and it worked out beautifully.

Isaac was the oldest. He was more practical, he wanted a nice solid house but not at a great expense. Wood was the natural choice. Jacob had some design input as well. It was easy to construct, and it did the job.

Jacob was fascinated by all branches of science, engineering and architecture. He studied ravenously. He wanted something grand; something that would stand the test of time; he also wanted a refuge for quiet contemplation and work. He went with brick fired in a kiln of his own design. This allowed him an unprecedented level of customization. Every single nook and cranny were to his exact specifications. A lot of it was beyond Isaac and Eli but they chipped in where they could, or where Jacob allowed.

It was a beautiful house, it could withstand the elements or even a small catapult. His workshop in the basement was even sound proof, he hated disruptions when he worked. Now he wouldn't hear a thing, not a blessed thing. Not unless the door chime rang, he installed one, he wasn't completely antisocial.

On one such day Eli had promised to help him with an experiment. He would be Jacob's 'guinea pig'; he loved that joke, however it always sailed over Eli's head.

The door chime rang. Jacob climbed the steps to the first floor.

"I'm coming." He said.

He installed a spy glass lens in the door to see who was there. He thought it was a clever idea. Sometimes he liked to keep his brother waiting just for fun. Except it wasn't Eli. Jacob had heard the legend of Big Bad Wolfric, but there he was for real on the other side of his door.

Jacob froze. He was too scared to make a sound. His hand fidgeted for the dead bolt and he gently slid in into place. It made a dreadful scraping noise as it slid. Wolfric looked directly into spy hole and smiled.

"Little pig, little pig, please let me in."

Jacob found no words.

"Then I'll huff, and I'll puff, and I'll blow your house in." Wolfric turned back down the steps. Jacob hoped he was leaving, but he stopped and turned. Big Bad Wolfric planted his feet and started to blow.

At first, he felt nothing but as the wind intensified his whole house shook. The shutters rag-dolled against the windows and the deadbolt bent under the pressure. Jacob planted his foot against the door and bared his substantial weight against it. He held on for what seemed like forever; his screams were drowned in the terrible disturbance.

And then it stopped.

For about an hour he clung, white knuckled to the door before he had the courage to even peek through the spy hole. When all seemed clear he reluctantly ventured outside and, with great trepidation, looked next door.

There was absolutely nothing left. Isaac's house was a pile of debris, Eli's hut was just a hole in the ground. He called out to them but there was no reply except his own echo.

Jacob's knees crumpled; he stayed on that spot for the rest of the afternoon, into the evening.

His analytical mind took over and he tried to sooth himself in reason.

He imagined Eli's hut proved a laughable challenge; and that his brother, ever the peace maker, would have tried to reach an understanding with Wolfric.

Isaac's house would have flexed a bit, but the brute force of the blast would have brought it down eventually. He pictured Isaac trying to bargain with the wolf, perhaps he tried to direct him to a better source of food or a more long-term solution to his hunger than just this one impulsive snack.

For the life of him he couldn't fathom why the wolf just stopped. Perhaps the king's men came by and chased him off. Perhaps he wasn't the easy meal the wolf had hoped for, and he just got bored and left. His house was still standing though, that was for sure. There it was, solid and alone.

He kept busy; he worked on the house, modified it, improved it. It became somewhat of an obsession. He enlisted in the war, his technical knowledge proved an asset to the King and Merlin. It was at the castle he first met Red. She taught him some basic combat techniques. He may have lost two brothers, though he brought the best of them forward through him, but he gained a sister.

"Jacob." The voice barely registered.

'Why now?', he thought. 'After all this time.'

"Jacob?" A hand gently turned his shoulder

It took some time for Jacob to recognize Red and Braum. Of course, he knew them, but sometimes he got so absorbed in something to the exclusion of all else.

"Red?" Jacob said. His eyes lit up as he returned to reality. "What are you doing here."

"We were paid a visit by one of Wolfric's lapdogs." She said. She put her arm around Jacob. "Is everything alright?"

"As a matter of fact," he said, "I had a visitor too, but he just left."

"We need to get to the castle." Red said, "It's got something to do with Merlin; we don't have any details, but we fear the worst."

"Yes, of course." replied Jacob, "Let me pack a few things."

CHAPTER 4:
'YOU HAD ONE JOB!'...

A deafening silence hung in the throne room, the pack was assembled before their Alpha; Gale and Shifter stood front and center; their tails between their legs and their heads down. Shifter's wounds were still in the process of healing; Gale was lightly charred with a subtle plume of smoke rising from his shoulders.

Wolfric's frozen contempt bored through them. Gale raised his head as if to speak but abandoned the idea to examine a chipped nail on his paw. Eye contact would have been career suicide; on top of that it would have been actual suicide.

William sat just off to the side of Wolfric's new throne; he literally had never been happier.

He hated Gale and Shifter on a visceral level. Being born a mute, they figured he was a defenseless target for ridicule. There was the always hilarious 'cat got your tongue' remarks; the talking louder to him like he couldn't hear what they were saying; and just a general attitude that they were somehow better than everyone because they were from the other kingdom. He couldn't talk back, so they always got the last word. When Wolfric first brought them over he tried to be friendly, he tried to be tolerant. Wolfric would give him the pep talk; that he was the oldest and therefore his brothers' keeper; that they hadn't been afforded the same opportunities in life as he had. They were younger and given a certain amount of leeway; the learning curve as Wolfric called. Fortunately, as time went on, their stunning ineptitude shone through. He would have loved to grab them both by the face and render them slobbering simpletons, but Wolfric hadn't ordered it, yet. Besides, how much dumber could he possibly have made them?

At that moment he was engaged in the mother of all stare-downs with Timmin.

He found her captivating; in their sharing she had seen the worst parts of him and she didn't even flinch. Timmin, of course, could never flinch as fairies don't blink. He had her caged in an ornate lantern of glass and iron. Fairy magic doesn't work on iron, so she was effectively trapped.

Timmin was patient, however, she could wait until stars burned out; and, actually, had on at least two occasions. She was hide and seek champion of her village for two centuries straight. The only one better than her was her cousin, Fern Greenleaf, a woodland brownie.

For brownies, hide and seek is more than a game, it is a profound spiritual devotion. To completely lose oneself in their environment is considered an achievement of the highest order. Generations would pass before some of the great masters of the game were found. Brownies don't observe the 'Olly Olly Oxen Free' rule, that is for quitters. Some, like Fern, are never seen again. It should be noted however, brownies are, for all intents and purposes, insane.

Even if she wasn't trapped, Timmin loved William's sad eyes, like a puppy's. He was an old soul, like her; more than that, his gift had allowed him the combined experiences of countless old souls. It made him extremely thoughtful, it had given him perspective. It was a quality she rarely saw in anyone not fairy.

"I gave you two these powers," Wolfric said, "because I thought that, even with your rudimentary intelligence, it would give you some kind of strategic advantage."

"To be fair," Gale said. But he quickly remembered where he was.

Wolfric leaned forward and gave Gale his full, undivided attention. Gale found it hard to breathe.

William and Timmin and him exchanged smirks. Was Gale about to be decapitated? Would he even notice.

"You were saying, Gale." Wolfric prompted. "I beg you, please finish your thought."

Shifter shrank a couple inches, almost imperceptibly. He was terrified and exhilarated.

"Shut up, Gale," he whispered. "Shut. Up."

Wolfric got up from his seat; his gaze fixed unflinchingly on them both.

They shut their eyes, an interminable duration between them and then ... nothing.

Gale risked a glance; he opened one eye just a crack. The throne was empty.

"Shifter." He whispered.

"Gale, shut the hell up." Shifter said.

"Shifter." Gale insisted.

Shifter slowly opened his eyes; no Wolfric.

A searing pain took them at the base of their necks. Wolfric's head emerged between them.

"Boys," Wolfric said, he dug his claws deep into their shoulders. "A pig and a girl.

You really couldn't handle a pig and a girl?"

He lifted them of their feet. A small stream of urine trailed down one of Gale's legs and puddled on the floor. The brothers fainted (Shifter smiling) and dangled limply in Wolfric's hands.

"You've got to be joking." He said. He shook them, but they didn't revive. He cast them aside. They slid across the polished marble floor into a heap against the wall.

Wolfric hated surprises and despised mysteries; his mind spiraled deeper and deeper in a frustrated corkscrew of possibilities. His facial features twisted with his bitterness. He felt a tap on his shoulder. When he spun around and saw it was William, he didn't maul him to death. He liked William.

William didn't like to touch Wolfric's mind when he got like this, it scared him and tested his loyalty even more than it already had been. But the Alpha always listened to his suggestions.

Wolfric placed a gentle hand on the side of William's head.

"Of course, you're right William.", he said, "They will get curious and come here to investigate. And when they don't find anything, they'll seek out Merlin for us."

Wolfric's sense of calm was restored.

"Wake your brothers," he said. "We probably don't have much time."

△ △ △

Red, Jacob and Braum crept to the edge of the forest, just out of sight of the castle and down wind. Jacob pulled out his spyglass and scanned the castle walls.

"Do you see anything?" Asked Red.

"Not a soul." Jacob said.

"I don't understand. Wolfric goes through all this trouble just to abandon the castle?"

"Maybe he didn't," Braum said. "Maybe he doesn't consider anyone a threat."

"I hate to say it Red." Jacob lowered the spyglass. "We're going to have to go in there for a closer look."

They all knew he was right.

"We'll wait until nightfall." She said.

A few hours later they made their approach. They kept under the cover of bushes as much as possible until they reached the edge of the mote. They eased down into the water. It wasn't far, but it was dark and slow going as they pushed through some sort of unidentified debris.

Red thought it was too soft to be tree branches. She reached down to shove a piece out of the way and stifled a scream. Her hand had touched a face. She swept her arms around the surface of the water; she felt a hand, wet cloth, and a leg. Bodies, they were wading through dead bodies. No one dwelled for long on the grim realization; after a small eternity they reached the base of the wall. The moon came out from behind some clouds but none of them turned around to confirm what they already knew.

The drawbridge was raised, and the bank was too smooth to climb. Jacob went into his bag and pulled out what looked to Red like a modified crossbow with a grappling hook on it.

"Alright, grab on you two." Jacob said. Red and Braum held on to his arms. He shot the grapple to the top of the wall. When he released the trigger, the cable attached instantly retracted and pulled them up; Red and Braum climbed over first and then helped Jacob up.

"Do you suppose I could get one of those" Braum asked Jacob.

"When this is over it's all yours." Jacob said.

The moon lit the courtyard and as far as they could see all was clear. Red had never seen the castle so deserted, not even during the war. She couldn't count how many hours she sat up along the wall as a child and watched the knights spar. Or the afternoons spent in the stables reading to Midnight, her favorite black stallion. Her voice seemed to calm his high-spirited nature. Midnight, another casualty of Wolfric.

"I don't like this." Jacob said. "It's way too quiet."

"What do guys want to do?" Asked Red.

"It's your call." Jacob said. "You might be the last duly appointed officer of the court left. We're both with you."

Red hadn't been back to the castle since the presentation of Prince Eric. And even though she no longer lived there, Merlin always kept her room ready for her just as she left it.

Red took a moment to consider the situation.

"There could be prisoners inside," she said. "the King and Queen even. A small group has a better chance of at least checking things out. If we need to we can come back with more men. We should go in."

They cautiously descended the stairs to the courtyard. There weren't many obstructions to hide behind if there were to be an ambush. All the same they avoided being out in the open and hugged the walls to the main entrance.

Except for some bones on the floor, the throne room was empty. Jacob lit a torch from the wall, it provided weak illumination; the surrounding shadows loomed and seemed eager to devour them. A glint of light caught Red's attention. There was something on the floor by Arthur's throne; it was the crown, crushed and folded flat.

"He wasn't even interested in the crown," Red said "this was revenge, pure and simple."

"So, the king and queen are dead." Braum said.

"Let's not give up hope just yet. There may be prisoners in the dungeon."

The dungeon cells were vacant; their doors widely ajar. It was rare the cells were occupied at all; and even then, it was seldom anyone more dangerous than a thief serving his time or a weary traveler who wasn't particularly fussy where they lay their head so long as there was a roof over it. A lot of the time they were simply used for storage.

Red couldn't restrain a disheartened sigh. Braum placed a hand on her shoulder.

"There's still plenty of castle left to search." He said.

She nodded and forced a reassuring optimism to her face.

Each room greeted them with shadow and silence; until they got to Red's. Her perfectly preserved room screamed a derisive accusation of her failure. She could vividly picture her younger self on the bed glaring back at her with tear-soaked condemnation.

'Where were you?' cried Little Red Riding Hood, 'They might have stood a chance if you were here.'

"Everything alright?" Braum's voice was a thousand miles away

"What's that?" She said. "Oh yes. We should check Merlin's room."

Merlin's chambers were just as Red and Jacob had remembered them. The room was disheveled, and one might have been tempted to conclude there were signs of a struggle, but it had always looked like that. Books of arcane knowledge and scrolls were strewn across every useable surface. As Merlin would often remind them, true geniuses were differently organized.

"Search everything." Red said, "perhaps Merlin left us some sort of clue."

It was here Red first learned to read; she was a little behind the other children in her classes and Merlin had taken it upon himself to give her some extra tutoring. She had a hard time focusing on poetry and an even harder time comprehending the work of someone named Shakespeare Merlin kept insisting on. She would often get distracted by the sounds of the knights outside the window on the grounds below; so, Merlin decided to run with that and taught her to read through great heroic epics and the codes of chivalry. He taught her the mathematics and geometry involved in archery and catapults. Occasionally, when he was too busy, Merlin would have Jacob tutor her.

They ended their search in the King and Queen's bedroom. A draft blew down the chimney and had scattered ashes all over the floor. The king and queen's bed was overturned, the prince's crib rocked back and forth eerily in the breeze. Excalibur was absent from its cradle above the hearth.

"Whatever happened here, happened fast." Jacob said. "This whole castle just reeks of wolf."

Jacob's sense of smell was a gift and a curse. It rivaled any wolf's nose and often gave him a tactical advantage in staying down wind or tracking. But the stench in the castle was nearly unbearable.

As in every room, he sniffed around but found nothing useful. He crossed the bedroom and twisted an unassuming candle stick. The hidden staircase once again revealed itself.

"How did you know that was there?" Asked Red.

"Who do you think designed it?" Jacob said. He stuck his tongue out at Red impishly.

Red returned with her own rude gesture and threw a pillow at Jacob's head.

Jacob knelt on the first step and sniffed.

"Fresh tracks in the dust and it's Merlin's scent." He said. "Looks like he went this way. But where would he go?"

"The sanctuary?" Red said.

"The sanctuary." Jacob agreed.

"Of course, the sanctuary." Braum said. He nodded confidently with his arms crossed over his prodigious chest.

Red smiled at Braum; it was charming of him to try and participate.

"We'll explain on the way." She laughed.

The passage way closed behind the trio.

Wolfric and the pack emerged from the shadows in every corner of the room. It was one of the harder spells Merlin had taught him. It wasn't like turning invisible, it was more like an elaborate camouflage. They had been present in every room the three heroes had searched.

He twisted the candle stick and the passageway opened.

"Shifter," He said. "You know what to do."

"Already behind them." Shifter said. A tentacle protruded from his tail and down the stairwell.

"If you lose them," Wolfric said, "the rest of you can stay gone too."

Shifter bared his teeth, slightly, his entire mass slithered down the stairs, his head lingered just a little longer.

"Ladies and gentlemen." Wolfric said to the rest of his pack. "After you."

Shifter was a brilliant tracker; Wolfric didn't like to praise anyone too much, it kept them hungry for his approval but even he would have to admit Shifter at least always found his quarry. Shifter stayed, more or less, under his target at all times. Part of him burrowed under the ground and would surface just out of sight, up ahead. As the targets passed by, his rear would burrow up front and take the lead; in this way he was always on either side of them at any given time. He relayed any pertinent conversation or changes in direction as they happened to Wolfric. Going through a forest made things easier; Shifter would surface up ahead in the form of a tree. He was great at trees, no one looked twice at a tree.

△ △ △

Half an hour later Red, Jacob and Braum had cleared the tunnel. They traveled through the night until daybreak. Braum bagged a couple pheasants and they stopped for breakfast. Jacob and Braum slept for a few hours while Red stood watch. Merlin had taught her a meditation and breathing technique; she could go long periods of time without rest. She didn't sleep so much as go inactive while remaining completely aware of her surroundings.

The Sanctuary always seemed to Red a very out of the way place for Merlin to go for privacy; of course, he never had to walk there. He insisted on making her traverse the physical distance; that it would teach her self-reliance and patience. She knew the way well.

She found a slightly elevated vantage point in a tree and curled up on a big branch. She let her mind go lax and just took in her surroundings. Her breathing was slow but unstructured. The treetops gently rustled on the breeze. Red could swear she detected some movement in a tree not too far off. Possibly an animal, but that was another issue. The forest was oddly quiet, too quiet. Often, when she meditated, animals seemed to just gravitate around her, but there was nothing. No birds, no squirrels, not even crickets. After a few moments she dismissed it and woke the others. It was time to carry on.

They walked deeper and deeper into the woods. The oldest trees in the kingdom lived there and they were very particular about who they allowed in their midst.

The air was heavy, and the path was overgrown with thorny vines. It had been ages since Red had come here but she didn't recall it being so dark. There was something nearby the trees didn't care for.

Finally, there it was. Merlin had grown the cottage out of a mighty oak. He guided its development and worked with it to form rooms between the roots. The oak allowed him to attach a door and windows and it bent to accommodate them.

The sanctuary was on a hill overlooking the whole forest and one of Merlin's favorite pastimes was to curl up in some of the highest branches and read or meditate. On a clear day he could even see the castle. He had only ever allowed two other people to enter the sanctuary.

Merlin had brought Jacob here to discuss engineering projects around the kingdom. It was also here that he taught Jacob the mysteries of black powder and secrets few blacksmiths knew; secrets that leant an enchantment to anything they forged. Jacob was more interested by the science of it all, but Merlin didn't hold that against him.

Red was often brought here for quiet study but a lot of times it was to keep her out from under foot at the castle. She had an insatiable curiosity and a tendency to wander. Merlin was often charged with minding her, but he didn't mind at all.

Red knocked on the door and waited a few moments. She couldn't hear a sound from inside.

"Merlin?" she called out.

A few birds startled from their perches and the steady song of a cicada were the only response.

She looked back at Jacob and Braum. Neither had any suggestions.

Red tried the door handle, it was unlocked. Merlin kept the sanctuary as 'differently organized' as his chambers at the castle. A million memories washed over Red.

She wandered passed his bookshelves. How many hours had she lost herself in those volumes? Tales of adventure and far off places. She traced her finger across the spines until she landed on one, she didn't recognize.

"The Once and Future King." She read aloud. "by T.H. White." She picked it up and thumbed through the pages.

"I didn't realize there was a book written about Merlin and Arthur." She slid the book back into its spot on the shelf. "Strange."

She pulled the one next to it. "English Fairy Tales by Joseph Jacobs." She said.

It appeared to be a collection of short stories. She was just about to put it back when she came across a tale called 'The Three Little Pigs'.

"Jacob." She called out.

Jacob looked up from the drawer he had been searching.

"You're going to want to see this." She said.

She held the page open to him as he approached. His face lost some of its colour. He took it from her and read.

Another book caught her eye. "Grimm's Fairy Tales." She opened and flipped through again, she had a strange feeling.

'Snow White," she read out loud. "Cinderella. Snowy and Cindy would flip if they saw this.'

And then, there it was, Little Red Riding Hood. A wave of chills washed over her.

She had barely begun to read when the book began to glow. A strange vibration surged up her arms. Red dropped the volume, and everyone backed away from it. It continued to glow more brightly, and a beam of light shot up from the pages. The familiar image of Merlin appeared in the center of the room.

"Merlin!" Red exclaimed.

"I'm sorry, child." Said the image. "It's not really me. You can think of this like an echo of my true self."

"What's going on?" Red asked.

"If you're seeing this, I can only assume Wolfric has come after the both of you to find me. I'm so sorry to have brought this on you."

34

"What are you talking about? You couldn't have known." Red said.

The image looked down and sighed a deep breath.

"Once upon a time," he said, "There was a child born, a little different. More wolf than man. I was gathering herbs for spells and remedies when I happened upon the infant; he was swaddled and left in a blanket in the woods. I searched the area but never found a soul; it was clear he had been abandoned. He was defenseless and nearly starved to death; I brought him back to the castle and, with Arthur's consent, he was allowed to stay.

I named him Wolfric and I raised him like he was my own. He grew up happy, at least at first, but there was a wild streak in him I couldn't seem to tame. I taught him the code of chivalry and the ways of a knight to try and channel his aggression to something constructive. He showed great promise as a student, he was particularly gifted in magic.

I showed him glamour magic, the ability to assume any shape he wanted. I thought, at first, if he could look like everyone else it might help him to fit in. I showed him how to read minds to gain a better understanding of people. I tried to guide him down the right path, but that darkness always remained. People were uncomfortable around him; he developed a particular obsession with Gwenevere.

I dismissed it at first, young boys tended to be unruly and given to infatuations. Then the livestock went missing; one or two at first. The townsfolk naturally accused him but there was no evidence. I tried to reassure them there was no way he could be responsible; finally, to put the people's minds at ease, and at Arthur's urging, I confined him to his room. He didn't like it, but I assured him it would help prove his innocence. He denied he had taken anything of course and I believed him, perhaps I just didn't want to see it. Cattle continued to disappear, and in greater numbers. The strange reports of wolfmen increased. Arthur ordered Wolfric be confined to the dungeon; and as much as it broke my heart I agreed. Wolfric just smiled at me when he was locked behind bars, that terrible smile. As it turned out he had been shapeshifting and coming and going at his leisure. One day he got out and never returned. I think he only ever came back to gloat that he could escape at will. Then children started to go missing. And then the war came."

"What are you saying?" The colour had run from Red's face.

"I tried to tell you so many times before, but I lost my nerve." Said the image. "I am as responsible for Wolfric's reign of terror as he is. I'm responsible for what happened to both of you. When I took you in I thought it might make up for things in some way."

For Red, it was a punch to the stomach; she found it hard to breath or look at him.

"I'm sorry, to both of you." The image repeated.

"What does Wolfric want?" Asked Jacob. His objectivity and civility were sorely tested.

"With you?", said the image, "nothing. The war had escalated. His forces got stronger with each encounter. Against Arthur's wishes I went to Wolfric's camp to try to reason with him. Try to find some trace of that child I raised. He laughed, of course. But I knew there had to be something he wanted. Something that would appease him. As it turned out there was."

"What did you do?" asked Red, reproachfully.

"I did what had to be done to save countless lives." He said.

"What did you do?" she demanded.

"It was nearly the same situation as with Arthur's father King Uther, you know. Wolfric wanted a night with Gwen, and the child of their union. In return he promised to cease all hostilities. I arranged for Arthur to leave the castle for one night. Wolfric came to her disguised as Arthur."

Red threw every book within reach at the image of Merlin, they all passed through.

"How could you make that choice for Gwen?" Red shouted, "She trusted you, Arthur trusted you."

"People were dying, the war was already lost. It was his only term and he agreed to leave forever." Said the Image.

"And you trusted him?" Red said.

"It's hard to see right now in the short term, but sometimes larger choices have to be made for the greater good. Besides, I never planned on giving him the child. I saw great things in store for the prince."

Red turned away, she had no idea who this man was.

"Where are you?" Asked Jacob.

"That's a little complicated to explain." The image replied.

"Try!" Red said.

"Your kingdom is one of many other, let's call them worlds." Said the image, "The events that happen in one land have an impact on another. In some cases, the very existence of one land depends on that of another. I'm from one such place. "

"The books." Red said. "Those books aren't from here, they're from your world."

"That's correct" replied the image. "You were always very bright."

"How do they know what happens here?"

"You misunderstand. They don't merely know what happens here, they cause what happens here."

All three looked blankly at the image of Merlin.

"Who are you? Really." Demanded Red.

"My name really is Merlin. Your Arthur and Gwen were inspired by the real Arthur and Gwen in my world. Ages ago, over there, magic used to be a lot more commonplace. Not so much now. After my Arthur died there didn't seem to be really any place for me in the world. I traveled around on my own for a while, aimlessly.

Purely by accident I opened a door to this world. Imagine my surprise; Arthur, still alive. Along with a host of other characters both familiar and strange to me, all living and breathing here. I traveled back and forth and studied the relationship that existed between both worlds. I noticed time virtually stood still here but in the other world years had passed since I had last set foot there.

Suffice it to say, that's where I am now, back in my world. I brought the prince with me, I had hoped to return in a relatively short time with the prince and a plan to stop Wolfric. There is a power in the prince greater than anything Wolfric could hope to possess.

Unfortunately, if you're watching this, it also means that plan has failed. I was created as a link for you to my real self, but a short time ago that link was severed. I don't know what has happened."

"Perhaps its best for everyone if you just stayed there." Red said.

"You have every right to be angry with me." He said. "But I do what I do with a larger image of things in mind."

"Ha!" Red said. "Do you hear yourself? Did you honestly think he would keep his promise to you?"

"Me keep my promise?" Wolfric stood at the door with Gale, Shifter, William and some of the pack. William cradled the lantern with Timmin inside, more so than ever to simply keep her safe.

The pack entered the room and surrounded Red, Jacob and Braum.

"If anyone reneged on our deal," Wolfric said, "it was the ghost in the room right there. Do you people have any idea what this sweet old man really is? Playing chess with people's lives. He's not what he pretends to be."

He walked over and stood face to face with the image. "Give me my son."

"The prince is beyond your reach Wolfric. I made sure of that."

"Oh, Father," Wolfric said. "Nothing is beyond my reach."
Wolfric raised his hand, closed his eyes and concentrated. The air across the room rippled followed by a vibration and an audible hum. The space in front of them twisted into a circle and a deep swirling hole appeared.

The image of Merlin was visibly stunned.

"How did you know about the portal?", it said.

"Seriously, Merlin." Wolfric said. "Where do you think I've been all this time?" he laughed. "How do you think I won the war?"

"You killed Arthur and Gwen, you have an army of offspring. Surely this is enough revenge for even you."

"You never understood." Wolfric said. "My real family understands me."

Merlin's image took a last glance at Red. "Find me", it pleaded to her. It ran straight into the vortex and vanished.

"Dammit!" Wolfric said. "He's going to warn his real self. Gale, Shifter, follow him."

They looked at one another for a moment but neither one moved.

"Problem, boys?" Wolfric said.

"Well," Gale said, "It's just the tunnel makes us queasy. Couldn't we go back through the other door in the for-"

Wolfric seized them both and threw them into the vortex. They screamed as their bodies were torn apart and drawn out like sand down some great drain.

William walked up to the door and gave it a casual inspection. He looked at Timmin who gave him a reassuring nod. They stepped through together.

"Well if it isn't the one that got away." Wolfric eyed Red up and down. His smile turned her stomach with a combination of rage and disgust.

"And hello, I'm blanking on your name, Bacon was it?" Wolfric teased. "How's the family? Still dead huh?"

Jacob clenched his fists and took a step forward. Braum stopped him with a hand on his chest. Jacob found his composure once again; Braum was right, of course, charging at the sadistic beast wouldn't help them.

Wolfric came eye to eye with Braum. "You, I don't know. I never forget a face, but there's something familiar about you. Have we by chance met somewhere before?"

"I'm afraid I haven't had the pleasure." Braum said.

"I'm sure it will come to me later." Wolfric said.

Wolfric turned back to the pack. "Kill them as soon as I'm through. We don't need them anymore." He bowed genially and allowed himself to fall backwards into the tunnel; he smiled and royal waved goodbye.

The pack closed in on Red, Jacob and Braum. The vortex suddenly became more violent. Some of the pack were drawn in, others changed their focus to holding on for dear life.

"What do we do?" Shouted Jacob.

"We don't have a choice." Red said. "We can't leave any world at the mercy of that lunatic."

Red held up her staff, both Jacob and Braum grabbed on to it. They charged the wolves and shoved them into the tunnel. They grabbed on tight to each other and dove in as well.

The tunnel closed behind them and the sanctuary returned to stillness.

CHAPTER 5:

A LAND OF DISENCHANTMENT...

ric stared at his screen; the clock in the lower right corner had shown '2:55 P.M.' for what seemed longer than his eight-hour shift, in fact it may have even gone back to '2:54'. He knew he wasn't getting out of there at '3:00'. It was as certain as death and taxes and made him pray for the former. That obnoxious beep from his headset would diddle his nerves and he'd have to take a call.

He worked at a technical support hotline for gLobo-Tech High Speed Internet. The job started out alright, the advertisement was certainly enticing; 'a rewarding career with advancement potential, good benefits, flexible hours, be a part of a winning team.' A few years later, every single day felt like he was tethered to the desk by his head and forced to play a sadistic game of customer service roulette.

'2:56 P.M., 'You're killing me.'

It had been a fairly average day in hell. He walked in the door 7:00 AM, bright and early. Well, early anyway. Well, he walked in the door at the very least. He sauntered indifferently passed the disappointed eye of his team leader. Eric didn't care, they couldn't fire him. He had one of the highest customer satisfaction ratings on the whole floor. He passed by Rose's cubical, just two down from his. She was already on a call. He mussed her beautiful red hair all the same. She gently squeezed his hand and let go. She smiled sweetly and waved without missing a beat with her customer.

Rose had started the same time as Eric, they sat next to each other in the same training class and became fast friends. She was the only thing that made the job bearable; more than that, he lived for the moment he got to see her each day. They took breaks and lunch together, they chatted for hours on the company's instant messaging service. All manner of frivolities or deeply personal conversations, there were almost no taboos subjects. He was a willing sounding board for all her problems and the recap of her dismal romantic life. Eric had subtly implied at times, perhaps too subtly, that perhaps the guy she was looking for was right under her nose. She always deflected him in the nicest way possible. As nicely as anyone could stab another person through the soul. Often times between calls he would steal a glance at her when she wasn't looking. His heart would ache and melt all at once. If he could only make her love him, but subservience wasn't love. He would sigh and return to his screen or get startled back to reality by another call.

Some days were dead, you could volunteer to go home if you wanted to. Eric usually opted for that even if it did cut into his pay. Money didn't always appeal to him so much as his free time. Other days were a complete shit storm that made his salary seem inadequate. Some days he would put a customer on mute and let fly a relentless diatribe of profanities while they bitched about the first world issues destroying their lives.

'2:57 P.M., does anyone have a bottle of Vicodin?'

Between Rose and him, Carol was having her third, daily, bowl of yogurt and granola. The irritating, methodical clink of metal flatware on glass had made him even self-conscious of his own eating. He searched online for silicon covered forks and spoons to deaden the sound or else favored finger foods. He wondered how many calories were to be gained in that final trace of yogurt residue she incessantly scraped the bottom to get every, last drop. He wanted to ask her, so many times, if she wouldn't mind eating anything else for the love of God. He wanted to steal her bowls, but she would probably just buy new ones. He fantasized about holding her face down in her Raspberry Greek till she stopped moving. He'd done it hundreds of times in his mind, but he supposed that would have to be enough.

'2:58 P.M.' There was a beep in his headset, it startled him each-and-every single time. He prepared himself, shook his mouse to wake up his screen. But there was nothing. The phone line cut off. The call had dropped. Oh, merciful father in heaven, the call had dropped. He looked up at the queue screen, he was at the back of the line again. He was getting out of there on time.

'2:59 P.M.!'

Eric packed up his things and put on his coat.

"Hey there, Eric!" It was the cheerful voice of death. "Got a favor to ask you."

His eye roll concluded its arc behind him and came to rest on Sheila's sweet lifeless smile; he answered with his own well practiced façade.

Sheila was a corporate liaison from the head office, the CEO's go-to girl; she toured the facilities regularly and liked to interfere, or 'pitch in' to put it more diplomatically, wherever she could. She didn't even work there but it was a classic example of overreach.

"Well, hey there you!" Eric beamed. *'Son of a...'* "What can I do for you?"

"We're experiencing a higher than expected call volume and we're just going around asking if people wouldn't mind taking one more call before they go. It would really help our customers!" She placed a friendly hand on his shoulder. Her hands were always like ice. Eric didn't know how she functioned, but he was positive she was an advanced form of A.I.

'Say no! Say anything, come up with anything!' His mind screamed.

'3:01 P.M.'.

"Well, I..." 'Words! Say any words!'

Sheila's smile widened; Eric could see bits of children's dreams still stuck in her teeth.

"Sure." he said, "No problem." 'Turn your balls back in to the human race, you sicken me.'

"Thanks!" Sheila said. She had already moved on to the next imposition.

'Well at least Carol isn't getting out of here either'. Eric took his satisfaction, no matter how petty, where he could find it.

Carol smiled at Sheila; Sheila at Carol; they both laughed. Then Carol got up from her seat grabbed her bag and coat and wished Sheila a good night.

'Burn in hell Carol'.

The familiar sound of Carl from workforce management buzzed in Eric's headset. "We need you to get back in queue to take another call, are you ready to go?" he said.

"Yes." Eric said, hissing the last consonant through clenched teeth.

The beep once again intruded on his peace of mind.

'Well, at least I'm getting the call over with now'.

One hour and sixty five percent less self-esteem later, Eric logged out of his phone and shut down his terminal. He had gotten a talker. She wasn't so bad or angry, just wanted someone to tell their life story to. He could have 'accidentally' dropped the call and gotten out of there, but it wasn't in him to be so cold. He could hear in her voice she appreciated it, even if it was a wrong number and it took him the last twenty minutes to hint that it was time to go.

If he was fast, he could still make the bus. Half way though the parking lot, another voice beckoned his attention.

"Eric?" it addressed him softly.

Not just any voice, her voice; Rose's voice.

"Hey." He said. His heart palpitated. "what's up?"

Her infectious smile and dazzling green eyes completely owned him every time.

"A bunch of us are going to Dooley's for drinks later." She said. "Interested?"

'Interested? Interested she asks. Absolutely. But, instead of a group could it just be the two of us? And instead of Dooley's could it be my place or your place? And instead of drinks could I cater to your every desire for all eternity?'

"Sounds great." Eric said. "I have a couple errands to run but I'll text you."

Errands to run, that was a laugh, but he didn't want to seem like he was completely devoid of a life.

"Great!" Rose said. She ran up to him and gave him a great big hug. She smelled amazing; that red hair caressed his cheek. Eric wasn't sure what conditioner she used but he was pretty sure it was the same one used in the creation of Himalayan kittens. He heard the bus go by him on the street. It was fine, there would be another one in... who cared?

An hour later his bus dropped him off in front of his building. He was still lost in that embrace however and didn't distinctly remember even getting on the bus.

He rented a studio loft above a convenience store. In addition to it being rent controlled he offered his services to the landlady for a further discount. He took out the trash, minded the store on occasion and shoveled the sidewalk in the winter.

He dropped his stuff off just inside the door, grabbed a beer and flopped on the couch. His cat, Dr. Stephen Anderson, scurried over and jumped up in his lap. Eric stroked Stephen's head and steered it back and forth by alternating scratches behind his ears. Stephen purred and rubbed his nose into Eric's hand.

"Hey bud," he said, "How was your day?" Eric wanted to believe this was affection, but he had read somewhere that cats simply marked their territory through scent glands on the nose. If nothing else, he comforted himself with the knowledge he was possibly Stephen's prized possession.

He picked up his remote and searched his PVR. None of his shows seemed to have taped due to some news story he wasn't even remotely interested in. He turned off his television and stroked the good doctor's tummy.

Eric's cell phone lit up in his pocket and vibrated; he lip-synced to the ring tone he chose specifically for Rose.

'Lady in red, is dancing with me. Cheek to cheek. There's nobody here, it's just you and me...'

Rose invited him to Dooley's, he had nearly forgot. Did he feel like going out? He just got home, he was comfy.

'But it's Rose. This could be your big chance.'

Her theme song stopped, and the room was silent once again.

'What if she thinks you're blowing her off?' He thought.

'She knows I'd never do that.' He counter-thought. *'Doesn't she?'*

'Sorry,' he texted Rose, 'I was in the bathroom.'

'TMI, Eric.' She replied. 'So, you comin out?'

'Raincheck?' He said. 'Not feeling so hot.'

'Lady in red, is dancing with me. Cheek to cheek. There's nobody here...'

Eric accepted the call.

A panic settled in Eric's stomach and cranked itself up to eleven.

"Everything ok?" she asked. "Do you need some company?"

A wave of tingles washed over him from head to toe.

'Rose?' He thought, 'Over here?'

A million fantasies had started just like this; in each one he was a take charge kind of guy, a man's man, a romantic warrior. But who the hell was he kidding? He didn't even play himself in his own fantasies.

"Thanks," Eric said. "I'll be fine. You guys have fun, I'll see you tomorrow."

"Alright," she said, Eric detected a note of disappointment in her voice, or wanted to. "Well get some rest and feel better. If you need anything you got my number. Take it easy, big hugs."

"Thanks, you too." He said.

He ended the call.

'You don't deserve a Y chromosome.' he scolded himself.

He flopped face down into a couch cushion; maybe, if he was lucky, he would smother himself to death.

CHAPTER 6:

THE STRANGE CASE OF MERLE LYNDSAY...

"And this is the secured wing." Dr. Joseph Reid swiped his ID badge; the lock to the reinforced steel door clicked. "After you." He said.

Alan took a few timid steps into the wing. No one had mentioned anything in his job interview about a secured wing; his self-defense training wasn't exactly comprehensive.

"Is anyone in here, you know, dangerous?" said Alan.

"Oh, no," said Dr. Reid, "most of the patients in here are simply incapable of rational thought. They can't legally make decisions for themselves."

"Ah, I see." Said Alan.

"Don't worry, for the most part if you're calm around them they will be calm around you."

Just past the door was the common area. Two patients on the couch stared at the television; 'Police Academy 2' was playing, Alan knew it well. Another man sat alone and completely still at a table with a fully set-up chessboard in front of him.

"That's Hank," said Dr. Reid, "You should sit and play him some night, undefeated."

"It seems pretty quiet." Said Alan

"For the most part it is. Even in the daytime there isn't too much fuss."

"Well that's good."

"All the same, I should introduce you to Merle."

"Merle?"

They passed through the common area and continued down to the end of the corridor. Through the windows of each door Alan spied patients on their beds, they slept or read.

"Tell me something, Alan," said Dr. Reid, "do you have a pacemaker or startle easily?"

"Um, no," said Alan. It was an odd question, a little disconcerting. "Fit as a fiddle. Why do you ask?"

"No reason, just making sure."

They stopped at the very last door. The light was on inside.

"Oh good," said Dr. Reid, "he's awake. Well, he's always awake in some way shape or form."

"Insomnia?" Alan asked.

Dr. Reid laughed. A little too hard, Alan thought.

He looked in the window and pushed the intercom button on the door.

"Good evening, Mr. Lyndsay?" He said. "Is this a good time?"

"Hello, Joseph!", replied a cheerful old voice. "Yes, absolutely."

"Merle, I'd like to introduce Alan Wilkins, he's going to be working night security with us."

Alan peered through the window, an elderly gentleman smiled amiably back at him. He was sitting on his bed holding a book.

"A pleasure to meet you, Alan." Said Merle.

Alan scratched inside his ear canal; for a moment it sounded as though the voice came from behind him. A warm gentle touch came to rest on his shoulder. Alan shrieked, spun around and back peddled to the wall.

Merle was right behind him.

"What the hell?" shouted Alan.

"Alan," said Dr. Reid, "meet Merle Lyndsay."

Alan looked back into the room, Merle was still on the bed. He spun around to find the hallway empty.

"Oh, ha-ha, very funny," Said Alan, "gag on the new guy. I get it, nice one."

"It was Doctor Reid's idea." Said Merle from behind him once again.

Alan shrieked and then laughed.

"Twins, right?" Said Alan. He turned, Merle wasn't there. Alan scanned the hall and checked the closest door handle; it was locked tight.

"Merle's the one and only," said Dr. Reid, "and he never left his room. Not really anyway. Or was he ever in his room?"

Alan carefully studied the old man who had gone back to reading his book.

"That doesn't make any sense." Said Alan.

"Exactly." Said Dr. Reid. "I wish I had an even a remotely adequate explanation for you. Merle's been with us twenty-seven years. I was still in the middle of my internship when they brought him in. He was prone to manic outbursts, so they kept him sedated most of the time. No next of kin; a child that was in his custody until he was taken by child protective services. Then, one night an orderly forgot to give him his sedative. He got out of his room, he was disoriented, raving; he demanded to know where the child was. That's when all hell broke loose. The secure wing door blasted off its hinges. (After that night they reinforced it). Staff members and security were tossed aside with the slightest gesture from his hand. We have it saved in the security video archives, it's incredible stuff, you should watch it. Anyway, I managed to sneak up on him and shoot him with a tranquilizer dart. The chief of medicine at the time decided radicle electro-shock therapy was called for. I wasn't so sure. But it calmed him right down. He never spoke of the boy again; he claimed he didn't even remember a boy. Things were quiet for a time, and then the bilocation started happening."

"The what?" Alan may not have been the most well read but that word sounded made up.

"Bilocation," said Dr. Reid. "The ability or state of being in two places at one time. Orderlies would find him out of his room, wandering the halls. Disoriented. They'd escort him back only to find he was still there and when they turned around he wasn't with them in the hall anymore. The former chief of medicine thought it could be a great source of funding and prestige for the hospital if they could document and study his unique gift."

"How does he do it?"

"Experts were brought in to verify the claims, but Merle here didn't like to perform. It almost cost the old chief his career. He hated Merle for making a fool out of him. Anyway, he retired, and I took over. I decided things were best left as they were. Nice and quiet. So, we just collect data on him as it happens. Serious scientists don't seem that interested in his case, the odd paranormal investigation group or, excuse the term, nut jobs write us for the latest information, to post on their blogs. That's alright with us. We don't know what he's capable of. The board feels it's best to keep him happy and passive."

"Has he ever escaped?" asked Alan.

"Once." Said Dr. Reid. "He did more than bilocate, he teleported. He was just suddenly in the main lobby; his hands were on the door. Security was about to rush him. And then he just stopped..."

"Stopped?"

"Yeah. We asked him if he was okay, but he didn't answer. A sort of strange bitter sweet smile was all. I walked him back to his room."

"Weird."

"Yeah." Said Dr. Reid. He checked his watch. "Anyway, I'm almost done for the day. I'll show you the break room."

Alan glanced one more time at Merle, he was absorbed in his book. Dr. Reid lead Alan back down the hall.

△ △ △

It was his favorite book. The Wisdom of Insecurity, by Alan Watts. He must have re-read it couple dozen times. He found comfort in Watt's astounding clarity. Even though Merle's past was a white washed canvass, and the uncertainty of it all was terrifying, at the same time it was also a starting point. When you didn't know where you've been and had no idea where you were headed you could go anywhere.

Merle took solace in his room, his reading and the present moment. After all, wasn't everyone, memories intact or not, just as confused about their place in the universe?

He liked it at the hospital. There were **regular** meals, the staff was friendly, he had a full library to explore and, once Dr. **Reid** showed him how to use the internet, he found that to be just marvelous. No substitute for a good book, of course, but it wasn't without its uses. He could explore the grounds whenever he felt like it; go out and get some sunshine. Doctor Reid preferred he not do that; but, honestly, what could anyone do to stop him?

He wasn't certain how he did it either. If he was calm and focused and envisioned it clear enough in his mind, he could just 'be' wherever he wanted. He respected Dr. Reid's wishes for the most part, but he couldn't help but explore the limits of his gifts. He may, or may not have, on occasion attended local theatre productions of his favorite Shakespearian plays. On more than one occasion he may have gotten a craving for authentic Cantonese and went to this wonderful restaurant he discovered in Guangzhou. Technically, however, he never left his room, not entirely.

One night as he read, he found he could turn the pages without touching them. With practice he was able to levitate the whole book, then a stack of books, and then his bed with him in it.

He did the bulk of his experiments in the evening, free from prying eyes. Mediation seemed to be the key to it all. The more placid his mind the easier it was to manifest his will. The more he let go, the more control he seemed to have. He read everything he could find on the occult, philosophy, spirituality. Some of it he found to be complete nonsense but the ideas that resonated with him he kept in journals.

At first, he hid them under his mattress but over time it looked suspect to the orderlies. He piled them in front of him one night, it was a ponderous collection. Where could he hide them? In his mind he pictured a room, a great study lined with bookshelves. He lined the journals up on an empty shelf then opened his eyes. They were gone. He visualized a specific volume, reached out for it and pulled it back into reality.

"Now, this has potential." He remarked.

From then on, that pocket universe was his sanctuary. Over the years he filled the

47

shelves with his own journals and his favorite books. He expanded it with room upon room of wonders and one hell of a swimming pool. It was a safe place to practice; whatever he desired he could call into physical reality from the sanctuary. It seemed he could do anything; anything except remember.

△ △ △

There was nothing on television that time of night except informercials and bad movies. Alan had finished his book and hadn't brought another one. He watched the security footage of Merle, but it was digitized from old VHS tapes and he couldn't be certain what he was seeing at times. He thought, perhaps, there might be something worth reading in the library. He glanced once more at the security monitors and decided to do his rounds early.

Merle was in the elevator when the doors opened. After a few weeks of it Alan barely jumped anymore. He was used to it. No one would believe him anyway, so he just made peace with the reality.

"Hey Merle." He said.

"Good evening, Alan." said Merle, "What's the good word?"

"Living the dream, Merle." He said. "Four, please. Going to check out the library."

"Certainly." Said Merle. "What do you read?"

"Usually true crime." Said Alan, "action, suspense."

"looking for a little adventure in your life."

"Something like that. My eyesight wasn't good enough for the police academy, so security was the next best thing. It was always the dream though."

"It's never too late to follow your dreams."

"Maybe."

A 'muzak' version of Air Supply's 'Lost in Love' filled the lag in conversation. Alan thought it was possible the original version could be considered 'muzak' too; regardless, he couldn't help but sway his head gently and lip sync.

The elevator stopped, and the doors opened. A gust of wind entered the elevator and blew Alan against the wall. Merle was completely unaffected. The common area was a scattered mess of furniture and papers; in the center, there was a big swirling...hole; or was it a tunnel? Alan had no frame of reference for what he was seeing.

Standing at the mouth of the gateway was a glowing man. Alan was glad he had the chance to get used to Merle or he felt like he could have really lost his shit just then. The glowing man looked exactly like Merle.

"Merle, are you doing this?" shouted Alan. He felt like it might be time to renegotiate the terms of his salary.

"Thank goodness, there you are!" The Glowing man approached them. He remained fixed on Merle and only gave Alan a passing glance.

Merle didn't respond; he stared at 'other him'.

"They're coming!" he said to Merle. "They know you're here. Where's Eric?"

Merle scanned the glowing man from head to toe. He backed up further into the elevator.

"Quickly, close the portal." He exclaimed. "Wolfric is on his way through!"

"Did I make you?" Asked Merle.

"Quickly!" exclaimed the glowing man.

"Who are you?" Merle demanded.

He raised his hands to the glowing man and the wind died almost instantly; dust and debris collided with an invisible boundary in front of them.

The glowing man suddenly looked a little crest fallen.

"You don't have the slightest idea who we are." he said as he drew closer. "Do you?"

Merle contorted his face and intensified the shield, but the glowing man simply walked through.

"We don't have time for this!" He raised his finger to Merle's forehead.

"I don't have all the answers," said the glowing man, "but I can give you what you left me."

At the glowing man's touch his entire form dispersed and surged into Merle's forehead.

Merle screamed and clutched his temples, he slid down the elevator wall to the floor.

"Merle!" Alan crouched next to him. "Merle, you alright?". He turned his head to face him.

Two new figures stood at the gateway. To Alan they looked as much animal as man; wolf-like. One was short and burley, the other was skinny and hairless. "Merle!" Alan shouted.

Merle dropped his hands and a serenity came over him. There was an entirely different look behind his eyes, a look Alan had never seen before.

"Actually," replied Merle Lyndsay. "the name is Merlin."

A much larger figure had joined the two at the gate; It froze Alan to his core to look at him. He shrunk away around the corner in the elevator. He had a feeling whatever was about to happen, Merle or Merlin could handle it.

Merlin got to his feet. "Wolfric." He hissed.

"You have not aged well." Wolfric said. "This might actually be a mercy killing."

"You'll never find the prince." Merlin said.

"My son? Semantics. But I'll find him eventually. I just can't have you interfering."

Merlin brought both hands together, electricity danced between them. As shaken as Alan was it was also one of the most awesome things he had ever seen. The discharge intensified until a bolt of lightning struck out towards all three of them. They retreated into the tunnel.

"This isn't over, father." Wolfric said.

Merlin advanced and applied the same force to the outer edge of the tunnel. He feigned a squeezing motion and the doorway slowly collapsed on itself.

"Be gone from this place!" Merlin commanded. The door exploded into energy.

Alan felt a jolt rush past him as it was dispersed.

'Lost in Love' continued through the speaker. Alan conceded to himself it was possible he may have peed a little. He got up off the floor of the elevator and joined Merlin at his side.

"Who were those guys?" Alan struggled to catch his breath.

"I have to find Eric." Merlin said, indifferent to Alan's presence.

"Who's Eric?" Asked Alan.

"I can't remember." Merlin said.

Merlin vanished from his side. An extensive search of the grounds revealed he had really gone this time.

CHAPTER 7:

RUNNING WITH A NEW PACK...

"Attention, guests," A recorded voice announced, "the zoo will be closing in ten minutes. Please make your way to the front gate. We thank you for visiting us and we hope to see you again soon."

Clifford smiled and waved as the last few stragglers left for the evening.

"Thank you." He said to each one as they passed by, "Thank you, have a pleasant evening." He felt like he would develop a cheek spasm if he had to flash his pearly whites for a second longer. Finally, he closed and locked the gate.

"Jesus." He sighed.

Clifford (Kip to his friends and family) was new; he had only worked there a few weeks. He wasn't much of an animal person, but a job was a job and the pay was adequate. He wasn't much of a people person either. He loved the isolation of the night shift. He liked it quiet, he liked it dark and he liked to keep to himself with minimal supervision.

He was one of the night maintenance crew, not security. He was, however, to report anything that seemed out of the ordinary to security and they would deal with it. This suited him just fine. Let them wander into the gorilla habitat and have their arms ripped off, better them than him.

Around 10:00 PM, Kip liked to take his break on the far side of the zoo, near the timber wolf enclosure. Smoking was strictly prohibited on the grounds, but he stumbled on a blind spot in the security camera coverage where he could light up without anyone being the wiser. He even managed to catch a few winks on occasion. Most things were asleep that time of the night. Sometimes the wolves would be awake and watched him intently, but they kept quiet.

"Evening fellas." Said Kip with a slender king-sized pursed in his lips. On that particular night however, the wolves paid him no mind.

The five were gathered in a semi-circle around a newcomer, a sixth. Kip strained to see the new addition in the dark, but he couldn't quite make him or her out. All he could see were its eyes glowing among the shadows.

'They must have added a new one today.' He thought to himself in passing. He really didn't care. He was a little unsettled but not enough to cut into his break. All the same he hurried through his smoke, crushed the butt under his toe and added it to his garbage collection. If security discovered the slightest trace of his private spot they'd install a new camera right on top of it.

"Welcome to the new guy and good night fellas." Kip said and resumed his rounds.

△ △ △

William watched the man leave. He had awakened there, though he had no idea where there was. Obviously, given his surroundings and the fences he was in some sort of menagerie, but his last memory was of walking through the portal in Merlin's cottage. But where was Wolfric? Where were 'Windbag and Shiftless' for that matter? Well, they were no big loss, but it may have been the first time since Wolfric found him that they had been completely separated.

'Finally.' He thought. Was that ungrateful of him? It was the truth.

Wolfric rescued him, clothed him, fed him, protected him, gave him a family. A dysfunctional one but still a family. However so had his mother, but she had done it through love.

In sharing minds with Wolfric there were many feelings, but love wasn't one of them. There was a relentless insecurity and will to dominate; even his revenge on Arthur hadn't seemed enough. Nothing was ever enough.

Perhaps a bit of distance from the pack was the best thing.

After a few moments the timber wolves had settled to William and Timmin's presence; they even became curious. William had never seen a pure wolf face to face. A pack member gingerly approached.

William reached out his open palm for introduction; the wolf sniffed the air and then his hand. There was an instant connection, William sensed an uncomplicated tranquility in the wolf's mind. He found it sad this proud creature had no memory of the forest. He was the alpha of this pack. William raised his head and howled a mute howl to honor him. The alpha could feel William's intent and howled along with him, the other four joined in. William had no idea where he was, and he truthfully didn't care.

Timmin had every idea where they were. It's a little-known fact of interdimensional travel that matter enters a state of flux as it is potentially in multiple plains at one time. A little-known fact that Timmin's people knew; A little-known fact that she exploited. Having found herself free of the iron lantern she hijacked the vortex, and William; and she closed that door behind them.

The wolves gathered around William and nuzzled him. They lay down around him in a huddle and for the first time, in a long time, William allowed himself to drift off to sleep without fear.

Timmin lay on his shoulder and counted the stars, she wasn't familiar with this sky.

CHAPTER 8:
ERIC'S UNEXPECTED GUESTS...

Eric toyed with the idea of quitting his day job to pursue his writing full time. It would have been a monumental risk but perhaps it would also have lit a fire under his ass. Most nights he was too drained to sit at his keyboard or practice his drawing for that matter. It was a long-term aspiration of his to write and publish his own indie comic or graphic novel. Some nights after work he was too tired, other nights his work shift was all the motivation he needed to want to get out of that hell hole and make something of his life. But those times were rare. Like most times, the events of his life conspired against him to make any real progress.

In a corner of his apartment was his writing desk, $50.00 at a thrift store plus $25.00 delivery. It was a heavy pig of a thing he was glad he didn't have to bring it up two flights of steps. Next to his desk, his drafting table and easel, both he constructed from old pallets that were up for grabs at work from shipments of paper. They weren't the prettiest to look at, he eyeballed all his attempts at construction, but they were level and did the job nicely. His studio apartment literally was his studio and his sanctuary.

The project that currently had him inspired was a graphic novel, an adaptation of popular fairy tales and legends. It was based on stories his grandfather told him as a child. Crazy as the old man was, no one could spin a yarn like him; he really brought them to life, like he had been there. If he had stayed with the old man, Eric imagined he might have turned out just as crazy as he was. Perhaps that would have been a good thing for a writer.

As a kid Eric never questioned it, of course. People tend to accept the reality they grow up in as normal. His grandfather was all the family he had ever known. He was a sweet old man but seemed keen on keeping a low profile. When people came to the door of their apartment, he made a game of it to be as quiet as possible until whoever it was stopped knocking and left. But someone must have been paying attention because they didn't stay under the radar for long.

On Eric's seventh birthday he insisted on going to an amusement park. His grandfather said no, but Eric pushed, and the old man relented. They were no further than the sidewalk when a big black car and a grey van came to an abrupt halt in front of them. His grandfather was tranquilized with a dart and carried into the van; child protective services ushered Eric into the car. It all happened so fast. He never saw the old man again, nor was he ever allowed to.

There was a solid year of absolute hell after that. Psychiatrists, psychologists, therapists, peer counselors, they all tried. By his teens he practically had his degree in pop-psychology and was a walking reference of self-help dogma. If all his answers were in him then why did he have to talk to anyone? He had been adopted by a nice family, the Princes; they meant well and largely left him to his own devices, which Eric thought was nice of them. He escaped into his fantasies whenever he could.

It wasn't all wasted, he did really well in high school English without really trying; particularly creative writing, he always got his best marks when the teacher left the writing assignment up to him. Those 'busy work' assignments doled out while the teacher was tending to personal business, nursing a hangover or just didn't feel like teaching. He managed to get some supporting roles in Drama Club productions, he had always been a little theatrical. His guidance counselor suggested he might flourish in some kind of artistic career.

A couple options appealed to him; Animation and Television. He registered to take the entrance exam for the animation program at a local community college, but when he showed up with his portfolio and saw that one drawing from another enrollee that made everything he did look laughable, he excused himself to the washroom and never came back.

So, television it was. He watched enough of it, he knew what was good, he could contribute something. All his friends said he had a gift for writing, television needed writers. Besides, all his friends had chosen their post-secondary paths and Eric already had to do a victory lap to pick up credits just to graduate. How would it look if he was still hanging around for another year?

Two hard drinking and fun filled years later he graduated and came to the realization he had to find a job. Everything was contract work. He decided to work a Joe-job, just to pay the rent, until something more permanent came along. Then the economy tanked. It seemed like every other year he got laid off. Alright, mistakes were made at some jobs, he didn't like to finger point, especially at himself, but more often than not it was just his bad luck. For a decade he was a career temp. It kept things interesting.

'Good life experience to draw on when he wrote his book', he would always tell himself.

That book that followed him from apartment to apartment in the form of half-finished ideas jotted in a stack of dollar store note books. Until one day he spotted the ad in the paper for the call center, He accepted the reality he was no longer in the television industry. Hell, they were all taught using video tape and had only the briefest introductions into digital. His skill set was stale. It was time to settle into a job; although the irony of the situation wasn't lost on him. As much as Eric shied away from the temporary nature of the jobs in Television, his career had been anything but permanent. He could have just taken the leap.

The call center offered benefits, the possibility for advancement and the salary was great. And it was also kind of in television. It was customer service for a big internet and cable giant. It afforded him a nice apartment, okay, it afforded him an apartment. And, he met Rose.

Ever since that day he had felt a lot more inspired to write and draw, if only just to make her think he was interesting.

That night the magic wasn't happening; he was blocked. So, he did what he always did; he switched gears to drawing. He found when he sketched or painted his characters it seemed to bring them to life; their stories, their histories became more vivid in his mind. His graphic novel was called 'Big Bad Wolves', a working title admittedly. The premise excited Eric. He imagined the Big Bad Wolf from all those different stories was one in the same creature; he wondered how he would have affected the lives of the characters he terrorized. What would Little Red Riding Hood's childhood trauma turn her into? How about the Three Little Pigs? Could they become the hero of their own stories or a victim of their past?

At the moment he was working on his interpretation of a fully grown Little Red Riding Hood. He saw her as beautiful, of course. Feminine and sexy but not frail or dainty. She was a frequent subject of his; a bit of an obsession, the unattainable woman of his dreams.

It wasn't often Eric managed to impress himself, but it was one of those times. Painting the human figure wasn't normally one of his strengths, but this one had surpassed all expectation. The eyes, her hair, the hood, it all looked so real. All his attention seemed bent toward the canvass; indeed, everything seemed to bend inward to the portrait.

Eric rubbed his eyes and cracked his neck. Perhaps it was time for a break. He looked around the room, but everything appeared as it should. He got off his stool and stretched. He backed away a few paces and looked at Red's picture from a fresh perspective. He hadn't imagined anything; his perception was tunneling into picture; the immediate reality bent around it.

Dr. Stephen hissed and, after a frantic false start to gain traction on the parquet floor, bolted into Eric's bedroom.

A breeze picked up in the apartment, it tossed papers and knocked over the easel as it gained strength; the anomaly twisted like water in a drain and a dark ... hole...opened. It gave Eric the impression of tornados or hurricanes as viewed from space.

Something shot past his head and very nearly took it off. Eric let out an effeminate shriek as his whole body tensed. A large grapple, or possibly a spear, had embedded in his wall and a long chord trailed from it back into the tunnel. A jumbled, shadowy mass travelled up the cable towards him.

'Did I leave the lid off the turpentine again?', He thought.

He made out two, no, three figures traveling up the tunnel.

"Hold on!" a voice shouted. "We're almost there."

Eric backed up to the spot on the wall he leaned his baseball bat. His hand found the handle without even looking. He wouldn't have categorized himself as a paranoid man, the bat was simply a common-sense precaution in the city. One never knew, for instance, when a singularity would open in your living room and one would be forced to defend oneself... with a piece of wood. He dropped the bat and slid along the wall to his authentic katana blade. His co-workers ridiculed him for getting into an online bidding war over it one lazy evening shift.

'Who's the idiot now, Terry?' He hated Terry, so smug.

He drew his polished, deadly Japanese steel from its holder on his makeshift Buddhist shrine; he went through a whole eastern Zen phase one time, he meant to get back into it.

The three figures cleared the tunnel entrance where gravity seemed to change and allowed them to stand upright. The doorway closed behind them and the tempest in his room subsided.

Eric didn't move, he barely breathed. He was afraid to blink just in case every time he did, they got closer; he'd seen a movie like that. So far, however, the trio hadn't taken any notice of him.

'Maybe they'll just leave.' He thought.

The blade of his sword fell from its hilt and clattered noisily on the floor.

'Shit.'

The three turned their attention to Eric. He gripped his bladeless hilt with both hands, ready for action.

"Hello." One of them said, she was beautiful.

For the moment, Eric couldn't place her, but she looked remarkably familiar. Next to her was some sort of medieval warrior; next to him an anthropomorphized pig-man.

'Did they use lead in oil paints? Mercury?' He tried to remember if that was something he ever looked up online. It could account for the eccentric nature of some artists.

"Hello?" she repeated.

'Hello.'. Had he said that out loud or just in his head?

The three exchanged glances. The pig-man walked over to the wall and yanked the spear. Pieces of drywall crumbled to dust at the baseboard. The pig-man reeled the chord into the gun and hooked it onto his belt. He approached Eric.

"Hel-lo." He said slowly. "Do-you-under-stand-me?"

The room darkened, and Eric's train of thought stopped there for the night.

△ △ △

The morning sun soaked through Eric's eyelids. He was in bed with the covers drawn up to his neck.

"What a horrible nightmare." He yawned.

His blurry eyes came into focus on the stucco ceiling. It reminded Eric of a reverse nighttime sky, an eternal white void with dark stars; he saw faces in the patterns that he often sketched later.

Red came into his field of view and smiled beautifully down at him. Her golden hair fell around his face and grazed his cheek. Eric hadn't had this dream in quite some time, but it was quite welcome.

"I think he's awake" She shouted. "Can you hear me?"

'That's not how the dream goes.'

The pig-man's face joined Red's. His protruding lower teeth and giant snout were definitely never part of the dream.

"Do you think he's some kind of a village idiot?" The pig-man said. He looked deep into Eric's eyes.

"Jacob!" Red gently scolded. "Can you understand us?"

"This is pointless." Jacob said, "Merlin could be anywhere by now"

"Merlin." Eric repeated.

Red and Jacob both looked at him more intently.

"What do you say?" Asked Red.

"Merlin." Eric said.

"You know about Merlin?" Asked Red, she grabbed Eric's face and turned his attention to her.

"No." Eric said. He sat up against his headboard. He gently pushed her hands away from his face.

'Her eyes,', he thought, 'a person could get lost in those eyes.'

Dr. Stephen jumped from his bed into Red's arms. She cradled him, and he purred contentedly.

'Judas,' Eric thought.

Eric's breathing eased. Beyond his bedroom door the warrior was exploring the apartment.

"Hey, Red," he said. "Take a look at this." He came into the room holding one of Eric's canvasses.

'Oh no.' Thought Eric. 'Which one? Please, God, not the ones hidden behind the stack.'

Red's eyes widened, and her jaw dropped slightly. She flipped it around to Eric.

Eric was relieved to see one of the more tasteful portraits of Red; it was an action pose with her staff.

"Where did you get this?" She asked.

Eric's mouth dried, and his throat closed.

"I painted it." He whispered.

"I think you know more than you're telling us." She said, "How could you have possibly painted this? I've never seen you before in my life."

"I don't know, Red." Jacob said, "there is something familiar about him."

"I just made it up.", Eric said. "It's based on stories. Little Red Riding Hood."

"Red is fine." She said. "I think you better start talking."

Eric looked under the covers before he pulled them off. Yes, he was fully clothed. He led them back into the living room to his book shelf. He pulled his edition of The Once and Future King and handed it to Red.

"Merlin had this book." She said.

"Merlin," Eric said, "is a character in this book. Legends have been told about him for centuries. I'm not sure what you mean by trying to find him."

Braum looked through more of Eric's canvases leaned against the wall. He picked one up with the very spitting image of Merlin painted on it.

"Would you mind explaining this?" He asked. Eric had the undivided attention of all three of them.

'What kind of surrealist delusion is this?' He thought. 'The call center finally broke my mind.'

"I don't know what you want me to say." Eric said. "I'm an artist. I write and illustrate. That's a rendition of Merlin the magician. Eric had never noticed how much it looked like the old man, his grandfather. He couldn't fathom the Pandora's box he would open if he uttered that out loud.

Jacob picked up a sketch pad.

"Hey," Eric said, "You can't just go through my stuff like that."

Page after page there was a young Red, Jacob and his brother's, Arthur and Gwen, it was all there.

Red scanned Eric's face, she cupped her hands on his cheeks and turned it from side to side. Eric couldn't say he didn't mind that part.

"Tell me your name?" She asked.

Eric only partly heard her.

"Huh?" he managed.

"Your name?" She insisted.

"Eric." He said, He would have confessed anything to her.

"Is it really you?" Her face lit up.

"It's really me." Eric clasped his hands over hers and beamed right back at her.
"Who am I?"

△ △ △

He found himself sitting with them at his table telling them his life story over a round a drinks and reheated pizza. The pig man, Jacob, really enjoyed it; Eric was glad he hadn't ordered it with ham or pepperoni. After a few beers his heart rate had managed to settle down.

He wasn't sure how helpful he could be. His earliest memories were of Merlin and him. And while their family life could have been categorized as pleasant, his home schooling, in retrospect, was strange. Merlin taught him mathematics of course, and the old man had an astounding grasp of history; but more than anything else Eric was forced to memorize endless volumes of folktales and legends. His lessons dwelled on everything there was to know about The Big Bad Wolf. No matter how many nightmares it gave Eric, Merlin insisted. To this day Eric wasn't really even a dog person.

But good or bad it was the reality he grew up with; and when he was torn from everything he knew it was months before he could talk. He still tended toward isolation more than social interaction. Therapy had helped a great deal but there were no miracle cures.

'Maybe this is a relapse.' He considered. 'Do I have to go back to counseling?'

His foster family tried their best, and though Eric came to love them very much, he couldn't get out on his own fast enough. He called them every couple of months, visited during the holidays. But he was his own creature, best left alone.

"There's not much more to say." Eric said. "Child protective services was adamant I never have any contact with Merlin. I never saw him again. Although people who are considered a danger to themselves or others are typically confined to some sort of hospital. I wish I could be more helpful. It's not a period of my life I care to dwell on."

"I don't understand why he didn't use his sorcery to escape with you." Red said.

"He talked about magic on occasion,", Eric said, "but he was very keen on me developing my own talents, as he put it. I never saw any magic. Even though he didn't have a job and we always seemed to have food in the house. You tend not to question things at that age. As for escaping he got hit with a tranquilizer dart before we knew what was going on."

Eric's hand closed into a soft fist on the table.

"Wolfric could have found him by now." Jacob said.

"I wouldn't worry too much," Red said, "He's nothing if not resourceful. He might even manage to find us first. Although given what we know now, perhaps it was for the best Eric was taken from him."

"Merlin is the only one who can open the portal back to our world." Jacob said, "and Wolfric is still out there. Like it or not we need to find him."

"I suppose." Red said. "What does one do when they want to find someone in your world?"

"Oh," Eric said, "well, the police could be helpful, or an internet search I suppose."

"What's an internet?" Asked Jacob.

$$\triangle \ \triangle \ \triangle$$

A computer terminal blinked to life in the darkness. Frank snored away in his chair, his feet propped up on the console and an empty bag of Cheetos dangled from his limp fingers.

His supervisor didn't mind naps on duty; he was his supervisor. Frank was one of the finest computer programmers in the industry (he would say the world). And while he was technically an independent contractor, his benefactor paid him a very generous retainer and supplied him with anything he needed. He customized the computer system of his dreams; money was no object, legalities were 'handled'. He had carte blanche to use his system or pursue any projects or hobbies he wanted; there were only two stipulations.

First and foremost, the job he was hired to do was to design and run an algorithm that monitored every search engine on the planet; the algorithm would alert him when very specific key words or criteria were used, report those findings back to his employer. Second, he was to be on call 24/7; he was never to leave his department, anything he needed would be brought to him, anything. It was an introvert's dream. His employer even had him do a little hacking every so often; rival companies, prospective acquisitions, basic industrial espionage.

A moderate alarm and the light from his monitors gradually intruded on his sleep. Frank dropped the bag of Cheetos, mumbled and scratched himself. He tried to sit up, but his legs had fallen asleep; they flopped to the floor as he nearly fell out of his chair. He winced as pins and needles shocked his calves out of atrophy.

He wiggled the mouse and type 'ctrl-alt-del' to bring up his login screen; he scanned his thumb on the biometric reader, he hated passwords.

A red, rotary dialed, land line rang on the desk next to him. A few years ago, Frank had updated his boss's mobile phone with a notification if the algorithm had found anything; his boss liked to be kept in the loop, he insisted, he was very hands on and kind of intense. Frank had never actually met him in person. They had talked on the phone, they had played online chess occasionally, but he had never laid eyes on Rick Wolfe. Two of his associates came down from time to time to check on things. A lanky guy who constantly made inappropriate advances, and a short, barrel chested hot head. They were both quite stupid and they both gave Franks the creeps.

Frank took a deep breath, steadied his hand and picked up the receiver.

"Yes sir." Said Frank, "Yes, I was just about to call you. It's the strongest match yet and it seems to meet all your criteria. The IP is tracing, and I should have an address for you shortly.... Thank you, sir."

$$\triangle \ \triangle \ \triangle$$

Eric tried to explain how the computer and the internet worked (to the extent he understood the technology himself). Jacob was fascinated and desperately wanted to take everything apart to see what was inside, Eric promised they could do that later.

Red guided Eric with possible search criteria; Merlin, Arthur, Eric, The Big Bad Wolf, they got lots of websites about fairytales, but nothing came together in any significant way.

Eric looked at the clock, it was almost 11:00 PM.

'Christ', he thought, 'I have to be at work in seven hours.'

Thank God it was Friday, things were slow on Fridays; there were less calls and people barely showed up. He suggested it might be better to resume their search in the morning. They all agreed.

Eric was concerned how long he would be playing host. He still wasn't completely convinced it all wasn't some kind of psychotic break.

He got Jacob and Braum set up on his pull-out sofa. Braum was the only part of this he couldn't reconcile to a delusion. Eric had never written about him as a character and he was certain Merlin had never mentioned him. All the same, there was something familiar and disconcerting about the man.

Eric gave Red his own bed and he took the cot he kept in the closet; he could handle it, but he would never subject guests to 'the rack'. It occurred to him every now and then that he should just toss that thing.

He was still a little hungry. Midway through the evening he had ordered more pizza as they all seemed to enjoy it. Red and Braum didn't eat much; Jacob devoured two large meat lovers. He wondered if he should have told Jacob what was in the sausage; but then again, he wasn't sure what the rules were with pig men from other dimensions or if it was even cannibalism. It was far too late, and he wasn't nearly drunk enough for a philosophical debate of that magnitude.

He bid them all good night and turned out the lights. But sleep never found him and all night long he stared at the ceiling.

CHAPTER 9:

LAYING DOWN ROOTS...

The morning sun reached the wolf enclosure early; a beam of light caught William's eye and gently roused him from his sleep. His newly adopted pack nestled snuggly around him; he couldn't recall ever feeling more at peace.

He felt no such closeness in the other pack, Wolfric's pack; least of all Gail and Shifter. He didn't know most of them personally. The vast majority were conscripted from this world, bitten and turned. A lot of the younger ones they abducted (liberated as Wolfric preferred to call it), William felt a strong sense of responsibility for, and a tremendous amount of guilt. Rose and the others hadn't asked for any of it. When you read enough minds, you gain a larger perspective. There was so much he felt like he had to make amends for. Despite all that he felt honor bound to Wolfric, who was nowhere around at the moment.

He looked down at his chest, Timmin's eyes were already fixed on his and she smiled a good morning. He felt a momentary but distinct butterfly in his stomach. She traced her fingers through his fur. The tip of his tail unconsciously began to flit.

The moment was interrupted by a loud metallic clank and the shrill squeal of the enclosure door opening. The pack sat up and hid William from view. From behind them he saw a man enter the cage and drop pieces of raw meat on the ground. Despite William's domesticated life, his mouth still watered.

He waited until the man turned to leave then leapt over the pack and grasped him by the head with his long fingers. The man gasped, not even getting so much as a scream out. William drew from the man's mind, the layout of the Zoo, a working knowledge of the city and anything useful about this world; his name was Tim.

William took Tim's keys; the park would be open soon and they had to leave. He wanted to liberate his new friends however he suspected they were safer right where they were. The pack agreed not to eat Tim and to allow his people to collect him. William bid them a heartfelt goodbye and vowed to return for them one day.

△ △ △

The zoo was on the edge of a wooded area; beyond that, towering over the tree-line, the city. There were shining monoliths of glass the likes of which neither William nor Timmin had ever seen, but there were also buildings of stone that looked more familiar. Wolfric had told him stories of this world but he was never allowed to go; something about William's connection to him that allowed Wolfric easy passage back, but William never believed that. Gale and Shifter were born here world and were permitted to travel with him; something about Wolfric not trusting them unsupervised. That part William believed.

When they were first brought over William tried to get along with them; for his Wolfric's sake. He was the first born and they were family, after all; but they were more like the annoying little cousins whom, at best, you promised not to throat punch. They constantly tried to win Wolfric's favor; who neither gave it to them nor discouraged the attempts. It was sad and cruel; even William managed to pity them at times. They were the youngest, however; it afforded them a lot of leeway. They were spoiled, as far as William was concerned; at least he wasn't expected to be his brothers' keeper. His connection to Wolfric would always be stronger than theirs.

Could Wolfric still feel him now? Was it a matter of time before they were discovered? William found himself starting to hope he could stay hidden, just a while longer.

Timmin knew what was on William's mind; it was highly unlikely they would be found. She had devoted a considerable amount of concentration to shielding them both from any detection. With a little practice such a spell became a permanent background function like a heartbeat. Besides, it was no time to worry about such things when they had an unexplored forest right in front of them.

Timmin was always ready to make the acquaintance of new trees. She flew in ahead of William who stood there, still pondering the scale of the buildings. When he heard the flutter of her wings stop, he rushed to her side.

She was on her knees amid the orange pine needles of the forest floor. He touched the small of her back and reached out to her mind.

'What's wrong?' He asked.

'This forest is too quiet.' She replied.

'Dead?'

'No. It's just, not alive.'

The trees, the animals, nothing responded like it should; none of it had that spark. Everything around them was cold and silent. That simply would not stand in Timmin's mind. Everything had a right to live, really live.

'Don't move.' She said.

William looked down and she smiled as their eyes connected.

She performed a series of deep stretches, a form of fairy yoga, and flexed her wings. She had never attempted what she was about to do but as she saw it she didn't have a choice.

'Oh,' she said, 'and I'll need some of your lifeforce.'

'What?'

'Trust me.'

She took to the air and started slow laps around William. She kissed his nose on one pass. He tried to follow her as she went by each time but as she got faster it just made him dizzy. He trusted her.

He felt a breeze as she picked up speed; her trail of light became many trails the faster she went until he was cocooned in her radiance. William had the distinct impression he was being lifted off the ground, he didn't fight it. An invigorating warmth washed over him, followed by complete euphoria. He instinctively raised his hands to touch the wall of his cocoon. He felt an aching drain, but just as much a willing release of energy to Timmin. The chrysalis exploded at his touch and William fell to his knees. The forest was bathed in a brilliant glow as Timmin circled wider and weaved around every tree. Her wings beat with a fury she could have never achieved on her own; a fury that climaxed in a spectacular shower of pixie dust.

It fell like snow all around them; William held out his hand to catch some. Every speck hit him with a jolt of excitement. He felt like he could fly, which he could have done if he were aware of it at that moment. The pixie dust disappeared into the ground, into every tree and into every curious animal who stood by to watch. None of the creatures knew what was happening, they were all about to scatter when everything changed. They gathered around William and Timmin. The trees rooted deeper, they looked heartier and lusher as they opened up to the experience. Moss grew thick on rocks and vines twisted around anything they could find. Life multiplied and took notice of the two strangers.

Through Timmin, William could hear the entire forest rejoicing. She landed on his arm, she was more beautiful than ever. There was a wisdom and a quiet grace to her he hadn't truly appreciated until just then. She smiled and winked at him. The animals approached them without fear; Timmin and William mingled with their new friends as they strolled through the newly enchanted forest.

At length they emerged at a clearing. They bid their new friends farewell. All along William and Timmin's path, pods sprouted from the ground. Inside the pods, small wispy lights flickered. Timmin knew very well what was in them. She couldn't, after all, leave the forest without guardians. She hoped they would return to check on their progress, but she knew they could handle things.

They were their children, after all.

CHAPTER 10:

THE SEARCH BEGINS...

M erlin decided to be on a bus traveling into the city; he didn't need to be, but it gave him time to think. He had trouble reconciling the information given to him by his image. There were vague images of a king and queen, a band of trusted companions, and an infant; he assumed that was Eric, but the child could have looked like anyone by now.

'Unless,' He thought, 'of course!' His personal effects would still be at the hospital. It hadn't occurred to him before since he couldn't remember anything before the hospital. He pulled a carboard banker's box out of the air and sat it beside him; the name M. Lindsay was written on the side in black marker.

Merlin looked around to see if anyone was looking. Everyone around him on the bus was still asleep. He had put them to sleep so he didn't alarm them with his sudden arrival; however, he woke the bus driver when they almost steered into an oncoming tractor trailer.

Just inside the box, stuffed down on top, was a long grey coat. He admired the garment and immediately put it on; it suited him, presumably because he had picked it out. Plus, hospital pajamas might draw unwanted attention. There was an old pipe and a pack of tobacco, he put those in the inside breast pocket almost instinctually. He found a small handwritten journal, inside was what appeared to be spells, he put it aside for the moment.

Lastly, at the bottom of the box was a wallet. There was eleven dollars inside, no identification and a picture of a smiling young boy.

"Eric." He whispered. That was it though. He strained to remember more but it was all a clouded blur just on the edge of his perception.

He pocketed the wallet and leafed through the journal. Many of the first pages had been torn out and the rest was completely blank. He wondered if anyone had the missing pages and if he should be concerned about that; or perhaps it was useless information he had destroyed all on his own. Was the book nothing more than a notepad?

The bus pulled into a depot just inside the city limits. The driver announced it was their last stop, however Merlin was already inside the terminal; he was studying a big map posted on the wall before the bus had even stopped. He passed his hand over the map, slowly, in the hopes his powers could divine a location; nothing jumped out at him. He wondered if he could even do what he had just attempted. The powers were still relatively new to him, but he was always open to experimentation.

He needed a computer; he liked computers, magic seemed to blend well with technology; energy was energy no matter what form. He spied an unattended information booth. He put himself in front of the computer terminal; no one paid him the slightest bit of attention, he willed them not to.

He wasn't the most tech-savvy; however, he had some experience with computers, properly supervised, at the hospital. He unlocked the screen with a simple gesture; a lock was a lock, be it a door or password.

On the desktop there was a virtual globe of the earth. If that didn't suffice as a map, Merlin didn't know what would. Perhaps he would have more successful than with the map on the wall.

He retrieved the picture of Eric from his wallet and focused on the boy's face. He wished he could remember anything. He placed his other hand up to the screen and concentrated. The digital globe rotated against its virtual backdrop of stars.

"Eric," he whispered, "where are you?"

The view over the map zoomed in; North America, then Canada, further down into Ontario, then Toronto and finally settling on a street and an address. Merlin sensed the stop and opened his eyes. He could see the rooftop of what could have been any building in the city. There was a button on the screen that brought up a curb side view of the building and an address. He made the screen print.

△ △ △

Frank's control room blinked to life a second time in as many days. He didn't know what to think of it besides the horrendous timing. He was in the middle of a campaign in 'Call To Valor'; and that kid in Norway was going down. He had the perfect sniper location picked out, he was, absolutely, untouchable. Ok, so he hacked the game to give himself the vantage point and unlimited ammo, but that little prick, Lars, was not to be underestimated.

The alarm persisted.

"Dammit!" Frank cursed.

He brought up the window for his algorithm on a separate screen. Someone had just searched out the same address he had provided Rick. He was surprised the curtesy phone wasn't already ringing. He was about to make the call himself when, across the war-torn landscape of the game he spotted his quarry.

"Guten tag! You little prick." Said Frank.

He took careful aim with his rifle and smiled.

It was late, he could inform Rick in the morning. It would be fine.

CHAPTER 11:
MR. POPULARITY...

ric's mental state notwithstanding, Jacob's freight-train of a snore made sleep virtually impossible. It was 5:00AM, Eric had to be at work in two hours; or did he? Did he dare leave his 'guests' alone in the apartment? Would the let him leave at all? What if they couldn't find Merlin? Was he off the hook? Would they leave him alone?

The doorbell rang.

'Who the hell could that be?' Eric thought. 'Rumpelstiltskin? Stewart-Friggin-Little?"

Jacob and Braum sat up; Red was at the bedroom door, staff in hand.

The 'Amazon Warrior Princess' 'The Huntsman' and the 'Pig-man'. How on earth could Eric explain them to anyone? Perhaps there was a ren-fair in town; or a comicon; maybe they were all going 'LARPing'.

There was a loud knock at the door, more of a pound. Eric frantically motioned for the others to get in the bedroom and begged their silence with an adamant finger to his lips.

The mystery caller pounded three more times in slow succession. Eric composed himself and took a deep breath. He peered through the spy hole in his door.

"Hey." Jacob said, "I came up with that idea too."

Eric shot his head around and desperately pointed them back into the room out of sight.

It was a police officer, of course it was. Who else could it have been? Eric cracked the door as wide as the chain allowed.

"Good evening," Eric said, "I mean, good morning officer. What can I do for you?"

The cop smiled a broad toothy grin but there was a distinctly cold demeanor in his eyes, his freakishly big eyes.

"Eric Prince?" Said the officer.

"Yes, eye-fficer... I mean Officer?" replied Eric.

"Could you please undo the chain, Mr. Prince?"

"Is there something wrong, officer?"

The officer's smile tensed, and his eyes squinted subtly.

"The chain please, Mr. Prince."

'Shit.' Eric nodded and closed the door. His hand trembled as he undid the chain. He became a little light headed. Did he have to open the door? Didn't they need a warrant or writ or something? He took a breath and opened the door to shoulder width.

"How can I help you, officer?" He said.

"Are you the same Eric Prince who was once in the custody of one Merle Lyndsay?"

'What the hell?', Eric thought.

"Yes." Eric said, "I mean it's been years since I've seen him."

'Not a coincidence. Not a coincidence at all.'

"Has he tried to contact you at all?"

"Can I ask what this is about?"

"Absolutely. It seems Mr. Lyndsay has managed to escape from the Acrewood Psychiatric Hospital a couple days ago. Would you know of his whereabouts?"

It might have been Eric's imagination, but the cop appeared to edge closer; uncomfortably close into his personal space bubble. He also glanced over Eric's shoulder into the apartment numerous times.

"No," Eric said, "Honestly I haven't had contact with him in years. Did you need me for anything?"

"No," said the officer. Eric found it very strange he didn't have a name tag. "we're just covering all our bases. You understand."

"Sure." Eric said.

"If he does happen to contact you, you'll be sure to notify us?"

"I will do that."

"Excellent, well I'm sorry to disturb you at this hour of the morning."

"Hey, anything I can do to help our men in uniform." Smiled Eric.

"Hey, I don't suppose I could trouble you for a glass of water." Said the officer.

Eric paused for an incriminatingly long time.

"What?" he said. "Oh, um, of course."

Eric backed away from the door, Officer Nobody pushed forward almost immediately.

"Hey, nice place you got here." He said.

"Um, thanks" Replied Eric. His heart was nearly bursting out of his ribcage.

The leftover pizza and plates were on the table; the cot was still in the middle of the floor.

"Having a sleep over?" The cop asked.

"Ha..." Eric fumbled for a glass in the cupboard. He ran the tap over his hand until it was cold and filled the glass. He restrained a trembling hand long enough to hand it to the officer.

"Thanks, you are a life saver!" Said the Officer. "It's been so dry out there, have you found it dry?"

Eric smiled and nodded. The officer slowly downed the water, not breaking eye contact once to even blink. He smiled with a satisfied gasp.

"Thank you so much for your time, and the water." He said. "I really should be going."

The officer half turned to leave but stopped himself.

"Oh, there's one other thing." He said. "In cases like this, when a dangerous offender is involved we would be remise if we didn't do our due diligence. Our cyber division tracked certain key word searches back to your IP address. You wouldn't happen to know anything about that, would you Mr. Prince?"

Eric frowned in thought for a moment, trying to come up with anything to respond. Nothing came. He bolted from his apartment in nothing more than his jeans, a t-shirt and one sock; somehow, in the middle of the night he always managed to lose one.

The officer dropped the pretense and Shifter finished his glass of water. He walked it over to Eric's sink, rinsed it out and dried it thoroughly. He made a lucky choice of cupboard on his first try and replaced the glass with the rest of them. He loved it when they ran. He jogged on the spot a few times and stretched; which, for him, was a wholly inadequate description.

"You're not taking him."

Shifter had already smelled the girl, the pig, and what's-his-name, in the apartment. He was glad, all the way over he was afraid there would be absolutely no challenge in this at all.

"Well," Shifter said, "it doesn't look like he felt too safe with you guys either." He laughed and turned. Red had her staff at the ready, Braum had his bow trained on Shifter's head and Jacob bared an axe of substantial heft.

"Tell you what." Shifter said. "You call to him, and then I'll call to him. And whoever he comes to can take him back to his forever home.", he really cracked himself up.

"You guys wait here, I'll go get him." He leapt across the room and smashed through a window. Two arrows stuck in the wall just behind him.

Shifter landed on all fours, on the sidewalk below. His blood pumped; the chase, it was what he was bred for. The scent of the boy's fear was absolutely intoxicating. Shifter homed in on Eric without any trouble. He was nearly across the street; he narrowly missed the front bumper of a tow truck before he ducked down an alley. Shifter hopscotched across the roofs of two passing cars as he crossed. It was a pitiful challenge; if he had any sense of fair play he'd have almost felt bad for the kid.

Red, Jacob and Braum (after a few wrong turns in Eric's building) finally emerged from the front door. They froze in their tracks in the middle of the street. The sun had come up and their eyes strained to adjust in the morning light. Jacob, in particular, was absolutely gob smacked; the massive multileveled structures; a road, flatter and smoother than the finest roads he'd ever seen; and the strange horseless carriages that sped passed them, he had died and gone to technological heaven. A particularly large carriage came to an abrupt stop next to them. A mighty horn sounded. There were over a dozen people inside the carriage and the driver did not seem pleased; he waved with a strange single fingered gesture the three of them were not familiar with. They waved back and crossed the street. Another carriage screeched to a stop, this one came in the opposite direction. The driver cursed at them in a strange dialect and offered up the same gesture.

"Everyone here seem to be in a dreadful hurry." Observed Red. "And they're very rude."

They cleared the path of the carriage and the flow of traffic resumed. This new world was loud and smelled strange.

"Which way do we go?" Red said.

Jacob had already started down the alley. His nose never lied.

"This way." He shouted, already far ahead of them.

Eric reached a dead end. He tried all the doors, each was either locked or had no handle. He tried to push a dumpster under a low hanging fire escape ladder, but he couldn't budge the thing; and besides he couldn't even do a chin-up, it was a fitness goal of his... had he ever went to the gym. He thought his membership had expired but they were apparently still taking money out of his account, he had meant to get around to dealing with that.

"Hell-ooooo!" A voice echoed around the corner and turned into a howl.

Eric saw limited options, he climbed inside the dumpster and closed the lid. The smell was rank. Over in the corner a raccoon paused, mid apple core, and studied Eric with a confused glare. Eric backed himself into his corner hoping they would each respect their mutual boundaries. He spied the alley through an old rust hole near eye level.

Shifter skipped around the corner with a smile on his face and death metal in his heart. He casually sauntered into the vicinity of the dumpster.

"Oh, no." He said in a dull cadence of enunciated words, "It would appear my quarry has eluded me."

It didn't take very powerful deductive reasoning, even for Shifter; Eric's scent was unmistakable, the dumpster notwithstanding. And while mercy wasn't one of his virtues, patience was; he loved to twist the knife, his ego insisted on it, he could derive pleasure no other way.

Besides, he had bet Gale $50.00 he could capture the human all by himself.

"Pay up, blow-hard." He called up to the roof tops.

"Wait for it, numb-nuts" A reply echoed back down.

Gale, and a small band of the pack (they were all kind of a clique), followed Shifter's progress from their vantage point. He almost wanted to help the girl and the pig and what's-his-head, but he was a wolf of his word; that and they were just about to come around the corner anyway.

"Where's the prince?" Red said. The three of them had fanned out to cover the exit.

"Hey, Red.", Shifter said, "be with you in a second. Gale!"

The trio closed in on him.

"Okay, Gale." he repeated, "Stop kiddin' around. You win."

"One hundred dollars." Gale said from up above.

"I swear to Dog, Gale!"

"One hundred."

The trio were practically on top of him.

"Fine," Shifter said. "a hundred."

The trio spread out to circle him. Shifter backed up against the dumpster. The woodsman's bow was trained right at his head. Shifter was both terrified and slightly aroused. There was still no sign of his brother.

"Gale!" he hissed.

"Anyone who'd pay a hundred," Gale said, "could most certainly swing one twenty-five."

"You are such an asshole." Shifter said.

"Tick tock stretch."

"Fine, one twenty-five."

A steady wind picked up behind the trio as Gale gently descended on his breath. He blew the off balance as the rest of the pack scaled down along the walls.

Eric shrieked as the hairless, mutant-wolf-thing slammed down on the lid just over his head. All the same, there was something familiar about him and his companions.

His back pocket vibrated, and he jumped a second time; was he hit? His pocket buzzed again. It was his phone, he still had his phone on him. He reached under himself to grab it; it was a text from Rose.

'See you in a bit', she messaged, 'extra-large double-double?'

Eric almost laughed; he was most definitely going to miss work.

'Sorry,' He replied, 'I don't think I'm going to make it in, feeling like trash.'

'Oh no. ☺ '

'Yeah. Pretty down in the dumps right now.'

Eric watched the gutter brawl that was going on though the peep hole.

'It would be a struggle for me to get there.' He replied.

'That's a shame,' Rose said, 'The big man himself is touring the facility today.'

'Rick Wolfe?'

'None other. You sure you can't make it in?'

'That actually would have been cool', Eric thought; The man was basically a rock star. Though she was tight lipped on the subject. Eric sometimes got the feeling she knew him. She absolutely lit up when the subject was broached, and she seemed to have more than casual insights about him. Sure, perhaps Eric was a little jealous, on the other hand the guy was very handsome and in the interviews he saw, charming as hell. There was an energy to him people just responded to. It could have been the billions of dollars as well.

'Feel better,' Rose said, 'I'll miss you, maybe I'll swing by later.'

Eric exhaled a wistful sigh. How could you not love her?

'She'll probably take her breaks with Terry today; smug-ass Terry, dick.'

Someone, or something, slammed against the dumpster and Eric was shaken back to reality; he screamed again.

The raccoon seemed a little distressed as well.

"Don't worry, little buddy." Eric said, "We'll get out of this."

The raccoon gawked blankly through its furry, black mask, dropped the apple core and escaped through a small opening rusted into the floor of the dumpster.

Gale pounced at Jacob; Jacob deflected, tripped Gale and tossed him into the side of the dumpster. Gale blustered back and sent Jacob against a wall.

Red had dispatched some pack members, but the rest had taken a stand with Gale to defend the dumpster.

Shifter's tail opened one of the trash bin lids. He extended his neck down inside for a better look. There was Eric, phone pressed to his ear; the horror on the boy's face was priceless.

"Hey, buddy!" Shifter said.

"Yes, I'd like to report a, a... gang war." Eric said into the phone.

"Now why'd you have to go and do that?" Shifter said.

His tail snatched Eric's phone.

"The alley near Eleventh and Bleeker!" Eric shouted as it left his grip.

Shifter crushed the phone and constricted his tail around Eric's torso.

"Get your, whatever the hell, off me!" Eric struggled.

Shifter's tail found Eric's head and covered his mouth.

"Shh," Shifter said, "there will be time for that later.

Braum had ran out of arrows and continued to fight hand to hand with his bow. Jacob was preoccupied with three small pack members; he slammed himself against a wall with the hope of checking them off his back and shoulder; they were small, and not particularly strong but they were persistent.

Shifter leapt to a wall and proceeded to climb to the roof, Eric in tow. Perhaps he wouldn't owe Gale the one twenty-five after all. He giggled to himself and hummed a merry toon as he scaled the brick.

A police chopper appeared overhead and a squad in full tactical gear came around the corner to block the exit. Everyone was momentarily distracted; Jacob and his three assailants halted mid-skirmish.

"Nobody move!" shouted the squad leader. None of the officers knew what they were looking at.

Shifter paused for only a moment and continued his ascent. An overzealous tactical officer opened fire; a staccato of bullets pelted the wall with some of them hitting their mark. Shifter hollered in pain and dropped Eric to the ground. He reached the rooftop and scrambled away.

Gale sent a gust of wind at the officers and knocked them back; he turned his face to the helicopter and sent it crashing on a nearby rooftop. With one more breath he carried himself over the rooftop as well. The rest of the pack scattered up the walls or just seemed to disappear into the shadows.

Eric crumpled into the fetal position on the ground, writhing to refill his lungs with air.

The tactical officers regrouped and trained their weapons on the remaining suspects.

"Drop your weapons!" said the squad leader.

Red, Jacob and Braum looked at one another. These men were obviously some sort of knights or sheriffs; clearly here to maintain order.

"We mean you no harm." Red said.

"Now!" said the squad leader.

Red nodded to Jacob and Braum; all three complied with the order.

"Down on your knees with your hands behind your head!"

Again, the trio obliged.

Gale watched from the rooftop as Red, the pig, and what's-his-head were loaded into a van. The boy was carried off in an ambulance with a police escort.

Shifter stood over Gale's shoulder, his arms crossed.

"You let him get away." He said.

Gale thrust his fist backwards, and even though he didn't look, it found its target. Shifter let out a shrill yelp and fell unconscious into the gravel rooftop.

They hadn't been specifically ordered to go after the prince, but he was sure the Alpha would admire their initiative.

CHAPTER 12:

ALPHA KNOWS BEST...

"You idiots." Wolfric leaned forward in his chair; his elbows rested on his desk and his hands were clasped below his chin. His eyes delivered an equal measure of disbelief and contempt.

"Under no circumstances were you to go after him without consulting me." Wolfric said. "Now he's in police custody and you've been seen."

"But, boss." Shifter quickly rephrased, "My Alpha, don't you basically own the police?"

"So not the point." Wolfric said, still quite calmly. It was the calm that scared Gale and Shifter the most. The Alpha was focused and deliberate in his actions. He was patient and he seldom missed.

"He is pack, he is family, he's already an employee. He would have been at work today, I could have laid the ground work for a strong relationship."

"We couldn't risk the old man finding him first." Shifter said.

"The old man is nothing!" Wolfric slammed his hands on the desk.

"We stopped the girl and the pig from getting to him" Gale said.

"They are inconsequential. And that was complete luck, you had no idea they were there." Wolfric said. "I don't understand how it's possible they found him first."

Wolfric pushed the intercom button on his phone.

"Sheila, darling." He said, a charming smile engaged his face and voice.

"Yes, my Alpha?"

"Sheila, could you have Frank come see me in my office right away."

"Right away sir."

"What would I do without you?"

"You'll never have to find out."

He released the button. "You could learn a thing or two from your sister."

"You have a legion of followers." Shifter said. "What makes Prince so special?"

Wolfric stood up from his seat, it was easy for Shifter to forget how much he towered over them from behind his desk.

"The only two reasons you will ever need in your miserable lives are 'because it's mine' or 'because I said so.'"

Perhaps the most terrifying thing about Rick Wolfe was that he was always happy, always. His public image was laid back, even beguiling, but Frank had the ultimate backstage pass to everything; the digital footprints painted a very different picture. Frank was paid to get his hands dirty too, he provided Rick with all the insider information he could; Frank had no problem with that and would have slept very well at night, except that smile. Obtaining the information was the easy bit, It was what was done with the information after the fact; A CEO dies, a company gets purchased, a chilling pattern presented itself; the fact was Rick Wolfe Enterprises was built over the river Styx and Rick might just have been Hades himself. That smile, that terrible smile, it gave Frank night terrors. That was just on a screen. But actual physical contact with the man.

The elevator neared the top floor; Rick's office and penthouse all in one. He rarely left his tower. Frank felt like the pit of his stomach was somehow tethered to the ground floor; it sank deeper the closer he got to the top; until, of course, Frank finally arrived. He prayed for the cable to snap and to plummet to oblivion. No such luck, the doors opened. Reception was just inside off the elevator and beyond that was Rick's office.

The office was huge, Rick's desk faced the door, so he was the first person anyone would see when they arrived.

"Francis!" Rick said. "How the heck are you? Come in! Can I get you anything?"

"Uh, no thank you, Mr. Wolfe." Frank managed.

"Do you like wheatgrass?"

"Excuse me, sir?"

"Wheatgrass smoothies. Sheila introduced me to them, cleansing. I'm all about them lately."

"No, thank you sir."

"Well if there's anything I can get you, you let me know. Ok?"

"Did you want to see, Mr. Wolfe?"

"You're focused, you're on point, I respect the hell out of you for that. Of course, come on in, have a seat."

Frank took a seat on the massive sectional by the bay window that overlooked the whole city. It was an impressive view, perfect for Rick to look down on his domain, Frank imagined.

Across from Frank were Rick's two... assistants (henchmen?) Gale and Shifter; Frank assumed those were nicknames, or else they had a very unfortunate parentage.

Rick finished a text on his phone, got up from his desk and joined them on the sofa.

"So, Frank." He said enthusiastically, "how's things? You comfortable down there, do you need anything?"

"No sir," said Frank; the intense hospitality unnerved him.

"So, Frank, we have an issue."

"What sort of issue, Mr. Wolfe?"

"Well," Rick said, "that address your algorithm came up with. It belongs to a, well let's just call him an employee we're trying to talent manage. My two colleagues here paid him a visit recently and employed some aggressive recruitment tactics that I didn't approve. And I'll deal with them accordingly, I'm just curious how they managed to get the address. You didn't happen to share the information with them, did you?"

"Share it sir?"

"Hey, you look nervous, don't be, we can't help one another if we don't bring these things out in the open. Don't worry, you are a valuable member of the team."

"They said you wanted them to go over there and they needed the address."

Gale and Shifter's eyes remained unflinchingly on Frank; Gale's narrowed slightly.

"Ok, I understand," Rick said, "Obviously there was a miscommunication and I'll own that. Anyway, going forward, I'd much rather you report any information directly to me and then I will make the call if I deem it necessary to share, ok?"

"You got it, Mr. Wolfe."

"Perfect. You're doing a hell of a job down there. I just can't say that enough."

"Thank you, Mr. Wolfe."

Was that it? Frank's stomach loosened, and his breathing was easier. He stood up from the couch.

"One more item Frank." Rick's tone softened and his demeanor stiffened ever so slightly. "An interested third party from a 'rival company' was also present at that same address. It just seems highly improbable to me this group would have had the same information. You wouldn't be moonlighting your services on the side, would you Frank?"

"No Sir, Mr. Wolfe," Frank's voice waivered, "I would never."

"Of course, Frank," Rick said, "Of course, just had to be sure. You understand."

"Absolutely, Mr. Wolfe."

Rick stood up and put his hands on Frank's shoulders.

"Loyalty is very important to me Frank. Loyalty and honesty. Without Honesty you don't know who to trust, without loyalty you can't trust anyone." Frank felt a burning in his shoulders or was it a piercing. He looked down at Rick's hands, they were somewhat hairier than he remembered, his nails were in desperate need of a manicure; and Ricks five o'clock shadow seemed to really come in the last few moments. His smile was yellower.

"I understand Mr. Wolfe." Said Frank.

Ricks features softened once again.

"That's all I can ask." Rick beamed cheerfully. "Thanks for your time, Frank, I know you're busy as hell down there."

"Anything for you, Mr. Wolfe."

Gale and Shifter's eyes were still securely planted on Frank. He turned to leave while the getting was good.

"One more thing." Rick said.

Frank stopped, he felt himself sinking into anxiety once again.

"I'd like Sheila to job shadow you for the next little while if that's ok. Show her the ropes. I think you'll find she's quite the little 'hacker' in her own right. I'm sure you two would have loads in common. God forbid you ever took ill, I'd love to maintain the staffing levels in your department. Plus, now more than ever it's important to acknowledge the strengths of women in the workplace. You understand."

"Yes Mr. Wolfe." Said Frank. There it was.

"Sisters are doin' it for themselves! Huh, Frank? She will be down later this afternoon."

"Yes Sir, Mr. Wolfe."

"Perfect, Go easy on her." Rick pointed playfully at Frank.

"Absolutely sir."

Rick walked Frank towards the elevator with a friendly arm around his shoulders.

"You sure you don't want that wheatgrass smoothie? Change your life."

"No thank you Mr. Wolfe."

'So that's how it is,' Frank thought, 'Replaced.'

It was a good thing he had made backup copies of everything that could come in useful on a server he put together off site on the company's dime; in addition, he had consolidated fractions of financial transaction typically too small to keep track of. It had added up to a substantial nest-egg. No sir, you did not mess with Frank Wilkins.

Wolfric ushered Frank to the elevator and patted him on the back before the door closed.

He turned to Sheila. "Have you logged all his key strokes?", he asked.

"Yes sir." Sheila replied, "it won't be a problem getting into his system."

"All the same just see if you can get him to log in before you, terminate his employment."

"You got it."

"I'd be lost without you, Sheila."

"Don't worry," she smiled. "I'd find you again."

Gale and Shifter looked quizzically at their master.

"It would have to be done eventually," Wolfric said. "this is a family company."

CHAPTER 13:

'...LIKE THE CORNERS OF OUR MIND...'...

Merlin stared at the picture on the printout until it was the reality he now stood in front of. He pictured the apartment number and found himself outside Eric's door. The door was open. Merlin knew that wasn't a good sign. He knocked all the same.

"Hello?" He called out?

A cat scrambled from the couch into the bedroom and startled the old man.

"Sorry." He called out, but the cat didn't respond.

He wandered around the space for a time, placed his hands on random objects, but no impressions jumped out at him. He sat on Eric's sofa and took out the picture. He focused every ounce of his will on the image; he flexed his brain, or just strained his eyes, he couldn't tell which, all he got was a bit of a headache. He dropped his hands in his lap.

Did he fail this boy; had he continued to fail him? In all the years at Acrewood he had never been told about an Eric; and an Eric had never come to visit him. Did this Eric even want to be found?

His doppelganger left him with a swirling jumble of memories; too fast to grab onto and make sense of; they felt like memories of someone else's life. He wondered if someone was still that someone if they couldn't remember their former self.

It scared him when he woke up in the hospital; his first memory. Over time Merlin got used to it, though; after a while he even found it liberating. Besides, the doctors weren't very much help; they were either not permitted to discuss his past with him or they didn't know. In a way it was a fresh start.

Arthur would have accused him of overthinking the whole affair. As a matter of fact, one time...

'Arthur?'

Merlin didn't move, he didn't breathe; he treated the memory as though a rare butterfly had just landed on his arm. He observed it, remained open to it.

'Yes', he thought, 'Arthur.'

He thought harder, but nothing came; but that was the answer. It didn't come to him through effort at all. All the years of trying were fruitless, he had to let go. It's what Alan Watts would have done.

He curled up on the sofa and crossed his legs in seated meditation. He observed the in and out of his breath; at first in a regular pattern but eventually he allowed it the freedom to do as it would. He tried not to try, but that was a tricky proposition because it was an effort in and of itself. The mental image of Arthur, once crystal clear, began to diffuse and degrade in front of his mind's eye.

Merlin jumped to his feet and rang his fingers through his hair. The answer was there somewhere. It had to be.

He happened to look over at Eric's drawing table and easel. He sat down in the rolling office chair and poured over the paintings and sketches. He knew all these people,

'Jacob, Red; I hope she can forgive me.'

"Forgive me for what?" He muttered.

It came in waves and flashes. The image of Arthur was once again as clear as ever.

'Gwen. She had every right to hate me.'

"Hate me for what?" Merlin stroked his temples; it was all out of order, frontwards and then backwards and then even sideways somehow.

Everything was over shadowed by that terrible wolf creature from portal.

'Wolfric.'

The name and his gruesome likeness were tangible even with Merlin's eyes open.

And then, suddenly, it was all there; his brain ignited with an inferno of memories and experiences he couldn't put out if he wanted to. He fell off Eric's chair and curled up in a ball on the floor. The clarity was deafening; he couldn't decide if his identity was being re-written or un-written. Lifetimes worth of awareness overlaid and intermingled with all he thought he knew. A mute cry became a full yell and then ecstatic laughter.

Lights in the apartment flickered; Eric's computer came to life as strange, garbled symbols scrolled by on the monitor.

'Of course,' He thought,' how could I have forgotten?'

Not just Eric, not just Red, Jacob, Gwen or even Arthur. No, his recollection spanned eons; before time was time, before he was him.

In the early days of creation, in the vast infinity of space and time, there formed an awareness. After an eternity it localized and developed a sense of self; as the consciousness grew, the 'self' implied 'other' and so it split and then split again; a collective consciousness grew. As the universe expanded, they were curious to explore. Where they all went, he didn't know; there was all spacetime to roam.

He became infatuated with a fledgling yellow star and decided to watch it grow. He tended to it as a gardener would a flower. Other worlds joined him on his endless waltz around the star; one world, in particular, caught his fancy, so he went in for a closer look. Her marveled over the endless variety of life, each with an intelligence that suited their needs, it was a wonderful dance of give and take.

One species, however, never quite seemed to find its rhythm. There was a lot of take and not so much give. They were smart, though, and so creative. They had tremendous potential if they could just get out of their own way. Sometimes they were a little too clever for their own good. It was clear they just needed help.

He had, as of late, been gripped by a terrible loneliness; he missed the company of the others; he took the form of the species called man. Merlin was positive, with his guidance, they could rise to greatness.

It was hard for him to integrate, they were a distrustful race who preferred their familiar groups to outsiders. On top of that he had certain gifts they did not possess which only made them more fearful of him. Oh, but when one of them needed something, an advantage or favor, that ambitious soul welcomed him with open arms.

Usually it was to help in one of their wars. Merlin had the hardest time grasping the concept of war; The differences between them were exclusively in their minds; they feared the unknown, they feared differences like the superficial color variations of their skin, they feared they would starve if they didn't control land or resources. If he could show them the subatomic level, it was all particles, waves, energy and nothing, but their minds weren't ready for that. If they could only see the truth, the way he saw things, surely, they would be better off. It was clear that it was up to him to guide them, out of love, for their own good.

Merlin toyed with the notion of just doing the job himself; set himself up as a god-king or emperor, but forced compliance wouldn't have been a true change, they had to want to do it of their own free will; besides, he wasn't a god and they were already fighting over plenty of those. They needed one of their own, an example to follow. But who? A man or a woman? Don't even get him started on the gender issue, it was ludicrous. It was like arguing which side of a raindrop was better, but he had to start somewhere.

After some false starts he observed a potent spark of leadership in the one they called Uther Pendragon. With his ponderous list of faults, Uther certainly was no role model, nor was he worse than most. Merlin figured one of two things would happen; the people would unite under him or they would unite against him.

Predictably, Uther ignored Merlin's council in most matters, and he saw Merlin's power only as another sword to wield on his quest to become absolute ruler. His ambition was matched only by his avarice and ego. When Uther lusted after the wife of another man Merlin knew it was time for a change. Uther was the rightful king, it would be harder to start again from scratch, but no one would dismiss an heir.

He agreed to help Uther obtain the object of his obsession, the Lady Igraine, wife of his sworn enemy Gorlois. In exchange, Merlin asked for the child of their union; not being a family man, Uther agreed. Merlin transformed Uther into the spitting image of his enemy. On the eve of battle when Gorlois had left his castle, Uther came to Igraine and fulfilled his darkest fantasies.

After that Merlin abandoned Uther to his fate; he was overthrown and for a time, the land was without a king. Gorlois died in battle the night Uther came to Igraine, Merlin saw that Igraine and her daughter Morgan Le Fay were taken care of but in no uncertain terms, her son, Arthur, was coming with him.

Merlin realized a true leader should be able to identify with even the lowest of his subjects. He placed the boy in the care of Sir Ector where he grew up as a squire; but Merlin was never far from Arthur; he kept a close watch and waited until the time was right.

To ensure the right person ascended to the throne, Merlin orchestrated a small test; he forged the sword Excalibur and thrust it into a stone. Only a person who was worthy, who had the right characteristics Merlin was looking for in a leader could draw the sword from the stone and wield it. With Merlin's help Arthur would be that chosen one. Surely if he started the boy's education early enough things would turn out perfectly.

And it was perfect, for a time. Arthur led the people into a golden age. He founded the kingdom of Camelot. He married Gwenevere, the love of his life and the kingdom finally had its queen. Merlin found a willing apprentice in Morgan Le Fay; he shared his mystical knowledge with her, which really was rather straight forward once you got your head around it. She was a natural at it, Merlin saw tremendous untapped potential in her, something he could never teach even Arthur.

However, unbeknownst to Merlin, but soon to be abundantly 'knownst', Morgan harbored a simmering resentment towards her teacher and his bastard creation, her half-brother, Arthur. She was also not too fond of Gwen. With a little magic and trickery, she conceived a child with Arthur, her own heir to the throne. Mordred. She sowed the seeds of descension in Arthur's own knights and amassed an army which she set upon Camelot. She drove a wedge between Arthur and Gwen, or perhaps Arthur had done a good job of that himself. She left with Sir Lancelot, never to be seen again.

Though Morgan's army and Mordred were eventually defeated it was at the expense of Arthur's life and all he and Merlin built. Mordred died by Arthur's hands, Morgan disappeared.

After Arthur was laid to rest, Merlin wandered the earth alone. He kept the sword with the hopes one day someone would be worthy to wield its power again. History became legend and myth. Magic became the stuff of superstition and nonsense. Merlin observed humanity from the shadows. Had he failed them? Was he only making it worse? He helped out where he could in smaller ways, wherever he happened to be. He was a voracious reader and quite a prolific writer, artist and inventor under various assumed names to earn some extra money. He was particularly proud of the work he did after settling in Vinci.

But, with all he could do it forever eluded Merlin why he couldn't interest humanity in the truth. They really were so close, but nothing was real to them unless it could be quantified and labelled and owned. He was just about ready to give up; he had a strong desire to return to the stars, seek out the others, see how they made out. The problem was he had spent so much time in his current form he had forgotten what it was like to be any other way. He could shape shift, change states, but those were still all variations on physical being. He conducted experiments in his sanctuary. If he couldn't return to how he was he would try to open a door to find one of them. He visited other worlds, other times. He wasn't certain how he'd recognize the others if they had changed as much as he had in different ways. Soon, he even began to lose hope in that.

Then one day, behind one door, he found something remarkable.

Merlin raised up off the floor of Eric's apartment. Lights flickered in the room and outside in the streets. Papers flew of the desk and swirled around.

All the pieces fell into place, the whole picture was clear.

"Oh!" Merlin giggled as he watched himself dissolve. He opened his arms wide and let the wind take him.

"Woo-hoo!" he hollered as he vanished.

CHAPTER 14:
SECOND CHANCES...

A
t the edge of the forest, at the edge of the city, underneath a huge collection of overpasses was the shanty town cynically nicknamed Camelot. The Forest, the overpass and Camelot were bathed in the buzzing, amber glare of street lamps which, regrettably, drowned out all but the brightest stars. But what could you do?

Jared and John typically held watch most nights. The digital clock on a billboard timed the slow passage of their evening.

"So, there I was, cornered in an alleyway." John barely kept his balance on top of a stack of milk crates. "twenty werewolves were walking towards me. They said they just wanted to talk. But I knew better than that."

John's stories, lately, all seemed to feature werewolves. Alcohol might have been a factor, Jared could smell it off him, but he also suspected John had some kind of mental illness. He toyed with the idea of clocking John over the head and dropping him off at a hospital for his own good, but he really liked John, he served with John, and he meant well. He refused to see his friend end up as another statistic of a healthcare system that failed the veterans it claimed to serve.

It wasn't all John. The wolf legend had gained some ground over the years and people had gone missing from the street, people they knew. But Jared wasn't one to believe urban myth and superstition; and society didn't take notice if one of their kind disappeared, they were invisible anyway. All Jared could do was his best to look out for his own.

Still, John's tale got better every time he told it and Jared couldn't help ribbing on his ever-evolving narrative.

"I thought it was only ten wolves." Jared said.

John stopped, crest fallen. Jared was too nice to mess with him and backed down.

"You know what?" He said. "I was thinking of something else, go ahead."

John's face instantly lit up and he continued; his hand gestures could take out someone's eye if they got too close.

"Where was I?" asked John.

"The alleyway." Replied Jared.

"The alleyway." John voice trailed off and his attention was focused off toward the edge of the forest.

Jared followed his friend's petrified stare to the dark hooded figure who had somehow arrived without warning. A light balanced on the stranger's shoulder; it appeared to be moving.

"Can we help you with something?" Asked Jared. His hand found the trigger of the sawed-off twelve gauge under his long coat.

"Are you lost pal?" Jared believed in being nice until it was time to not be nice; admittedly he stole it from the movie Roadhouse, but it was a solid philosophy none the less.

John pulled a switchblade from his pocket. His hand was shaking so much Jared was afraid John would cut himself more than anyone else.

"Easy John." Jared's hand came to rest on John's, his trembling eased somewhat. He sat his friend back down.

"Alright," he returned his glance to the stranger, now a foot away from him. Jared pulled the shotgun out from under his coat but the stranger took him by the head with his long bony fingers. A momentary panic flared but just as quickly subsided. He heard a voice inside his head.

'We mean you no harm.' It said.

The figure did the same to John who was too petrified to move but relaxed soon after.

The figure dropped his hood. It really was a wolf; a wolf and a fairy. She curtsied to both Jared and John in greeting.

"Told you." John said.

"Sure, why not?" Jared said. After William touched his mind the shock of the situation was nonexistent. "Are you guys hungry? We don't have much but..."

Jared was nearly drowned out by a commotion behind him.

He followed the chain reaction of voices behind him to see an immense banquet table, lit by candelabras, and practically overflowing with every sort of food imaginable.

The 'Camelites' were, at first, hesitant to approach the feast even though there were plenty of chairs for everyone; but one by one their stomachs got the better of them and when they saw they had nothing to fear everyone dug in.

Conversation around the table soon turned to laughter, and laughter to joy. By an astounding twist of fate, a guitar and fiddle rested near the table and as luck would have it a couple people knew how to play. The music started out gently but livelier tunes and even dancing followed.

Even the wolfman seemed surprised by the display. But the fairy leaned against his neck with a strange, satisfied smile.

She gestured to Jared and John as if to say, 'What are you waiting for?'

It was a fair question, and one they didn't spend very long debating.

$$\triangle \ \triangle \ \triangle$$

Frank was busy backing up data on a fistful of jump drives. If he was fired, he was taking them down with him, perhaps even cut a deal with the feds. If they were planning on making him disappear then he'd make sure all the dirt made it to the press.

"I couldn't agree more," a voice said behind him. It was soft but very cold. "it's absolutely essential to save your work."

Frank turned. It was Rick's assistant Sheila.

'Sheila... what was it again?'. Frank thought.

"Cornwall." She said.

"I'm sorry?"

"My last name. It's Cornwall."

"Okay...".

Frank wasn't aware he had said that out loud.

"You didn't." Sheila assured him. "Look I'll just get to the point. I would like to apologize for Mr. Wolfe's rash behavior. He means well, but he doesn't always see the larger picture. That's why he has me. I don't believe in throwing away good talent at the slightest transgression."

"You don't?" Frank prided himself on his ability to calculate multiple variables, but he honestly didn't see this coming.

"I'll speak to Rick, don't worry, you can consider the matter closed."

"Thank you, Ms. Corwall."

"Sheila." Her smile was possibly even more chilling than Rick's.

"Thank you, Sheila."

"I might have some other jobs for a man of your talents. There's a substantial bonus in it for you. Interested?"

"Um...very."

"Splendid."

She approached casually, her hips swayed with the mesmerizing grace of a dancer. Frank unconsciously backed up against his console until he could go no further.

Sheila took Frank's hand in both of hers, massaged between his fingers and then gave it a proper shake to seal the deal. She brushed a few stray hairs off his brow.

"I'm so glad we had this chat. I'll be in touch." She said softly. Her voice echoed around inside his head. She picked up the flash drives and pocketed them.

"You won't be needing these." She said.

"Whatever you say."

She turned and strolled out of the room. Frank stood motionless and watched for a full half hour after she was gone.

Perhaps, he had been hasty.

CHAPTER 15:

ARRESTED DEVELOPMENT...

Detective Santino was a twenty-five-year veteran of the force and had very nearly seen it all. Granted, the costumes didn't normally come out until devil's night, Halloween or unless there was some kind of convention in town, but he had seen plenty of that too. They weren't usually as pretty as the woman in red they placed at his desk; normally it was some crazy cat lady or a 'voice of my own god' whack job.

"Alright, Miss," he began, "Please state your name."

"Emily." She replied. "I usually just go by Red." She smiled back at him.

Santino was a sucker for a pretty face, but he regained him composure.

"Address." He said.

"Address who?" she replied.

He looked up from his screen, he couldn't tell if she was trying to be smart with him, he was usually a good judge of character. He gave her the benefit of the doubt and rephrased.

"Where do you live?" He said.

"Oh," she said. "I live in a small cottage in the north woods of the kingdom of Camelot. The court of King Arthur and Queen Gwenevere. Former king and queen"

'And it's whack job by a nose!' He thought; but it had been such a long day, and he was clocking out soon, he just went with it.

He took a closer look at her clothes and it all just clicked.

"You wouldn't happen to be 'Little Red Riding Hood', would you?"

"Well, it's been ages since anyone called me that. Have we met before?" Red asked.

"Sure." Said Santino. Was he being put on by some of the other officers? They had some pretty creative ways of breaking up the monotony. There was a curious sincerity to her, but lots of delusional people believed what they said. Still, he played along. "It was at Cinderella's wedding reception, I was talking to Snow White."

"Were you there?" Red's eyes widened. "I'm afraid I don't recall, we were making rather merry that night. If you know what I mean." She laughed.

"Sure do." He said. "Perhaps the four of us could get together and go out for a night on the town." He said.

Red tilted her head and replied with an impenetrably blank, but pleasant expression.

"So," he resumed, "What were you and your associates doing in that alleyway?"

"My friends and I are here to find Prince Eric and Merlin in the hopes of stopping Wolfric The Big Bad and save our kingdom."

"Merlin." Said Santino. "The wizard."

"Yes," she replied, "You know a lot of people where I'm from."

"I know lots of fairytales." He said.

"Fairies don't tell tales." She said. "They are usually very grounded and practical."

The comment flew past him as incoherent babble, whatever she had smoked must have been some top-quality shit.

"If I may," she said. "I have nothing but the utmost respect for a knight of the realm, such as yourself. I understand you have a duty to protect the people of your kingdom, but it's imperative that my friends and the Prince are allowed to continue our quest."

"Eric," he looked up the last name in his file. "Prince, was roughed up pretty bad. He's being looked at right now. We still have some questions for you and your friends, we'll see what we can do once we get this all sorted out. Ok?"

"Alright." She Replied. "Thank you."

She smiled the most beautiful smile he had ever seen. His demeanor softened.

Why did he always like the crazy ones? Was there something fundamentally wrong with him. He couldn't help but have a soft spot for her.

△ △ △

Jacob was in a cell of impressive construction; even when things were at their worst he had to acknowledge quality craftsmanship. The bricks were shaped and laid with exacting precision; the bars and the door were machined to meticulous perfection and when he shook them, even with his own considerable strength, there was no play in the hinges at all.

His cell mates observed him from the other side of lock-up, huddled in frozen terror. The guards also could not help but stare. Jacob, who had never been self-conscious, completely ignored them.

He didn't recall being read a list of charges, perhaps the knights of this kingdom were merely being cautious. He gave them the benefit of the doubt. He glanced to Braum across the hall in another cell, he leaned on the door and raised his eyebrows in response. For the moment there was nothing to do but wait.

$$\triangle \ \triangle \ \triangle$$

It was just like on tv; the interrogation room, the table and chairs, the big (presumably) two-way mirror. Eric tried not to look at it, he felt paranoid enough. He tried to breathe but it was impossible to tell himself to calm down without also reinforcing the fact he was nervous. No one had been in to talk to him yet; he mentally prepared for the hardnosed detective with a bad suit and worse breath, or the good cop bad cop routine.

His ribs ached but the doctor who examined him said nothing was broken. The wind had been knocked out of him, but he was none the worse for wear.

"You ain't gettin nothin, copper!", he muttered to himself. He enacted various scenarios in his head that saw him play the role of the badass. He couldn't imagine how he would even begin to explain all this without getting fitted with a buckled blazer and put away for a very long time.

'Let's not dismiss that too hastily.' He thought. 'Would it be all that bad? Free room and board, unlimited time to write and draw. Mad basket weaving skills.'

The door opened. A man with a briefcase and very expensive suit walked in.

He smiled at Eric, a little too intensely.

"Mr. Prince?" He said.

Eric's stomach knotted, and he shivered with goosebumps. He couldn't shake the feeling there was something familiar about him.

"Yes?" He managed after an awkward silence.

"Bob Franklin. I'm your attorney." Bob thrust his hand out to Eric.

Eric looked at the hand and back at Bob.

Bob sat down in the chair across the table from Eric. He opened his briefcase and shuffled through some papers.

"What have you told them?" He asked.

"Told who about what?" asked Eric. "Have I been charged with something?"

Bob smiled and, not so subtly, ignored the question.

"It's really best if we get you out of here now.", Said Bob. "I can take you to a secure location."

"I haven't even met with a police detective," Eric said, "what's going on here?"

"We have a car waiting, I can explain on the way." Bob said without the slightest delay.

"I'm not going anywhere with you." Eric said. "Help!"

Bob's arm stretched out, wrapped around Eric's head and covered his mouth. Shifter emerged from Bob.

"Why'd you have to go and do that?" He said. "We could have done this the easy way. Although."

Eric struggled against Shifter's grip as his muffled screams went unanswered.

"Shhhhhhhh." Shifter put his free hand and finger to his own lips.

"I'm not going to lie." He said, "This is going to get weird."

Shifter grunted a slow, morbid chuckle. He melted in front of Eric.

Eric felt something grab his feet and then a pressure glided up his calf muscles. He looked down to see an amorphous blob envelope him from the floor. He struggled harder, but it was no use. The arm around his head expanded and the room went dark. His chest was restricted; he felt buried alive, he couldn't breathe, he couldn't scream.

An Officer came into the room.

"Everything alright in here?" he asked, "I thought I heard a commotion."

"Just fine," Shifter said through his deranged caricature of Eric.

"You're free to go for now." Said the officer. "Don't leave town or anything. We'll be in touch if we have any questions."

"Thank you, officer." Shifter said.

The officer paused just a moment but shrugged it off and went on with his life.

Shifter had done this to several victims in the past. It sent tingles all through him to feel someone or something struggle inside and gradually stop. He never thought it would actually be useful for something one day.

He walked through the precinct without so much as a second glance from anyone. Eric's struggling got weaker and he could feel the human's heartrate slow, he hurried out to the car. The Alpha did want him alive after all.

He got in the back seat of the limo and receded away from Eric to a seated position next to him. Eric gasped for breath and coughed.

"You ok there, sport?" asked Shifter. He was absently flipping through the newsfeed on his tablet.

Eric collapsed to the side and passed out.

"Yeah, you take five." Shifter said, "It's been a long day."

CHAPTER 16:

THROUGH THE LOOKING GLASS...

"Eric?", the gentle, distant voice echoed in the darkness. It was a familiar voice, the sweetest voice ever. Eric was almost certain he was dreaming. He opened his eyes, the blurry world gradually focused into a face he often dreamed about.

"Rose?" Eric back peddled until his head bumped against something soft. He was on a sofa. Rose sat over him with her arm on the backrest.

"Welcome back, sleepyhead." She smiled.

"Told you he wasn't dead.", a voice said from across the room. A familiar voice. A voice that couldn't possibly be in the same company as Rose.

"Shifter, oh my god, shut up." Rose said.

"How are you feeling?" She stroked Eric's forehead and cheek. "You should have come in to work, He really wanted to meet you."

"Who wanted to meet me?" Eric rubbed his eyes and scanned the room. He was in a spacious penthouse office, a bay window overlooking the city spanned the entire side of the room. "Rose what's going on? Did they get you too?"

On the sofa across from him, chewing the last remnants of meat from a ham bone, was the other one from the alley, the barrel chested one. He locked eyes with Eric, annoyed, and stopped.

"Help you with something?" he said, quite intelligibly despite the ham bone wedged in his mouth.

"Don't mind Gale." Rose said, "he's just hangry."

Shifter intruded into Eric's field of view. "I can still feel you inside me.". He laughed.

"Shifter!" Rose snapped. "You are such a creep, get out of here!"

"You really wore me out." He laughed "Get it? Because you wore me, and we walked out!"

He licked Eric's nose and flopped next to Gale on the sofa; he grabbed a remote and activated a giant tv built into the wall, in actual fact the tv was the wall.

"Why don't we all just back away from Mr. Prince and give him a moment to acclimate?" The voice came from the desk. Eric recognized the face from his countless interviews and appearances, as well as his holiday greetings to all company divisions. It was Rick Wolfe.

Rose squeezed Eric's hand and smiled with delight.

"Surprise!". She said.

Eric was 99.999% positive he'd had a stroke. It was the only explanation for the overwhelming incongruity of the past few days.

Rick got up from his desk, sauntered across the room and sat next to Rose on the sofa. She leaned in, put her arm around his shoulder and rested her head on his chest. Rick scratched her head gently. Rose closed her eyes with pure contentment on her face.

"Great to finally meet you." Rick said. "I believe you know my daughter."

"I thought I did." Eric said.

Rose seemed surprised by the comment. She gave him a look that was part uncertainty, with a touch of hurt.

"She's told me nothing but good things." Rick said.

"Oh?" Eric said; it was a considerable effort to even make a sound.

"She said you're quite the artist and writer."

"She did..." He glanced from Rick to Rose. Her face was little more than a mask at the moment; a mask that hid a stranger.

'What?', she mouthed to him. She appeared annoyed

"I love creative types, Eric. This company was built on creativity. Creativity and the courage to implement it."

Eric scanned the room to latch onto anything that made sense. Shifter was watching YouTube videos, Gale continued working at his ham bone.

"Do you like it in the call center?" Asked Rick.

Eric's attention snapped back to Rick.

"Huh?" Eric said. "Oh uh, it's fine."

"You can level with me.", Rick said. "I know it's a shit job. A necessary part of business but no one was meant to stay in a place like that. Least of all someone like you."

Eric nodded and smiled timidly. He had to agree.

"You know, one of my first jobs just starting out in this world, was in customer service. I understand completely. I know how they look at you or talk to you. Like you're a servant, less than human; no better than a dog. You can't help but take that home with you. You can't help but take it to heart. If you let it, it starts to define you. Define your sense of worth. It undermines your self-confidence."

Eric still had no clue what was going on, but his tensions eased. somewhat.

"Would it surprise you to know I was adopted?" Rick said?

"Really?" Eric said. After a pause he volunteered, "So am I."

"I didn't want to bring it up, it's your own business, but Rose kind of filled me in. Yes, I didn't have the greatest of childhoods. My birth parents didn't want me. I'm sure my adopted father thought he did his best, but when the chips were down, when I needed him most, he sided against me. What kind of monster sides against his own child? I decided then and there, when I had a family, they would be everything to me and nothing was going to stand in our way."

Eric continued to nod. Rose took a hold of Eric's hand. He wanted to pull away, he very nearly did.

"It's all about family, Eric.", Rick said. "Friends come and go in and out of your life, if you're lucky a couple of them become like family; but in the end, there is a distinction between the two. You trust your family over some casual acquaintance any day."

"Absolutely." Eric was in agreement mode; it could have been survival, it could have been a very hard-hitting case of Stockholm Syndrome, but Rick started to make sense; even if it was all very Brando in Godfather. He hoped Rick wasn't about to give him the kiss of death or ask him to ice someone. He wasn't even sure where you could get a horse's head at this time of day.

"But I digress, listen to me prattling on." Rick said. "Eric, I bet you're due for a promotion. Am I right? Like I said I love creative types. You know we are always looking for writers and producers for original content on our streaming network. gLobo-Vision could use a guy like you. I just have to snap my fingers and you're hired. Forget that graphic novel you're working on, how about your own series? I know what you're thinking, but honestly, who has any experience before they just jump right in and get their feet wet? What do you say? Rose really spoke highly of you."

'What the hell is going on?' Eric thought. Was this guy for real?

"Monday, you start Monday! You know what, it's not even up for debate, I am taking you up to Mount Olympus my boy, you are going to live with the Gods, You and Rose can produce whatever you want."

"Today is Monday." Rose giggled.

"It is?" Rick shouted. "Then welcome aboard son!" He smiled an infectious smile. "We should get some champagne and celebrate". He reached behind the sofa to an intercom on a table.

"Sheila, darling?" he said.

"Yes, my Alpha." Sheila replied.

"Bring us a couple bottles of the good stuff. Oh, and a deli-platter, get a deli-platter too."

"You got it."

"You're the best, Sheila."

"I'm not the best, sir, but there are none better."

"Ha! I love it!" Rick released the button. "So, Eric, say something; you got this stoic quality, I'm digging it but it's hard to get a read on you. What do you think?"

Eric had a hard time forming any thoughts. Rick didn't take a break between ideas; he employed the bewildering pressure of a veteran salesman with near flawless execution.

"I know what you're thinking." He said, almost in answer to his own question, "There's more to this than just a job-offer. I confess, there is an ulterior motive in bringing you here."

"OH?" Eric said.

"Well two things really. We've actually been looking for you for quite some time."

"Is that so?"

"Once we found you, we tried our best to keep you safe but also give you some space to be yourself. When things got a little dicey for you, we decided to guide you into the fold a bit more."

"I'm sorry, I'm not following any of this."

"It's all a little hard to explain, you might even say it defies explanation. I hear you had some visitors."

"Um, ya."

"Despite what they tell you they cannot be trusted. An infinite number of random points of entry and they somehow landed with you. That's a remarkable coincidence, don't you think? And at the same time your former guardian just happened to escape from the Acrewood facility. Can you explain any of that?"

Rick's smiled remained, but his eyes went dark. Eric felt the room temperature drop a couple degrees. Everyone's eyes were on him, even Rose's expressed more interest than affection now.

"Look, I don't know what's happening." Eric said, "I don't know why everyone is suddenly interested in me. Three people, well two people and a pig, appeared through a magic doorway in my living room. Your shapeshifting hairless dog and his brother show up on my doorstep and try to abduct me. Now, seriously, I'd love for someone to tell me what the hell this all has to do with me."

"The portal opened up right in front of you." Rick said. "The odds of that are astronomical. Curiouser and Curiouser."

"You know," Eric said, "This is all a bit too much and I really think I'd rather just get back to my apartment now."

"You're right," Rick said, "I'll stop beating around the bush. I'm your father,

Eric."

All things considered it wasn't the weirdest answer he could have been given.

"Ok, I'm just going to see myself out." Eric said. "Thanks for a lovely visit. Rose, I'll talk to you later. It's been...well, it's been strange."

He stood up from the couch.

"Gale." Rick said. "Shifter."

Gale puffed Eric back into his seat. Shifter elongated his arms and bound Eric to the sofa.

"You know what?" Eric said, "The bus probably won't be by for another hour."

"Do you know how long we searched for you?" Rick asked. "This is a family run business. I'm going to say about 80 percent of my labor force are all my children. And after all this time to find out you actually work in one of my companies? What are the odds? It's destiny."

'So that means Rose is my...,' Eric couldn't continue the thought. 'Oh, dear lord.'

"Your sister," Rick said, "Rosie is an excellent judge of character. She's my eyes and ears there. People don't open up to managers or team leaders, they don't tell you the real stuff they'd tell a trusted co-worker. She was dying to tell you when she found out about all this."

"So how many wives have you had?" Asked Eric.

"Don't be so literal, my boy. There's a certain, shall we say, gift, I am able to bestow on people. But they are all as dear to me as if they were my own children, they are all family. Rose is adopted. Well, more rescued from a bad home. You are my only actual offspring, that I know of." His amusement with himself burst forth in a giggle.

Eric's conflicted feelings towards Rose drifted away in a wave of relief. Admittedly, it was an odd thing to focus on at that moment.

"You actually look a lot like your mother." Rick said, "If it's any consolation I loved her. If circumstances were different, she would be at my side to this day."

"The old man," Eric said, "Merlin, told me..."

"Merlin!" Rick's face changed at the mention of the name. It was darker, more angular, hairier. "I'm sure he filled your head with all kind of nonsense. Always consider the source son."

"That's enough. Let him go, Wolfric."

Everyone turned toward the source of the voice; Merlin spoke with his mouth full as he sampled a very nice jalapeno brie from the deli platter laid out by the door.

"Or do you prefer Rick Wolfe?" he said, "That's not even clever. Frankly, I'm a little disappointed in myself, more than you."

"Hello, Father." Wolfric said. "Gotta say, you're looking spritely. I was worried I'd never get to see the real you again. I am absolutely thrilled you dropped in."

"I'm not here." Replied Merlin. "I mean, I'm not 'not' here either. The here and now is everywhere; so is there and then." The wizard guffawed. His attention remained fixed on the deli platter; he stacked a sharp cheddar and chorizo salami on top of a rosemary-olive oil crostini; he took it in one bite and rolled his head back with ecstatic fulfillment.

He hadn't aged a day; a tide of memories flowed back to Eric. All he could do for the moment was tread water through them as he remained fixated on Merlin.

"Son of a bitch." Eric cursed silently.

"Aren't we all!" Laughed Rick.

Rose, Gale, and Shifter giggled.

"Sorry," he said. "Canine joke. I guess we can all drop the pretense now."

He let the Rick façade slip away and stood tall in his full lupine splendor.

Eric watched in horror as even Rose turned full-werewolf, albeit a cute, red furred one. Gale and Shifter's appearance made more sense to him at that moment, but they were still ugly.

He looked down at himself, he was unchanged.

"Gale, Rose darling," Rick said, "make our guest feel welcome."

Rose and Gale crossed the room and split up to flank Merlin from either side. Gale began his deep breathing stretches; a stiff breeze picked up in the room.

Eric wondered what tricks Rose had up her sleeve; she was smart, but in all the time they had been friends nothing stood out about her beyond the obsessive attention she gave her nails. She was always filing them during casual conversation or with clients on the phone; the headset kept her hands free. Those same nails that, as Eric watched, had grown steadily as she approached Merlin; those nails which were, now, six-inch claws.

'Ah.' He thought, 'that makes sense'; nothing else about her ever seemed particularly shallow or vain.

Sheila pulled an ornate dagger from a garter on her thigh, just under her skirt. Eric noted an intensity in her eyes that even Rick didn't have at that moment.

Rose pounced and swung a paw at Merlin. He vanished. Everyone looked around the room.

"For what it's worth, Wolfric" Merlin's voice seemed to come from everywhere. "I'm sorry. I truly am."

"Sorry you didn't kill me?" Wolfric said.

"I'm sorry I tried to make you something you weren't. In my efforts to help you fit in I fear I only singled you out more. I see that now. I should have accepted you and found a way for you to express who you were. And for that I am sorry."

"Are we having a moment, Merle? Why don't you show yourself and we can hug it out. Shifter, it's stuffy in here, open a window."

Shifter's hand became a sledge hammer, he shot out his arm and shattered one of the bay windows.

"You have until the count of three to show yourself or Shifter will throw Eric out the window."

"Daddy! You promised!" Rose said.

"Plans change, sweetie, learn to adapt." Rick said. "One."

"Look," Merlin said, "I said my peace."

"Two." Rick said.

"I know I promised you this boy, but it wasn't my promise to make. I see that now."

"Three."

Shifter raised Eric off his seat and brought him to the window.

"No!" Rose screamed.

She vaulted the room, her claws bared, ready to take Shifter's head off.

Gale blew her past Shifter and out the window. Rose twisted in the air and locked eyes with Eric.

Time slowed and the terror in Roses eyes played out for what seemed like forever. Eric prayed for a miracle, as messed up as everything was, she still had his back. Her face drew closer to his. Had it worked?

It hadn't. As promised, Eric had been thrown from the window to his death.

Rose reached out to him, she retracted her claws. Their hands clasped, and he pulled her into an embrace. The ground rushed up to meet them. Eric closed his eyes.

CHAPTER 17:

SOME ASSEMBLY REQUIRED...

Red had been moved to a holding cell. She was surrounded by an eclectic mix of women, all with their eyes on her; she did her best to be polite to her cellmates.

A nice looking, although scantily clad, young lady sat next to her. Red could appreciate the leather work of her outfit however it couldn't have been comfortable or practical to wear; she wondered how walking was even possible with heels that long on her boots.

"So," asked Red, "What are you in here for?"

"Hooking." She replied. "How about yourself?"

"It's against the law to fish here?"

"No, Prostitution."

Red returned a blank expression to the hooker.

"Wow, you're really fresh off the boat." She said. "Having sex with someone in exchange for money."

"Oh my!" Red said. "I am so sorry."

"Why? Do you think you're better than me?"

"Oh, I'm not saying that."

"You go to hell bitch!"

A moment before the hooker could scratch out Red's eyes, Red found herself on a bench next to Jacob in his cell. Braum ran to the bars across the hall when he saw her arrive.

"Red?" Jacob said. "How did you get here?"

A moment after that the three were seated on Eric's living room Sofa.

Eric was standing in the middle of the room screaming; in his arms he embraced a woman none of them had ever seen before.

Eric's voice trailed off and his eyes gradually opened. He was home. Rose had a death grip around his chest.

"Ahem!" Red said, gently.

Eric let out a tiny shriek, Rose twirled him behind her and adopted a defensive stance, claws extended and at the ready. She bared her teeth with a visceral growl.

"Perfect," Eric said. "You guys again. You know, don't think me ungrateful, but for once I'd love to go a day without someone kidnapping me!"

He put his hand on Rose's shoulder.

"It's fine" he said. "they're fine, they're the good guys. I think."

"Fine?" Rose hissed. "Do you know who that is?" She pointed emphatically at Red.

Her eyes threw daggers, but Eric managed to hold her at bay. Rose held firm to her defensive posture.

"Eric, who is this?" Asked Red. She appeared none too fond of Rose as well.

"Oh, this is a friend from work, Rose, whom I recently learned was a werewolf and minion of the Anti-Christ."

Rose stood straight and faced Eric; her eyes widened, and her mouth fell. Even obscured by fur and a partial snout the look of hurt in her eyes was clear.

"What?" Eric said. "It seems like something that might have come up in conversation."

"I didn't want to scare you away." Rose said, "it turns out to be a deal breaker with most guys."

"So, you had me abducted? To do what, exactly?"

"I had nothing to do with that. He assured me you would come to no harm and that I might be able to change you myself."

"Change me? Change me."

"If you wanted."

"Why do women always think they can change a guy? Change me into what? These aren't normal thoughts people have. And since when did you even care?"

"Never mind. Forget it." Rose said.

She crossed her arms, returned to her human form, turned to the window and brooded.

Jacob looked back and forth between the two of them, then to Red and Braum. The tension in the room was suffocating. He got up and went to the fridge.

"This is so messed up." Eric said.

He stormed off to his bedroom and slammed the door behind him. Only, it wasn't his bedroom; he was on the rooftop of his apartment building. Over on the ledge sat Merlin, his feet were dangling, and his hands were folded neatly in his lap.

"Hello, Eric." He said.

"Hell no." Replied Eric.

Eric retreated to the door only to find it was gone, replaced by brick. He touched the wall then knocked on it, it was solid. He pressed his forehead against the edifice and sighed.

"Sure, why not." Eric said. "Hey, Merlin, been a while."

"We need to talk." Merlin said.

"Nearly thirty years, nothing. Now, suddenly, everyone needs to talk to me."

"I am truly sorry about..."

"Don't!" Eric threw up his hands. "we are way beyond sorry."

He turned to face Merlin who was now standing three feet behind him.

"Dammit!" Eric jolted backward against the wall. "Would you stop doing that shit?"

"I recall you used to get quite the kick out of it."

"It was cute when I was 4. I spent years convincing myself none of it was real. The social workers said it was for the best. I always thought someday you'd come back. But you never did."

"I know," Merlin said.

"Do you know what kind of week this has been?"

"I have some idea but if you would let me..."

"I've been abducted three times! I was enveloped and walked around like a marionette. The owner of my company and everyone employed there are apparently werewolves, including the girl I love and..."

Merlin raised his hand and Eric stopped; he was frozen in time.

"Can I please explain?"

Eric's brow furled, and his eyes screamed with manic confusion.

"I'm going to release you now. Can we please have a civilized conversation?"

If a person's eyes could flip someone off, that's the expression that would best describe the look in Eric's eyes. No other part of his body could move or even twitch.

"Eric," Merlin said, "I can hold you like this until stars burn out. I've done it. Now I'm going to release you. Will you let me explain? Blink once for yes, twice for no. I highly recommend yes."

After a timeless, disdainful glower, Eric grudgingly blinked, once.

Merlin lowered his hand and Eric fell back against the wall.

"Thank you," Merlin said, "Now, perhaps a more comfortable setting."

In the next moment, Eric and Merlin were seated across from one another in easy chairs; between them was the deli platter from Rick's office.

"Where are we?" asked Eric.

The room was part library, part museum. Instead of a ceiling, a universe of stars, nebulas and galaxies cast an ethereal glow over everything and stretched upward into infinity.

"Nowhere really." Merlin said. "a pocket universe I like to call the sanctuary. I had a smaller one at the hospital but recently remembered this one and merged them together."

"Absolutely fascinating." Eric said. "Ok, first question. What, in the absolute flying hell, does everyone want with me?"

"That will take some explaining."

"I am all ears."

Merlin looked thoughtfully down at his hands, he wrung them anxiously, then after a time looked back up at Eric. The old man's eyes still had a sparkle.

"When I brought you to this world, my only plan was to escape; respect your mother's wishes and take you to a place Wolfric would never find you."

"Masterfully done."

Merlin waved his hand and Eric's mouth sealed shut. Eric protested in muffled screams as he frantically pawed at the skin where his lips used to be.

"May I continue?"

Eric rolled his eyes and blinked once again.

Merlin returned Eric's mouth.

"I had always sensed there was something special about you," Merlin continued, "but I had no idea how special."

In the air between them Merlin conjured a glowing cloud; inside the cloud Eric was astonished to see himself as a boy and Merlin in their old apartment.

"There was a television in the apartment we rented; dreadful things, I never should have let you watch it. You were almost three years old. Well, I mean, the time difference between both worlds is not chronologically in sync but let's just keep things simple for now."

"Focus." Eric said.

Merlin shot Eric a sideways glance.

"An advertisement came on for a stuffed teddy bear who told stories. You were spellbound by it, you couldn't take your eyes off it. Until one day I found you playing with it. I knew I hadn't conjured it up, so it was a minor mystery how it got there. As days passed your room filled with more and more toys. If I hadn't seen it for myself, I might not have believed it.

One night as I was reading, you were watching some children's program with puppets. I tried my best to tune out the noise but suddenly it sounded like one of the puppets had actually called you by name. I looked up from my book and there was a living, animated version of the puppet dancing and singing, physically in front of you.

You didn't know any different, you were clapping and giggling.

I called for you to come to me immediately. The moment you turned your head towards me the apparition vanished."

Eric vaguely remembered the television show and the teddy bear; he certainly did not remember it dancing in front of him. The reruns of his life displayed in the cloud were surreal.

"A plan formed." Merlin said. "I would teach you everything you needed to know, return with you fully grown and defeat Wolfric. With your power you would be unstoppable. In time I would have helped you cultivate it."

"So Wolfric wants this power in me?" Eric asked.

"To him, you are the trophy of his victory over Arthur, nothing more." Merlin said. "The world judged him; in his mind he has stood judged for his whole life and has forever tried to prove his worth. He doesn't realize the power you have. I don't even think you do."

"Oh yes," Eric mocked, "bow before my might."

"After you were taken from me they locked me away in an institution. They wouldn't allow me to see you. When I protested they performed shock therapy on me; but energy is energy whether it be electrical or magic, and when it contacted with my mind there was a bit of an overload and eons of memories were misplaced for a time. I knew I had pressing business out there somewhere, I simply couldn't remember what it was."

"Convenient."

"Believe it or not, it was probably for the best."

"How were the last 30 years of this life for the best?"

"There are worse lives you could be living in other parts of the world. You have a job, you have a roof over your head, you live in a democracy, you have friends."
Eric crossed his arms and leaned back in his chair. Perhaps it wasn't the worst thing in the world he was taken away from this man.

"If I had stayed," Merlin said, "you might never had realized your true potential."

"What are you talking about?"

"You wished me away. You wished I would leave you alone, forget all about you."

"That is complete bullshit."

"Is it?"

"I wished you away."

"In my effort to protect you and train you I kept you hidden, never let you go outside. I buried you in stories and legends, pressuring you with notions of your royal heritage to prepare you for a future of my choosing. You're telling me in all that time you didn't wish I would just go away?"

"You're out of your mind." Eric walked off to the edge of the room; there was no wall, simply the infinite abyss of the cosmos to gaze into. He never understood that expression until now, but it did seem to look back into him.

"Maybe once." Eric said. "Okay, maybe all the time."

"And when the power of that desire was strong enough it happened. Like magic.

And it was probably jarring to you but also probably a relief. You could live a normal life. No more pressure, nothing to live up to."

"Yes." Eric said.

"And your whole life since then, there has been nothing to live up to. Life on your terms."

"Well the job situation could be better."

"Could it? You wanted no responsibility, but you never considered the ramifications of such a wish. You're in a job where you are treated like a slave. All your decisions are made for you. You stay for fear of having nothing or having to live up to something. Fear of failing at something greater. You toy with working on your book but how long have you been at that? Your whole reality has been your choosing."

"Enough, Dr. Phil. I get it."

"The fact you ended up in a company owned by Wolfric is ultimate expression of denying your destiny for too long."

Eric kicked a stone on the floor off into space. He observed its path into infinity. He returned to the chair and picked through the deli platter, it occurred to him he hadn't eaten in some time.

"So how does my superpower of bad life choices help us?" He asked.

"You misunderstand," Merlin said, "It's precisely that power to choose that Wolfric lacks."

"Seems like he's had some pretty phenomenal success with his choices."

"No, no, no..." Merlin's voice trailed off as he walked over to a bookshelf. He traced his finger over the spines and pulled out volume after volume of Myths and legends. He brought the stack to the table next to the deli platter and sat down again. He tossed Eric a copy of English Fairytales.

"Time and time again, in countless mythologies around the world there is a Big Bad Wolf. He is destruction, he is the devourer, the trickster, the Boogeyman. For all intents and purposes, he is the devil."

Merlin held up an open page to Eric. An illustration depicted a giant wolf devouring the moon.

"In Norse myth a wolf, Fenrir, is responsible for bringing about the end of the world. Wolfric is simply another incarnation of this primal fear."

"He's terrifying, we've established this."

"Yes, he is evil, but he is bound to play the roll in which humanity conceived him. He is bound to fear. If you're afraid long enough fear makes the choices for you."

"If I'm from the same fictional world," asked Eric, "then how am I different?"

"They aren't really fictional." Merlin said, "But, everyone is fictional in a way, if you think about it. We're all a compilation of our life's experiences. They leave impressions on you. They inform our opinions of ourselves and the world. But it's all an illusion. Your past isn't you. You don't have to tell yourself the same stories for the rest of your life. Wolfric was conceived as the villain."

Another millennium of stillness passed between them.

"Huh?" Eric said.

"You never existed in any legend. The events that shaped you are a direct result of my interference in that other reality. You were born over there but your lifeforce is a product of this universe. The events of that other world are inspired by events in this world. If I had stayed with you, you would have simply grown up playing the roll I was trying to choose for you. But you decided against that. You took control and wrote your own story. And you continue to write it. Wolfric is still bound by the story that was made up for him."

"Again," Eric said. "Huh?"

"You have the power to influence both realities." Merlin said.

"So, what? I can unwrite him?"

"You didn't create him, you can't unwrite him."

"How do you know?"

Merlin laughed. He sat down and leaned forward to Eric.

"I've meddled in the affairs of others for as long as there have been others. With all the things I can do it seemed like a natural conclusion that I use my talents to guide humanity to a better understanding, a better way. But every one of my solutions just lead to another problem. I tried again and again, each time thinking there was some variable I overlooked, each time thinking 'this time will be perfect'. But it's all two sides of the same coin. The only variable I overlooked was myself. I couldn't have things the way I wanted them to be. As long as I stood in judgement of people all my actions would reap the same outcome. It might have come from a place of love or concern, but wanting to change someone, that isn't love. Just like manipulated events are not reality. I feared Wolfric's potential, everyone did. I thought I could change his nature, deny what he was and impose my own set of morals over him. But you can't fight fear out of fear. You can't run away from fear either. Anything you do out of fear only strengthens fear. It's the most devious trap in the whole universe; fear fights on both sides of any conflict and it only gets stronger. He's far too strong now. He's fueled by fear, he's not even really acting of his own free will. Like I said, two sides of the same coin; fighting fear acknowledges fear and strengthens it. Actively ignoring fear or inaction out of fear to get involved doesn't help either."

"You're not leaving us with a lot of options." Eric said.

"No, but what do we fear most? We fear loss, we fear impermanence and uncertainty. We fear losing a loved one, but if you could fix them in space and time, unchanged forever, they would cease to be the living creature you loved and simply become an image of them. You love them because they are alive and changing and

interesting. You can't give in to fear, but you have to embrace it just a little bit too."
The only thing Eric was afraid of, at that moment, was that the old man was starting to make sense. That or Eric's own logic had finally skewed on a tangent, straight to utter and drooling madness.

A brightly tailed comet streaked overhead.

"Is it true what he said?" Asked Eric? "Is he my father?"

"Yes." Merlin lowered his head and rung his hands together.

"What is it?" Asked Eric.

Merlin took a deep breath and sighed, Merlin fixed his gaze on Eric. There was a deep sadness in his eyes Eric found difficult to acknowledge but found it even harder to look away.

"I couldn't bring myself to destroy Wolfric." Merlin said. "I couldn't allow the war to continue either. He was winning. At the time his demand seemed like the lesser evil. Part of me felt like I had failed him; like I owed him this one thing. And the Arthur of that world wasn't really my Arthur. They were all fictional, after all. Like I said, I didn't show respect for anyone around me, my judgement was the only call that mattered. I arranged for one night with your mother to conceive you. Disguised him as Arthur. She always sensed though. She never looked at me the same way after that. I thought if Wolfric ever showed up to claim you, well, I'm not sure what I thought anymore."

"Wow."

The mental chatter in Eric's mind died. The word 'monster' felt inadequate for Merlin but no better words, or any other words for that matter, came to him. Somewhere in the universe above, entire civilizations evolved and perished in the span of silence between them.

Eric checked his watch. Both hands spun counter to each other around the face and the date display had a big question mark where there used to be numbers.

"So, what's the plan?" Asked Eric, "We should probably get back to the others. Rose might have eviscerated Red or Jacob by now."

"They're fine" Merlin said. "She really does love you, you know."

"Red? I thought she was with that other guy."

"Rose."

"Yeah, well, I liked her too. But there's been some rather extreme developments as of late."

"Don't be such an ass-hat," Merlin said.

Eric looked up, stunned at the old man.

"None of that is her fault." The wizard continued. "Wolfric has fed her a diet of lies her whole life. Don't forget, she got blasted out of a window trying to save you from her own pack. On the way down, you both seemed pretty close."

"She didn't have to lie about it."

"She didn't lie about it. She was scared. Is it that much of a deal breaker? True love is a rare thing in any universe, don't be so fast to dismiss it. Did you honestly want normal in your life? Were normal girls lining up at your door before all this"

"Wow," Eric said "solid burn."

"I used to hang out with Oscar Wilde." Merlin said. "Go to her. She needs you right now. They all do."

"You're coming too, aren't you?"

"I'm not sure that's the best idea. Red doesn't trust me anymore."

"That sounds like fear," Eric said, "We can't run away from fear." Eric's near spot on parody of Merlin's voice drew a head tilt from the wizard.

△ △ △

Rose sat in an easy chair on the opposing side of the living room from Red and Braum. Her arms were crossed, and she studied Red with an unshakable suspicion and contempt.

Red didn't care for how she was being looked at, least of all by a wolf; she refused to take her eyes off Rose for a moment. Braum, his hands folded neatly in his lap, looked back and forth between the two with an uneasy smile and sweating brow. There was something eerily similar about both of them, he just couldn't put his finger on. The tension between them could forge iron.

Jacob had constructed a sandwich using two slices of leftover pizza as bread and an assortment of meats and vegetables from Eric's fridge

Eric reappeared next to Rose. He scanned the vicinity with startled confusion. He was positive he hated traveling like that.

Rose acknowledged his presence with only the slightest of glances before taking out her file and cleaning under her nails. She flicked the dirt, dismissively at his feet.

"I'm sorry." Eric said.

"And?" Rose said.

"I'm an asshole."

"And?" She gave extra attention to a hangnail on her right index finger.

"Thank you for trying to save me."

"And?" She stopped manicuring and dropped her hands in her lap.

"You are queen of all that is."

"Say more things like that."

"I am but a lowly speck on the heel of your greatness."

Rose stifled an unexpected smile.

"One more," she said. "make it count."

"I love you." Eric said.

She leapt from the easy chair and into Eric's arms. He was unprepared and nearly dropped her; but she was light, and her arms held their embrace around his neck. She locked her legs around his waist and kissed him with all her animal passion. Her nails dug into his back, in a good way. Eric flushed, beet red; his knees gave out and they collapsed in a heap on the floor. None of this distracted Rose from the job at hand.

△ △ △

A breeze blew in from the broken window, but it was pleasant outside. Wolfric stared into the burning fire glass of the hearth along his wall. He sipped a glass of whiskey, neat; it had been a straight whiskey sort of day.

He leaned back into the understanding cradle of Sheila's arms as she massaged his shoulders and stroked behind his ears.

"Where did I go wrong." He asked. "Have I not given all of you everything you could possible desire?"

"You spoil us, Alpha." Said Sheila.

"Rose was one of my first children, did you know that?"

"She's an ungrateful wretch."

"Kids huh?" Wolfric turned the glass and watched the fire refract through the amber and crystal.

"Still," he continued. "Gale shouldn't have tried to kill his sister without my permission ." He downed the rest of his drink.

"Could you be a dear and get me another?" he said.

"Absolutely", replied Sheila.

He leaned forward so she could get up.

"How is Gale anyway?", Wolfric asked casually.

"I'll go check." Sheila left the couch and peered over the edge of the broken window.

Gale swung in the wind, tied up in a rope made from Shifter's stretched out body; Shifter held on to the window ledge by his teeth.

"He's still hanging in there." Sheila laughed.

"Oh, you and your puns," laughed Wolfric.

"Can I come in now?" Gale's voice reached them in a muted echo from a few floors down.

"Still deciding!" Wolfric snapped back.

"Whaa aa-out eeee?" asked Shifter. A puddle of drool had formed on the floor around his teeth and he could feel himself slipping. Rick had temporarily blocked him from changing any further.

"You?" Wolfric said, "You two are responsible for each other's actions. Your fates are inextricably entwined. So just hang tight."

Sheila strolled over to the bar and picked up a bottle of twelve-year aged rye.

"Has there been any word from William?" He asked.

"No one has seen or heard anything, I'm afraid Alpha." Sheila replied.

"Now there's a child that never disappoints. He must feel so lost out there all alone. Keep looking. I know where ever he is he's desperate to get back to us."

CHAPTER 18:

WILLIAM REACHES OUT...

William didn't want to be found, ever; for the first time in recent memory there was joy in his life. He, Timmin and their new friends had discovered an abandoned warehouse on the edge of town; and with a little imagination, and some magic from Timmin, they had managed to furnish it quite comfortably. At the very least it was a start.

The community was initially standoffish about William and Timmin, but it didn't take long to warm up to them; none of them had felt a spark of wonder in quite some time. Besides that, everyone trusted Jared and when he gave the all clear that was good enough for them.

He was an old soldier with an older soul. He didn't like to discuss his past too much, but when he touched Jared's mind, William had managed to sneak a casual glimpse of his mind.

He saw Jared seated at his little girl's bedside, she delighted at story time and the stories he made up. She usually insisted on hearing tales of the dashing knight and the lovely Princess Rose, her name. Her beautiful red curls glistened by the incandescent light of her night stand and framed her chubby, freckled, smiling cheeks. His wife listened fondly as she leaned on the door frame behind them.

The memory changed to a different bedside in a room that was unfamiliar to William. It lacked the comfort and warmth of the other setting; the walls were green, and Rose rested in a white bed with metal bars on either side. A strange liquid was piped into her arm from a clear bladder suspended above. Rose's cheeks were gaunt and pail and her lovely crimson locks was gone; oh, but her eye still sparkled as she basked in the soothing tone of Jared's voice. His wife stared despondently at the floor from a bench outside in the hallway.

The scene briefly flashed, almost too quick to register, but a funeral was a funeral, and William recognized that.

Finally, he saw Jared on the bedside next to his wife. She was laid out in her best dress, a look of serenity on her face; a small orange, empty bottle clutched in her hand. The vision flashed on the note she had left, but again Jared's mind didn't linger too long on the image.

He enlisted in the military; he had to get away, he hoped he could forget. He knew he was running; he was okay with that. During his tours of duty, he experienced horrors that were white noise by comparison. He hoped, perhaps one of those horrors would send him to his wife and daughter but none of them did him the curtesy. He returned home to a world that had no use for him and would rather forget he existed.

He lost himself on the streets with no expectations.

The first stray he picked up was John; despite Jared's best attempts to stay alone, John looked up to him and clung to him like a shadow. He loved to hear Jared's war stories, and Jared reveled in the absurd exaggeration of John's.

They encountered others, not just adults but children, even families. They rallied around Jared; for the life of him he didn't know what use he could be but, somehow, he would get them through.

With Timmin's help they had all the food they needed, and upon request she would turn things to gold for them to trade.

Gilding is a rather pedestrian skill for a fairy; used primarily for decoration. But the race of man seemed to value it so Timmin was always happy to oblige if it helped them in some way. Though she often questioned a people with priorities so incredibly skewed.

With every miracle, Timmin became more radiant, but William couldn't deny how much she had aged in the process. And despite how blissful their lives had become there were two inescapable conclusions; Wolfric's shadow forever loomed over them and Timmin was slowly dying.

There was only one hope for their freedom and one hope of salvation for Timmin. They had to find Merlin.

Plus, there was someone Jared should probably meet.

CHAPTER 19:
LONG OVERDUE TALKS...

Eric sat on his fire escape with Rose between his legs, one step lower resting on his stomach. They watched the setting sun dip below the buildings across the street as they passed a bottle of whiskey back and forth. It had been an entire bottle of whiskey sort of day.

Eric stroked her hair; when it was all over, he would also have to remember to ask what conditioner she used. He traced a finger around her right ear; it was a very pointy ear and he wondered how he could have missed it before.

"I'm sorry I had you kidnapped." She said.

"If I had a dime every time a woman told me that." Eric laughed and took a swig from the bottle.

"You'd have a dime?" Rose laughed and stroked Eric's knees; he was ticklish there but under the circumstances he didn't mind.

He let out a dry guffaw, "Yes, I'd have a whole dime."

He passed her down the bottle. Where Eric merely sipped, Rose downed a whole gulp or two. He was more than a little impressed by this.

"So how did all this happen to you?" He asked.

"The whole werewolf thing?"

"Yeah."

Rose turned the bottle over in her hands and started to scrape the label off with one of her claws.

"I don't really remember." She said. "I have a vague memory of when the wolves came for me. I remember Wolfric picking me up from the midst of them and protecting me. Before that, I don't know, there are flashes of almost memories. I was really young. I remember Wolfric's bite that turned me. I was scared but there was

117

one adopted brother who really looked out for me. It wasn't so bad after a while. I've been like this for most of my life."

"What's it like?"

"The world around me is a thousand times more radiant. Smells, tastes, sounds. At night everything shimmers like the whole world is made of silver. I can parkour the hell out of this town. I can outrun a deer in full sprint."

"That's hot." Eric said. "Have you ever..."

"Eaten someone?" Rose snickered.

"No! Well, yeah. I'm sorry, is that an offensive question? I feel like someone trying too hard to be culturally sensitive."

"It's ok." She said. "No, it's not like that. I've only hunted wild game. When your wizard friend showed up, my first impulse was 'who the hell is this guy' and to protect you; it was the first time I had ever confronted another person. I've heard the war stories where my kind were fighting for survival, but I was too young for that at the time. When we finally settled over here the Alpha promised us a better life. He talked about finding you so many times. The odds of us ending up working together, astronomical. That's just crazy. But earlier, no, my instincts just took over and I had to defend you."

"That is intensely flattering."

"You know, I could turn you."

"Um, thank you." Eric said, "I feel like my threshold has been pushed enough for the day, but we can revisit that idea."

"Cool." Rose handed him the bottle.

"So, who else is a werewolf at work?"

"Oh, well Sheila, at least I think so. Most of the team leaders, Sharon in accounts receivable, pretty well everyone... Terry."

"Terry? That tool is a werewolf?"

"Oh my God! What's wrong with Terry?"

"I don't know, just on a visceral level I never liked him. I physically hate him."

"Awww. Were you jealous because I got along with him?" Rose massaged his calf muscles and leaned in harder. "Maybe there's more wolf in you than you know."

"Yeah, about that, if I'm Rick's son, why haven't I turned?"

"Beats me." Rose said. "You just give the word babe, no pressure."

It was an enticing offer. It would be like getting superpowers. They could stalk the streets together dispensing vigilante justice.

"So, the blonde chick in the red cloak, do you know who she is?"

"Now who's jealous?" Eric passed her back the bottle.

Rose dug her nails into his calf.

"Joking, Joking." He winced.

Rose released her grip and resumed stroking.

"The 'chick'," Eric said, "is Red Riding Hood. The humanoid pig is Jacob, last surviving brother of the Three Little Pigs. The old man who teleported us here is apparently the actual Merlin the magician, as in King Arthur and Merlin."

"Wow," Rose said, "I was afraid the werewolf thing would weird you out."

"No, I'm pretty maxed at this point."

"Who's the other dude? There's something familiar about him. He's kind of cute too."

"His name is Braum, but I can't, for the life of me, think what story he's from."

"We have to ditch them. You realize that, don't you? You don't know what they are capable of. We can't trust anyone now."

"I'm sure it's fine."

The sun dropped below the horizon and the air started to cool off. Eric and Rose called it a night and went inside.

Dr. Stephen Anderson had finally surfaced and purred with ecstasy while receiving a vigorous head scratch in Red's lap. Eric felt at once betrayed but also a little envious. Rose would probably eviscerate him if he confessed that out loud; a dark alleyway of his nature found that notion intriguing as well.

'You need therapy'. He thought to himself.

'I'm aware of that'. He replied.

Jacob was, again, in his kitchen routing through the fridge. It was fortuitous that Eric had recently stocked up with a big Shop-Co run a few days ago.

Braum had become intrigued by the cable sports channels and was enjoying a soccer match.

'Go, Sports Ball!' was Eric's typical response whenever he was asked if he had watched such and such a game. 'The warrior archetype team really gave the ferocious animal team a run for their money.' Rose would often talk sports with the others at work and Eric always felt so left out and inadequate. He fantasized about impressing her with his knowledge on the subject. The only thing standing in his path was knowledge on the subject or the interest to acquire it.

Rose had curled up in his easy chair, her legs crossed in a perfect lotus position, filing her nails with the methodical beauty of a Japanese tea ceremony. Her posture was perfect, and every stroke of her emery board was practiced and deliberate. It was an incredibly random thing to swoon at, but Eric didn't dwell.

Merlin emerged from the bedroom. Beyond the door Eric could see the rooftop of his apartment. He wondered if he would ever see his room again; his favorite shirt was in there.

He walked over to the old wizard.

"Alright, Yoda, how do I access this, power." Asked Eric.

"I can't tell you how to access your power." Merlin said. "How did you do it before? How did you divert the vortex with Red, Jacob and Braum into your living room? That wasn't an accident."

"Nothing, I was writing, I was painting. I was..."

"Creating." Merlin said.

Merlin waved Eric onto the stool in front of his drafting table. The experience was jarring but he was getting used to teleporting. Besides, he was given very little choice in the matter.

"I've been drawing and writing for years. I've wanted things desperately before too and none of it just materialized in front of me."

"Like I said, it's your power. If you're not specific enough sometimes the universe works things out in its own way."

Eric picked up his favorite pencil and twirled it around his fingers. He had gotten quite good at it, fidgeting between thoughts.

"That's another thing, I never wrote Little Red Riding Hood or The Three Pigs."

"You didn't create them, you modified their paths; you expanded their narrative."

"I expanded on their stories but there's things they told me that happened days after you left their world with me. I couldn't have been more than two years old. How could I write things that hadn't happened yet but are a part of my story?"

"Like I said, there is a chronological incongruity between both worlds. From the outside looking into their world, time is virtually at a standstill, yet years will pass here. But if you know anything about quantum physics, an event can precede its cause."

"I dropped physics in high school."

"You shape your reality, future, present, and past. Do you follow?"

"Not even Einstein could follow you." Eric said.

"Einstein. bright boy," Merlin said, "a tad naïve perhaps."

"Why can't I just reshape the events that happened before this and stop Wolfric before he even starts?"

"Change history."

"Yes."

"Have you ever heard of the Prussian Global Empire?"

"No."

"Exactly. It took me decades to fix and that is why you don't mess around with the past. Events aren't inherently good or bad, they are just events. Good luck can turn to bad luck can turn to good luck. Two sides of the same coin."

Merlin and Red locked eyes across the room, he knew he couldn't delay the encounter any longer.

"Begin practicing." Merlin said, "There's something I have to attend to."

Eric watched as Merlin approached Red. She had eyes on him from the moment he appeared. Eric couldn't focus on drawing anything for the moment.

Rose mouthed "what's going on?" to Eric from her seat. Eric shrugged his shoulders, but it was obvious to everyone that silence and feigning obliviousness was the best course of action.

"Hello, Red." Merlin said.

"You're a monster." She replied.

"Would you permit me to explain?"

"I have nothing to say to you."

Merlin toyed with the idea of freezing her as he did Eric but decided a gentler approach was more appropriate.

"Please," he begged, "hear me out."

She stood to meet him eye to eye.

"Fine." She said.

Merlin raised a hand slowly in front of her.

"Would you permit me?" He asked.

Red consented with a solitary nod.

Merlin rested his hand on her shoulder. Eric couldn't be sure, but it looked like the two of them blinked out of sight for a split second.

Merlin dropped his hand to his side.

"I understand," Red said. She placed a hand on Merlin's shoulder, looked him in the eye and nodded before she returned to the couch next to Braum.

Merlin had a look of satisfaction as she walked away. Not eager satisfaction but it was a start. After a deep sigh, he returned to Eric's side.

"How come we just didn't do that?" asked Eric, "Instead of your endless metaphysics lecture in the twilight zone?"

"Where do you think Red and I have been this whole time?" Merlin said.

Eric slipped a fresh pencil into the electric sharpener. When he needed inspiration the most there was nothing like new pencil with a tip that could split an atom.

"Alright," Merlin said, "What was your mindset when you opened the vortex in your living room?"

Eric observed Red and his cat; she got more beautiful each time his gaze came to rest on her. Those eyes, those lips; the way her hair framed her face. She reminded him of Rose in a lot of ways.   Rose was watching television with her head propped up on one arm. Eric had stolen glances at rose for years, studied her features when she wasn't looking; Red and her really were alike, remarkably alike. More precisely, it was uncanny. Eric scanned back and forth between them.

"Oh my god!" He blurted out.

Everyone turned to look at him.

"What's wrong?" asked Rose.

"What's wrong?" asked Red, almost simultaneously.

Eric forced a pleasant smile through gritted teeth.

"Nothing." He replied. His voice was a full octave higher.

How did he not see it? He had based Red's appearance on Rose.

'Ok,' he thought to himself, 'don't panic. If neither of them have noticed yet there's no reason to bring it up. Is there?'

"Everything ok, babe?" asked Rose. "You look a little pale...er than normal."

"Fine, honey." He said, "just fine."

'Maybe she'd be flattered', He thought.

'Are you insane?' He thought again.

Rose was out of the chair and across the room before he could protest.

'Wow, she can haul it.'

Red stood up, still cradling Dr. Stephen Anderson and came over to investigate also.

'Oh, God, really? Both of them?'

"Everything alright Eric?" Asked Red.

"You know," Rose said, "It's fine, I got this."

She positioned herself directly in Red's path, nose to nose.

"Ok, I'm not sure why." Red said, "but ever since you arrived I've been detecting a note of, oh, let's call it animal hostility from you."

"Oh honey, you haven't seen hostile." Rose countered.

"Have I offended you in some way. Have I unleashed something?"

"I'm just saying it's covered, you can sit down now."

"Fine."

"Fine."

Red smiled politely at Eric and returned to the sofa, Rose retracted her claws.

Eric's breath shallowed; his eyes flicked back and forth between both women with such rapid succession he thought they might pop out.

'How are they not seeing this?'

Merlin placed a hand on Eric's shoulder and intruded into his thoughts.

'Eric, are you aware how similar Rose and Red look?', The wizard asked.

'Yes, thank you! What do I do?' replied Eric.

'Well, if they haven't realized it, I wouldn't bring it up'.

'Arthur was so lucky to have you.'

'I'd be more concerned about them realizing Braum looks like you.'

'What? He does not.'

'Look for yourself.'

Braum got up from the couch passed all of them on his way to the kitchen.

"Anyone want anything?" he asked.

Eric scrutinized him. Alright, perhaps there was a superficial similarity. But Braum was taller, more confident and built like a brick shithouse. Perhaps they looked the same around the eyes, and the nose, the cheeks, lips, chin.

'Oh my god. How?' Eric thought.

Merlin didn't respond, he had removed his hand from Eric's shoulder. He was faced towards the kitchen as Braum handed the wizard a bottle of water from the fridge. Eric latched a hand on to Merlin's wrist.

'How?' Eric asked again.

Merlin flashed a sympathetic yet quite amused grin at Eric.

'Fantasies are a creative process too.' Merlin said.

'It wasn't like that. They were just day dreams.', replied Eric.

"Eric, are you okay?" Asked Rose.

"It wasn't like that!" Eric exclaimed.

"What?"

"I mean, I'm fine, hon."

CHAPTER 20:

A DETOUR DOWN MEMORY LANE...

"And that's why gLobo-Tech is pleased to offer our valued customers unlimited data. We heard you and we listened. Download and stream all your favorite shows to your heart's content. I for one plan on a little binge watching to catch up on 'The Undying Dead', so no spoilers out there! Ok?" Rick laughed and smiled his practiced corporate façade.

He was a weekly guest on his twenty-four-hour news channel's late-night talk show. He felt it was important to keep in touch with the community. Never in person, of course, but he went live from the big desk in his penthouse. He had Sheila work the camera; she had a real talent for it and always seemed to capture his good side. Rick could monitor all the live programs from the big wall in his office and often gave real time direction to the producers in the control rooms. He enjoyed that level of control, or rather he craved it. The show host buzzed back at him through his ear piece, to be perfectly honest he was only half listening.

"Well, as always, it was my pleasure Terry." He said. "Everyone out there have a great evening."

His smile dropped the instant the live feed was cut. He had always read it took more muscles to frown but smiling didn't come completely without effort either. Besides, he never frowned, he just preferred his resting face.

Sheila took her headset off and powered the camera down.

"Great segment, as always, my Alpha." She said.

Rick knew she would praise him no matter what he did; at times it felt disingenuous, but his circle of loyalty had shrunk as of late. He trusted that the pack was, for the most part, too terrified to ever cross him. But that wasn't trust, that wasn't real loyalty. Sheila embodied the quality almost blindly. Was it too much to ask for everyone to be like that?

Sheila poured him his whiskey neat, as was his custom after a broadcast. He downed it without so much as a wince.

"Any word from Gale and Shifter?" Asked Rick.

"They are at the police station rallying up some troops, but they haven't left yet."

"Full blooded from birth and they are still useless." Rick said. "I blame society."

"Full Blooded?" Asked Sheila.

"Did I never tell you this?"

"I don't believe so."

"Oh well. I was born a wolf. As was William, Gale and Shifter. I have no idea what transpired – It's probably the greatest mystery of my life. Anyway, I found William in the other world when he was young. I found Gale and Shifter years later. In that respect they are probably more like brothers, biologically speaking. Anyway. I discovered by happy accident one day my bite could transfer this gift to others. Half-bloods I called them."

"I see." Said Sheila.

"Don't take offence my dear." Rick said. "I don't mean to diminish you in any way. You are a credit to the pack, and I couldn't be more pleased with you."

"None taken," said Sheila, "it's my pleasure to serve."

"Remind me again, dear," Wolfric said, "Where did I find you?"

She smiled and took Rick's hand.

"You remember." She said.

Rick's voice trailed off and he went into a daze.

"Of course," he said distantly, "... now I remember."

"Now," Said Sheila, "you were talking about William, Gail and Shifter. Where did you find them again?"

She let go of his hand and he snapped back to reality without missing a beat.

"They are an incongruity, aren't they?" Rick said. "William, I found first. He was older than I was when Merlin found me, but it was the same story, he was an unwanted child cast out like some feral animal. I escaped from the cell they kept me in, almost nightly, I needed to run free and hunt. One night our paths crossed chasing the same deer. He had spirit, he really wanted it; he looked like he hadn't eaten in days. I backed off and let him have it. He needed it more than I did. If I could say nothing else about Arthur's dungeon, I was adequately fed. Arthur was always so compassionate – quite admirable, really, misguided but admirable.

As time passed, I ran into William more frequently on the same game trail; we agreed to share the kill if we hunted as a pack. I gave him the lion's share.

I soon learned that while he could understand me perfectly, he was completely mute from birth. I taught him the same power of telepathy that Merlin taught me. At first it was just so I could talk to him, but the gift suited him. I could confide anything to William; there was no judgement because we knew each other's minds better than anyone. Besides you there's no one I trust more."

"What about Beavis and Butthead?" Asked Sheila.

A short blast of laughter escaped from Rick's mouth; it wasn't often he genuinely laughed but Sheila sometimes had the knack for bringing it out of him.

"That is an apt description." He said. "I discovered this world at the height of the war. There were multitudes of displaced, wayward souls looking for a purpose over here. If I saw promise in them, I turned them, and they joined the cause. After the war I took more time to explore this world. It was ripe with opportunity for a group such as ours. Besides, if I was going to be a father, I had to provide The Prince, and provide all of you, with an adequate home. I was sadly lacking in the currency of this world. But there was no shortage of people willing to pay for a unique group of motivated self-starters such as ourselves.

I learned there was some fast money to be had in a little-publicized, underground fight arena on the edge of the city. The arena champions were two brothers who were reputed to be unbeatable. I chose some of my best fighters to compete, but they were no match for those two. I admired their ferocity, their brutality, their willingness to cheat. They were thugs, pure and simple.

More than that I recognized them for what they really were; something I was surprised to find in this world of all places; two more full bloods. They deserved a better life than that. They deserved to be with their own kind. So, we liberated the place. It was our corporation's first acquisition."

"Gale and Shifter." Said Sheila blankly. "Arena champions."

"I know." Rick said. "Life is full of surprises. In retrospect perhaps, I expected too much from them. Oh, they are capable pit-bulls, but they lack a certain capacity to think outside the ring. I gave them their abilities in the hopes they would rise to the occasion. I think I spoiled them with this life of privilege, they lost their edge. At least they have a better life than they did."

"We're all better off with you, Alpha." Said Sheila.

"Thank you. You're too kind." Rick said. "I mean, you are better off, I just never tire of hearing it."

CHAPTER 21:
TIME OUT...

ric stared at the blank page. There was nothing so enticing or daunting as the blank page. Full of all the potential energy in the universe or the solid indifference of a brick wall. Merlin had manifested a book to read; this was taking more time than he anticipated.

A knock at the door silenced the room. Eric thought for sure the police had come to round them all up again. Red, Jacob and Braum formed a line and drew their weapons. Rose transformed and stood at the ready.

Merlin returned his book to the air and walked over to the door.

"It's fine everyone." He said. "Just some party guests arriving fashionably late." Merlin opened the door.

William stood out in the hall, his hands neatly folded in front of him. Timmin was perched on his shoulder leaning against his cheek.

"Billy!" Rose raced over to him and bear-hugged him off his feet. She squealed ecstatically and spun him around. Timmin momentarily took to the air to weather the reunion.

Rose quickly ushered him into the room with her arms around him.

"Eric." She said, "this is Billy!"

"This is your brother?" Eric replied.

"Yes!"

"That's Silent William." Red said, "Wolfric's interrogator and right-hand man."

She clenched her staff harder. Jacob raised his axe; Braum had his bow trained on William's head.

Rose extended her claws and stood her ground in front of William.

"Whoa, Whoa, Whoa!" Eric shouted. He got up from his stool and separated the factions with his hands futilely held up to both sides.

"Eric, get behind us." Red demanded. "Wolfric can't be far away. Your girlfriend is obviously a spy."

"Two hits, blondie." Growled Rose, "me hitting you, you hitting the floor."

"I'm right here." Red said. "Come here girl, come here!" Red patted her hands on her thighs and called Rose like a dog.

"That is it!" Rose charged.

Red swung her staff.

"Fetch, girl!" She shouted.

"Everyone JUST STOP!" Eric, dropped to the floor, his arms over his head. But there was nothing. The room was silent. He gradually raised his head and looked around.

Everyone in the room did just as he asked, everyone froze. Everyone except for Merlin and Timmin (who were beyond such tricks), and Dr. Stephen Anderson, (who never listened to Eric, ever); he continued grooming, perched on the arm of the sofa.

"Well done!" Merlin said.

"Well done, what?" asked Eric. "That wasn't you?"

"No, that was all you my boy."

"I didn't draw or write anything."

"Don't be so literal. The drawing is simply a tool to help you focus. You don't really need to."

Eric waved his hand in front of Rose's beautiful, if extremely angry, eyes. She didn't so much as flinch. Timmin flew into Eric's face and admonished him with a squelching noise that reminded him of a dial up modem.

"What the hell is that?" Eric backed up against his desk but Timmin closed the distance between them just as swiftly. She stung him with micro-bursts of lightening to the forehead.

"That's Timmin." Merlin said. "And, to paraphrase around the numerous expletives, William is her friend and she wants you to let him go."

"Tell her to back off and I'll try!"

"Fairies don't negotiate." Merlin said.

"Release William!" Eric shouted.

William remained unmoved. Eric's forehead was getting numb.

"William Release! William Come!"

"Now you're just offending her, likening him to a dog."

Eric slipped around Timmin and bolted over to William. He grabbed him by his shoulders and shook him. Timmin ignited into flame and slow-burned towards Eric.

"William!" he screamed.

William snapped out of his trance. Timmin tasered Eric out of the way and embraced William around the neck.

Eric rubbed his forehead, the numerous spots in front of his eyes had begun to clear. He felt like he had a handle of what to do. He put his hands on Rose's cheeks, and looked deep into her eyes. He focused.

"Rose." He said.

She reanimated and struggled with him for a moment.

"It's me, It's me." He said.

"What happened?" Rose was disoriented.

"Everything's fine, you're safe, you're safe."

"Eric, I don't trust her. We have to get away from them."

"It's fine now. They're fine. Everyone just needed a time out."

"We have stories about her too. Red Hood the Wolf Slayer."

"Rose, just calm down, it's going to be fine."

"No, we have to go."

William gently rested his hand on her shoulder. He closed his eyes. Rose settled down.

"What's he doing?" Eric became slightly frantic himself.

"He's showing her the truth." Merlin said.

Rose gently transitioned to her human self.

"What? That can't be." She struggled slightly, as though she were having a bad dream.

William released his hold on Rose and opened his eyes again.

"He lied" She said. "He lied about everything."

"Are you alight?" Asked Eric. He worriedly searched her eyes for any sign of unease.

"I'm fine." She replied. "That son of a bitch."

"You're good now?" Eric fretted.

"Yes." Rose said with a sigh. "Sorry I lost my shit. The aggression kind of comes with the package. Are you freaked out?"

"Yes." Eric smiled. "But we'll find an outlet for that. We'll get you into underground cage fights."

She punched him in the arm, and they held one another.

Timmin sighed from her vantage point on William's shoulder. It was all so incredibly romantic. She was relieved she didn't have to incinerate Eric.

"OK." Eric said. "You realize I'm going to have to release the rest of them, right?"

"Yes." Rose said with a slight eye roll "I told you I'm fine."

"Ok good."

"Bitch better watch her step, all I'm saying."

"Rose..."

"Last time."

Merlin suggested it might be wise to disarm everyone before Eric undid his enchantment. With their weapons safely stashed against a wall, Red, Jacob, and Braum were seated comfortably on the sofa. Eric and the rest gathered around the living room to perform their strange intervention.

Eric was about to speak when something else occurred to him.

"Merlin, could you bind them first?" Asked Eric.

"Done." Merlin replied.

"Ok."

He knelt in front of them, focused, and called them each by name. All three awoke and struggled to move.

"What is this?" Demanded Red.

"Ok," Eric said. "Don't freak out. We've reached an understanding."

"With them? Eric you can't trust a thing they say. Do you have any concept of the atrocities they've committed? Surely Merlin told you."

"I understand. There is a lot of bad blood here. But you are supposed to be the good guys though. You can't fight fear and hate with fear and hate."

Eric glanced over at Merlin. The wizard nodded with approval.

"You also can't paint everyone with the same brush. Rose and William have deserted Wolfric and are willing to share what they know. You just have to keep an open mind. If you want to blame anyone, blame me, I wrote your stories. Maybe I could even write that you come around to my way of thinking, but I'm not going to do that. Your lives aren't going to be swayed by the whim of my pencil or paintbrush anymore. We're asking for your help but it's your choice. Wolfric must be stopped, but we're stronger together."

Red forced a heavy sigh. She turned to Jacob.

"What do you think?" She said.

Jacob fixed a cold gaze on William and Rose. In every decision he always tried to imagine what Eil and Issac would have done. Everything except his revenge. It was always something he felt he had to do for them. But Eli, he could forgive anything. And Issac, he would have questioned the practicality of Jacob holding on to something so long that no longer served him. Both of them would want him to be happy, after he kicked Wolfric's ass.

"Let's do it." He said finally.

"Braum?" asked Red.

"I didn't really have anything planned today." He said.

"You know Eric," Red said. "Your father would be proud of you."

"Wolfric?"

"No, your real father. Arthur. His way would have been forgiveness too."

Eric smiled. Red returned it.

"Alright," She said. "we're with you, Prince Eric."

Rose wrapped her arms around Eric.

"Told you, you'd make a good team leader." She said.

"Maybe I just needed the right team." He held her tight and scratched behind her ear.

A police siren echoed from the street outside, it was joined by another and soon another.

"Well that can't be good." Eric said. "I think they noticed we're missing."

"First royal decision your majesty," Rose said. "We should hightail it."

"They probably have the place surrounded." Replied Eric.

The erratic thumping of tactical boots echoed from the hallway outside; a heavy pounding beckoned entrance at the door.

"This is the police!" the voice commanded, "Open up!"

"I don't think they're going to ask twice." Eric said. "Merlin can you barricade the door?"

"Absolutely." Replied Merlin.

With a gesture the door was reinforced with nailed planks and a buttress made from a solid timber.

"That's a temporary solution at best." Merlin said.

"Mind if we borrow your sanctuary?" asked Eric.

Merlin nodded and strolled up to Eric's bedroom. He closed the door, waved his hand over it and reopened it. Beyond the door frame everyone could see the dimly lit sanctuary.

"Everyone take what you need.", Eric said, "We probably won't be back."

The group filed through the door. Rose looked back at Eric and frantically waved him in.

"I'll be right there." He said. "Stephen! Where is that stupid cat?"

A loud repeating thud demanded entrance at the door. Eric suspected they were using a battering ram.

"Stephen!" Eric shouted. The cat was nowhere to be seen.

"Stephen!" Shouted Rose.

Dr. Stephen Anderson ran past Eric and into the sanctuary.

"You little shit..." He said.

He took one last look at his apartment, he was probably going to lose his security deposit. He ran into the sanctuary and slammed the door behind him.

CHAPTER 22:

COMMUNITY OUTREACH...

ric leaned on a bookshelf and stared out at the ceaseless expanse of the cosmos. A comet tumbled by on its unending journey to who-knew-where. "When I was younger, I could never get enough of this view." Red joined Eric at the edge of the room. "Actually, this very spot was one of my favorites. I used to beg Merlin to do our lessons in here. He was forever tying to compete with all of this for my attention."

"He's kind of like your dad," Eric said. "Isn't he?"

"Dad?"

"Your father."

"Oh, yes. I suppose. He raised me from the time I was a little."

"He seemed genuinely afraid of you hating him."

"I thought I did. I'm not thrilled with him and some of his choices at the moment. No offence to you being born as a result."

"None taken."

"The truth is, we were going to lose the war. Arthur knew it. He tried to keep a sense of hope alive in the kingdom, that was his job, but we would have eventually been wiped out. So, I understand the overwhelming responsibility Merlin felt he was wrestling with. I wish he'd have come to us, Jacob and I. Trusted us to find another way. I don't know. It's complicated I guess."

"He is hard to love but too wonderful to hate."

"That's a fair statement."

An asteroid collided with the comet in a blinding explosion of light and stardust.

"Whoa!" Eric exclaimed. "That was awesome!"

"What's awesome?" Rose sprinted over and aggressively wedged herself into the open space between Eric and Red.

"You just missed an asteroid hit a comet."

"Cool!" Rose said, "So what are you guys talking about?"

"Nothing, really.", Eric said. "I was just standing here thinking. I've rallied all of you together and I don't have anything even vaguely resembling a plan."

"I'm sure you'll think of something." Red reassured.

"Totally babe" Rose said, snapping at the heel of Red's statement.

A brief but no less unwieldy silence passed between them. Red rolled her eyes but smiled.

"I'll leave you too alone." She said.

"You don't have to go." Eric said.

"It's ok, I'm going to go see what Jacob is up to."

"Nice talking to you, Red." Rose grinned, her fangs slightly bared.

"You too, Rose." Red said. She placed a hand on Rose's shoulder and beamed the fakest grin she could muster before she left.

Rose rolled into his arms and obstructed his view of the universe. In the nicest possible way of course.

"I wish you two could get along." Eric said.

"I was totally getting along!" Rose said. "Didn't you see our bonding moment? She touched my shoulder, I didn't sever her arm."

"I stand corrected."

How could he not love her? Their flaws perfectly balanced each other's. On top of all that she was a complete and utter smoke show he had always believed to be way out of his league. And she was jealous over him; over him! If it was all a dream and he was really just in a room somewhere, drooling and catatonic, he was okay with that.

"So, what did Billy show you?" Asked Eric.

"What a lying piece of shit Wolfric is."

"Do you want to talk about it?"

"Not really. But maybe I should."

"Well, we apparently have all the time in the universe in here." Eric squeezed Rose tighter. She turned around in his arms and leaned back into his chest. For a few moments the cosmic ballet swirled in front of them.

"I remember a commotion. I remember the wolves, I remember being afraid. He came and rescued me. He told me my family was gone but not to be afraid, that he would take care of me."

Rose's voice broke and lowered to just above a whisper.

"But it was all bullshit. Wolfric was the one that had my family killed. For no good reason; it wasn't a fight for survival. I was some kind of trophy."

"We'll stop him."

"I remember someone telling me bedtime stories. It's a man's voice but I can't see his face. Some nights I almost can, and then it's gone. I think it's my father."

"Can we trust Billy, William? He was with Wolfric an awfully long time."

"Too long." Rose said. "He is absolutely wracked with guilt. He felt like he owed a debt of loyalty to Wolfric. He was never anything but sweet to me. That fairy, they've been together for a little while. I think he actually loves her."

"I see." Eric said.

"You trust me, don't you?" Rose turned; her haunting green eyes scanned his face. For a moment he tried to remember how to breathe.

"With my life." He said.

"He's met some people who might be willing to help." she said.

"Well, they are in luck; we are currently looking to fill several new positions in our lambs to the slaughter department. We can't do anything from here. Tell Bill to lead the way."

$$\triangle \ \triangle \ \triangle$$

The rental cube van backed up to the warehouse loading dock. Jared stood by the open door on the raised platform and waved them backward into position. John, always there to help take charge of a situation, mimicked Jared's hand gestures and posture.

He had the van stop just shy of the rubber bumpers. The driver turned off engine and leapt up to join them on the platform. Jared raised the back door and inspected the cargo.

"Good job." Jared said. "These will do nicely."

Pasta and rice filled the void, but it was hardly the basis for a healthy long-term diet. His people had become sluggish and just a little bit depressed. A truck full of fresh fruit, vegetables and meat would go a long way towards improving that.

With the gold their amazing new friends had left them they purchased a few large refrigerators and freezers. Under Jared's direction they had also set up a respectable kitchen. He had spent more than his fair share on mess hall duty in the army under disciplinary action. Under the circumstances it was time well spent.

A lineup of men and women formed in the loading bay. Jared picked up a box and handed it to John, who in turn handed it to the next person and so on. Their bucket brigade unloaded the truck in no time.

"Good job everyone." Jared said. "Eddie, return the truck. Everyone else let's get this stuff stowed."

Ashley, a skinny teenager, appeared from a door and rushed over to Jared.

"Wolfman and Firefly are back." She said.

"Oh, good, thanks for telling me." Jared said.

"They aren't alone."

A few moments later Jared entered the main warehouse with John and Ashley in tow. All activity had ceased, and the community had gathered in a wide circle around William, Timmin and six strangers. They had armed themselves with an assortment of baseball bats, axe handles and machetes. Strangers made them uneasy. The new arrivals stood back to back in a circle of their own.

"They just suddenly appeared in the middle of the floor." Said Ashley.

"Everyone ease up." Jared said. "Hey, William, who are your friends?"

Jared assessed them with a cautious once over.

"Um, hello." Eric said. He held up both hands and gingerly stepped out from the group. "We're sorry to just barge in. William said it would be fine. Perhaps a more gradual introduction might have been the way to go. That's my bad."

"What do you want?" Jared asked.

"William, said we might be able to help each other with a mutual problem. He tells us your people have been disappearing. Something has been taking them. We know what is... who is doing it."

"Ok." Jared said, "I'm listening."

"Thank you." Eric said.

"Are you hungry?" Asked Jared. "We were about to prepare dinner."

"Again, thank you." Eric said.

"I can help with that." Jacob said.

"Ashley can show you to the bunks if any of you are tired." Jared motioned to Ashely who responded with a wave.

The group followed her, Jared's eyes casually landed on Rose as she passed. He made a start toward the pantry to help take inventory but stopped and gave her a second look. It was the hair, he had only ever seen the shade of red one other time. He shrugged it off. When he started down that particular memory lane things just got too dark.

Rose's peripheral vision was outstanding. She felt Jared's eyes on her and gripped Eric's hand that much tighter as they passed. She didn't look back. Perhaps it had just been a long day. A lie down might be just what the doctor ordered.

With everyone's help, and some embellishment from Timmin, the banquet area had been set. She had manifested a huge round table for the community to gather around. It was an impractical use of space, but they had all the room in the world. Her people gathered in circles all the time.

Jared sat between Merlin and Eric. Rose sat next to Eric but insisted William sit on the other side of her, so she could be between her two favorite guys.

Jacob had temporarily usurped control of the kitchen. He spent the last few hours making his mother's famous Slop Stew, it was a one pot meal that was, usually, better than the name implied. Red quite enjoyed it, on occasion. It was generally thrown together with whatever was on hand and as a result the flavor profile was uneven from batch to batch. Jacob insisted each stew was a unique orchestra of subtle notes that were lost on the human palate.

Since he was a guest and they didn't want to seem rude, the community ate it without complaint; a lot of them had eaten much worse. He rolled a cart around the table and ladled a healthy helping into everyone's bowl.

Eric thought a little pleasant conversation might distract away from the meal.

"This is quite a place you got here." He said.

"Thanks," Jared said, "a week ago we were in a shanty town under an over pass. William and Timmin helped put this roof over our heads. I don't pretend to understand half the things I've seen them do; but we were happy for the help."

"It's been an eventful week for me too." Eric replied.

"I'm not sure how willing they are to get in a fight against magic and monsters. Your welcoming party is the most aggressive I've seen any of them. Petty fights, some run-ins with gangs but they aren't soldiers."

"We understand," Red said. "But we believe the whole world is in danger. Wolfric is up to something that goes beyond abducting people off the streets. He's wealthy and powerful, you might know him as Rick Wolfe."

"Really? I find that hard to believe. Rick Wolfe had done more to help the homeless in this city that any public official. The people love him. He's set up soup kitchens, methadone clinics, free needle exchange programs, free counselling. I was considering reaching out to his foundation for support for our community."

"He might seem like that on the surface," Eric said, "but the reality is much different, trust me."

Rose's heightened sense of smell and taste interpreted the stew differently than Jacob. The 'unique orchestra of subtle notes' was out of tune. She pushed her plate away and curled up to Eric. She heard there was some fresh steak in the fridge, blood rare. Her Pavlovian craving was almost too much to resist.

She felt Jared's eyes on her again. She engaged eye contact with him until he looked away.

'What the hell does he keep looking at?' She thought.

She was certain she had never seen him before in her life; there was, however, something very familiar about him. His voice, as unlikely as it seemed she had heard his voice before. Maybe it was time to get that steak.

"Excuse me please." Rose said as she left the table.

Eric watched her leave. He knew when something was bothering her and when she was just putting on a face.

"I'll be right back." He said.

Eric found Rose seated in the corner of the kitchen chewing on a raw twelve-ounce T-bone; blood dripped down her chin as her sharp teeth tore into the piece of meat.

"You ok there, hon?" He asked.

Though she was looking right at him, she replied only in low grunts and growls as the ripped the flesh from the bone.

"Need a plate? Knife?"

Come to think of it, she was five-time hotdog eating champion at the annual company picnic. He recalled one time, when she had finished all of hers, she started on the tray next to her. Jack, from accounting, must have outweighed her by 150 pounds, but the terrified look on the man's face when he almost lost a hand was unforgettable. Eric hadn't put much stock in the memory until just then.

Rose finished and picked her teeth with the pointed tip of the, now bleached, bone.

"What's wrong?" Eric tried again.

"I stress eat." She said. "Ok? Now you know my dirty little secret."

"That was your dirty secret. Not the lycanthropy." He sat on the floor beside her.

"You want to head for the hills now, don't you?" She asked.

Eric reached up for a dish rag from the counter, wiped Rose's face and then kissed it.

"What has you so stressed?" He asked.

"Oh, everything." She said. "But that Jared guy keeps looking at me. And for the life of me, I know I know him from somewhere."

"They've lived on the streets for quite some time. Is it possible you saw him in passing?"

"It's more than that. I've heard his voice before."

"Recently?"

"No, it was in the past somehow. It doesn't seem possible."

"Leave it be for now, come back to the table. I always find the brain keeps working on it when you let it go."

"I know. You're right."

Eric and Rose returned to the table. Jacob was going around seeing if anyone wanted seconds. There were few takers.

"Don't worry." Jacob said, "It tastes even better the next day."

Eric and Rose sat back down, she leaned on his shoulder.

"Everything alright?" Jared asked.

"Oh yes," Eric said, "Rose has...specific dietary needs."

"Rose." Jared said. "that's a very lovely name."

With some effort, Rose managed to return eye contact. There was no malice in his gaze; in fact, she thought she saw a touch of sadness.

"Thank you." She replied softly.

"It was my daughter's name."

Jared brought his attention back to Eric. He didn't like to dwell on his daughter, it was too painful. But perhaps he had lived in denial too long and her memory was coming back with a vengeance.

"So, what is your plan?" Jared steered his thoughts back to the present.

"To be perfectly honest I have no idea where to start." Eric replied. "I heard you were in the military. I could use a touch of strategic experience."

"Well, typically before any mission intel is gathered on the target; spies, aerial reconnaissance. You can't just march right in without the right intel. It sounds pretty basic, but if it were me, I would send someone in to find out what they can."

"Merlin," Eric said, "You were invisible before you rescued us. Could you just hang around his office and listen in?"

"I'm afraid it's not as easy as that." Merlin said. "Back in his office he was already aware of my presence; he wasn't scared, it was as though he didn't need to be. I taught him his powers and I have never felt him so powerful in his life. We need him to let his guard down. We need someone he wouldn't suspect in a million years."

William raised his hand. Timmin immediately flew from his shoulder and attempted to wrestle his arm to the ground. With his free hand he grasped her gently and she let go.

Timmin joined his mind.

'It's too dangerous.' She said.

'It's the only way.' He replied.

'He won't let you go once you're back. It's too suspicious.'

'There's no one he trusts more than me. It will work.'

Timmin grudgingly agreed, her head dropped further with each successive nod. William took his finger and raised her head and attempted to reassure her with a smile.

'I'm coming right back.' He said.

"Are you sure William?" Eric asked.

William nodded.

"I should go with him." Rose said.

"I'm sorry, what?" Eric squeezed her closer, almost holding her down.

"It'll work, Eric. Wolfric would be so happy to see us both it would keep him off guard."

"I seem to recall you forsaking them in an attempt to save me? Won't he be a bit perturbed at that?"

"I could sell him some b.s. story. I was confused, you kidnapped me. William miraculously came to my rescue, I returned home with him. There's a touching reunion. As long as we throw in the proper amount of pandering to his ego he's a pretty easy sell."

"And what if you're wrong?"

"First of all, I'm never wrong."

Jared burst with a laughter that even caught him by surprise.

"And if I am wrong." Rose continued, "you're going to rescue me."

"Rescue you."

"Uh-huh." Rose smiled.

"Storm the castle without the information we sent you in to get in the first place."

"Yup." She smooshed his cheeks together and kissed his forehead.

Eric shook his head, "This is insane."

'I'm never wrong.' Jared remembered his Rose would always say that. It was impossible to deny anymore; the word impossible had lost all meaning the past few days. It was her; somehow this was his Rose.

"Merlin is pulling you out the first sign of trouble." Eric looked into her eyes to confirm she understood.

"Agreed." She said.

"No problem." Merlin added. "Actually, I could use Timmin's help."

Timmin flew eye to eye with Merlin.

"You and William have a rapport. You could help boost a mental link to William and Rose to keep tabs on them."

Timmin agreed with a nod.

"My mind to your mind, yours to William and William holds hands with Rose; the connection would be complete. At the slightest sign of danger, we're there and we pull you out."

"When do we leave?" Rose asked, a little too eagerly for Eric's comfort.

"Probably best to leave in the morning." Jared said. "We have plenty of places to sleep here."

Everyone agreed; Eric reluctantly.

After the table was cleared, those of the community who could play broke out guitars and fiddles, another on a set of conga drums. Merlin materialized a cask of wine he had been saving for a special occasion, well over a hundred years. And, at least for a time, the shadows that hung over everyone were dispelled.

Braum presented himself before Red to request a dance with a formal bow and extended hand, she consented by giving him her hand. Others joined the dance floor.

Timmin felt the lighting was all wrong, she killed the electricity and lit candles around the hall; pixie dust hung in the air above them like a blanket of stars.

Eric and Rose slow danced to their own rhythm out of step with the music.

Jared watched them from across the room, moved to a point somewhere between joy and tears. She was so beautiful. This Eric boy seemed to genuinely care for her.

He had damn well better, for his sake. Jared wrestled with whether he should tell her or not. Would it be just for his own peace of mind? Would she vanish in a puff of mist if he tried to touch her? In the end, he was satisfied that his daughter had somehow continued and was happy.

Timmin dragged William to the dance floor. Literally (fairies can be freakishly strong). She twirled around in his hand. A bashful smile creeped onto his face and under his fur he blushed. Eventually he got over his shyness and their size difference and danced with his lady.

The party went into the late hours of the evening until, bit by bit, everyone turned in.

Eric and Rose found an unoccupied double sized cot. He spooned behind her, his arms around her waist and their fingers entwined. He held on to her for dear life, trembling. She turned over to face him and ran her fingers through his hair; she lightly grabbed his neck and pulled him in for a kiss. His trembling ceased.

The next morning everyone gathered on the loading dock to see William and Rose off.

Red walked up to Rose.

"This is either very brave or very stupid. But sometimes it's the same thing. It's possible I misjudged you."

Rose smiled, genuinely this time. "We still have a fight coming. Don't spoil it by being likeable."

"Wouldn't miss it."

"But you're alright too... Red."

Red punched Rose lightly on the shoulder. Rose bared her teeth and growled, playfully.

William, Timmin, and Merlin put their heads together to confer on last minute details; they joined hands to sync their minds.

"Timmin and I will observe everything that's going on from your perspective." Merlin said. "You were always the more gifted telepath, William. If Wolfric wants to read your mind you should have very little trouble blocking any memory of us or this place from him. The safety of these people depends on it."

William gave a thumbs-up. Timmin laid a kiss on his nose.

'You come right back.'

'Before you even know I'm gone.'

Eric gave Rose one more long and passionate kiss.

"I have to go." She said.

Eric reluctantly opened his arms to let her go.

William and Rose departed down the street toward the heart of downtown.

"Stay safe!" Eric shouted after them. "I really hate this plan!"

Rose blew him a kiss over her shoulder as they disappeared down the street and out of sight.

CHAPTER 23:

THE PRODIGAL SON, AND DAUGHTER, RETURN...

"So where are we on our timeline?"

Rick was seated at the table in his penthouse; his usual breakfast of an egg white omelet, fresh strawberries, a blood raw beef liver and a sweetgrass smoothie was set before him. He had always believed in the rejuvenating powers of a good liver; great source of iron.

"Asia is right on schedule. We have secured exclusive rights to provide broadcasting and internet support in every major market." A voice replied.

The table was positioned in front of Rick's wall sized screen; it had been split into the images of his various department heads; it really was the best way to conduct a conference call.

"India has signed on condition we base a majority of the international customer support centers in New Delhi and Mumbai." A lady said.

"Whatever they want." Rick said.

"Australia wants a guarantee of at least fifty-five percent Australian content in the programming." A gentleman said.

"Very particular for a nation founded by criminals. But, Dog love them, deal."

Rick guzzled his sweetgrass smoothie and lightly slammed the glass down on the table with a satisfied gasp.

"Sounds great everyone. Keep up the good work. We'll talk tomorrow."

Rich dismissed the screens via remote. He finished his liver and lapped up every trace of crimson from plate with his prodigious tongue.

Gale and Shifter vacuumed and dusted around the penthouse.

"Alpha, how long do we have to do this?" Gale asked.

"Boys, I have spoiled you. I will own that. Say what you will about Merlin but when I was your age, he taught me the sense of pride that came with a hard day's work."

"Alpha." Shift said.

"No, now hear me out." Wolfric continued. "It's been a pretty uneventful period. I grant you. Idle hands and all that. And city life tends to soften a man."

"Alpha." Gale said.

"But I promise you we are on the cusp of some very exciting things."

"Alpha." Gale repeated more emphatically.

"What, Gale? What is so important you need to interrupt me?"

Gale pointed in the direction of the door.

Wolfric turned around. He was rarely ever caught off guard, but it was one of those times. There was William, with Rose at his side. Sheila stood just inside the door and presented them.

"Alpha." She said. "We have company."

William and Rose both dropped to one knee.

Wolfric grinned from ear to ear and clapped. "There he is! Don't scare me like that! We have been tearing this city apart looking for you. Get in here you crazy son of a bitch. You must be famished." He embraced William and picked him up off the ground in a bear hug. He put him down and regarded Rose curiously. "Rose, this is... unexpected."

"Alpha." She said. "I'm sorry. I lost my head. I was confused."

Rose could cry on a whim. It really was her best performance.

"They treated me like an animal. Eric worst of all. They only wanted information from me. If William hadn't sensed me in the area and came to my rescue, I don't know what..." She fell to her knees at William's side.

"... I see." Wolfric eventually said. "It's alright child. We all do crazy things when we're in love. I laid waste to an entire kingdom. Well don't just stand there at the door come in and take a load off. Sheila get them something to eat."

"Yes, my Alpha." Sheila paused for a few extra uncertain heartbeats before she headed off to the kitchen.

William and Rose sat down on the sofa. Gale and Shifter sat across from them at a rare loss for words. Wolfric poured himself a whiskey before joining them.

"Welcome back your brother and sister boys." He said.

"Welcome back Bill." Shifter said.

William merely nodded.

"Welcome back Rose." Gale said. "Sorry about blowing you out an open window and stuff."

"Bite me." Replied Rose.

There was a profoundly awkward tension in the room.

△ △ △

"It's not working." Eric said. "They aren't buying it."

His hand rested on Merlin's shoulder, the wizard placed his hand on Eric's so he could 'tune in'. Merlin was in seated meditation with Timmin who sat in his other hand.

"Look," Merlin said, "this isn't as easy as it looks. If you can't relax you might want to wait in another room."

"I'm fine," Eric fidgeted back and forth. "Read my mind, I'm as fine as fine can be."

"Clearly." Merlin replied.

△ △ △

"So, William," Wolfric leaned back in the sofa and crossed a leg over his lap. "the stories you must have. The things you must have seen. Tell me everything. Where's that pixie you were carrying around? I have a few interested buyers. Do you know what you could get on the black market for some fairy dust?"

"She's gone." Rose said. "Apparently she escaped when he arrived."

Wolfric's glare fell on Rose. She had nearly forgotten he was the grand master of stare-downs; she felt a chill that resonated through the ether and even gave Eric a heart palpitation across town.

"Now Rose," Wolfric said. "We've discussed this, no interruptions while adults are talking."

"Sorry, Alpha". *'You sanctimonious son of a bitch. What am I, nine?'*

"Why don't you go give your sister some help in the kitchen. You can catch up on girl talk."

"Really? I'd much rather stay in here with you."

"That wasn't a request, sweetie."

"Ok then." Rose said, in a somewhat louder tone, "I'll be in the kitchen on the other side of the penthouse floor from your office."

Gale and Shifter exchanged glances. Gale wondered if perhaps he had hit her harder than he originally thought.

Rose stood up and released William's hand; William tried to hold on a few seconds longer.

△ △ △

Rose vanished from the telepathic link.

"Oh my god." Eric withdrew his hand and the connection was broken.

"Try to remain calm." Merlin said.

"Remain calm?" Eric paced the floor cradling his forehead. "They've been separated. And her banter. Oh man, she's beautiful but she is not subtle."

"Eric."

"What!?"

"Sleep."

Eric's head dropped; his eyes rolled up into his head and his eyelids slammed shut.

△ △ △

Wolfric finished his drink, stood up and held out his hands. William assumed his position as he had done for nearly as long as they had known one another. They placed hands on each other's temples and stood with their foreheads together. It was the deepest form of sharing they had with one another.

William felt their mind's join but rather than show him the truth he guided Wolfric through a maze of fiction. William hoped he wouldn't notice being lead around by the hand, so to speak, in his head.

It was the sad tale of an aimless, wandering nomad. A stranger in an inhospitable nightmare world, never giving up hope he would one day be reunited with his beloved master. William felt Wolfric's ego enjoyed the narrative.

It occurred to him he could probably fry Wolfric's mind on the spot and end things right there. It fascinated him how tyrants could stay in power; they were just one man. Couldn't the people just turn on them? Oust them from power?

He could do it so easily, he just had to push into Rick's mind and snuff his consciousness out like a flame. Gale, Shifter and Sheila would likely be a handful afterwards.

Things suddenly changed. William's mindscape grew colder, darker; he found it difficult to think. There was a pressure between his eyes. His inner monologue dissolved into silence.

'Oh, William.' Wolfric's voice was all there was. William's consciousness was suppressed to mere observation; a coma victim screaming that he was still alive inside.

'I'm surprised at you. I spare no expense trying to find you and you go and pull this shit?

But I don't blame you; you're just a puppet like everyone else he's encountered. He thinks he's above you and that reality should conform to his set of arbitrary standards.'

Wolfric pushed past William's mind until he was consciousness to consciousness with Merlin.

'You are getting predictable, old man. You know, I wish I had this gift you have; people will do anything for you. How many hapless disciples have you marched into the jaws of death for your cause? Your body count rivals mine. You can't help yourself. Chalk two more up in your tally.'

Merlin and Timmin pushed back in futility, Wolfric's presence materialized in their minds with an all too vivid tangibility. William hung by the scruff of his neck, limp in Wolfric's hand; his eyes desperately pleaded with Timmin.

'Is this where I was supposed to divulge my evil plan, Merlin? Hmm? You and your team of superheroes come riding in and save the day? You've read too many of this world's books. Humans are absolute basket-cases of neurosis and anxieties, but they love their stories. They love stories more than their own miserable lives. Oh, what the hell, you got me talking now, I might as well tell you.'

Wolfric manifested an easy chair; he always liked to be comfortable even if he was only thinking about it. He sat William on his lap and cradled him.

'When I was younger, I didn't understand why I was different, I didn't understand why people were afraid of me, but they were, on a primal level. It was something that went way deeper than any rationale. I didn't know what it was, but that fear gave me goosebumps, tingles, that fear would sustain me for days. Some nights, just for fun, I would sneak into a kid's room and do the whole monster in the closet thing, it's a riot. As you can imagine though, in a world full of fantastic creatures you can only defy expectation so much; a monster in a closet isn't really that big of a deal. I mean we literally have closet monsters back home. But when I first came over here. The air was different. That tingle was always around. This world is afraid 24/7, only it's a different fear. They don't believe in monsters- well some of the really interesting ones do, but what they really fear is the unknown. They'd rather cover it up with distractions, fantasies. They don't want to deal with it, and the more then deny it the worse it gets. But it's what they want; And who better than me to give them what they want?'

'I should have left you in that forest.' Merlin said.

Wolfric laughed a hearty, yet chilling belly laugh.

'That's not even the best part. They don't even want to have to think. With a media empire I can form their decisions, set their moral compass, tell them what to buy, sell them what I told them buy. They rally behind the banner of brand association. My banner! Even when they aren't conscious of it. There's a subliminal message embedded in all my programming and web content that directs just a little of their attention to me. Forget hiding among them in sheep's clothing, I'm the shepherd.'

Timmin grew restless in Merlin's hands; try as they might, neither of them could break the link.

'Fidgety little thing, isn't she? We're almost done here. Do you or the fairy have any last words for William? No? How about you William, anything to say to your friends?' Wolfric cackled and worked Williams mouth like a ventriloquist dummy. Timmin exerted her mind with every ounce of consciousness.

'Whoa! She's a scrapper. I can see why you like her William. Well, liked her anyway.' Wolfric got up from the chair and it vanished.

'Tell my son I have his girl here. She's alive and well, though for how long I make no promises. I'd really like to catch up with him. I've missed some birthdays; it's all so very 'Cats in The Cradle'. I'll keep a light on for you and a seat by the fire.'

Wolfric smiled; then he seized William by the head and broke his neck. Wolfric's smile remained unchanged. Merlin and Timmin felt a flash of pain and terror and then nothing. Their attention snapped back into the room.

For a moment, they sat in utter silence. Merlin felt a warmth in his hands that became hot and then burning. He released Timmin and blew on his fingers.

Timmin slowly drifted forward through the air. The room became a sauna; her glow brightened into a white-hot ember. Her once soft features became more angular, her wings elongated and fluttered around like whirling daggers.

Merlin slid backward to the wall. He pulled Eric, still sleep-standing, to the floor for his own safety.

"Timmin!" Merlin called to her.

She twisted to the direction of his voice in a sharp pirouette; her dead eyes pointed at him but looked through him.

She screamed; the windows of the room splintered and rained glass down on Merlin and Eric. She shot through the open window and took to the sky.

Eric woke from the sound; he coughed from the dust and debris.

"What the hell just happened?", he asked.

Merlin stared grimly skyward. "Timmin's upset." he replied softly.

CHAPTER 24:

FAMILY FEUD...

The rest of the community awoke to the commotion. Jared had serious misgivings about what he had invited into his people's lives. Sure, they had been living under an overpass and were randomly abducted by werewolves but... well he lost his train of thought after that. On the other hand, his daughter was out there; he wouldn't lose her again. A meeting was called around the table.

"I was afraid of this." Eric said. "We played right into his hands,

"That's the least of our worries." Merlin said. "there's an angry fairy out there with incalculable destructive potential."

"She can't take them on all by herself." Red asked. "Can she?"

"Not as powerful as Wolfric is now. Moreover, she wouldn't go it alone."

"But there aren't any fairies here." Eric said. "Are there?"

Merlin's face turned grim. "As a matter of fact..."

△ △ △

Timmin dropped into the middle of her forest. The orange carpet of cedar leaves at her feet caught fire. The trees delight at her arrival soon turned into terror. She sped up her wings, their low hum loudened and echoed off the trees until everything resonated with the same tone.

Her children shyly emerged from the canopy above and out from under shrubs and burrows. They were at once fairylike and lupine, with a soft blue glow; and though they had never seen her before they knew her and rallied around their mother.

'Where is father?', they asked.

'Your father was taken from us. I need you all to be brave and trust me. We're doing this for papa.'

Her wings pulsed and hummed; the rhythm increased in tempo. The wolflings closest to her flapped their wings and joined in. They burned as brightly as their mother. The pattern spread out like a brush fire from Timmin to her surrounding offspring, a thousand strong.

The forest floor burned and spread to the trees. A regrettable sacrifice, but a message had to be sent.

'Remember,' she said. *'let nothing stand in your way.'*

△ △ △

"Why don't we just let them finish the job?" Eric proposed. "Problem solved."

"I'm not sure you fully understand our situation." Merlin replied.

"Well please explain, I'm all ears." Eric flopped down in a chair at the table, folded his hands together and gave Merlin, if a tad sarcastically, his full attention.

"Fairies are a proud and, at times, quite stubborn people; but they are extremely close-knit and loyal to one other as well. A slight to one of them is a slight to the whole group. They are in tune with one another on a level you can't even imagine. The term 'mob mentality' doesn't begin to do it justice."

"Okay, so, they're a tiny little mafia."

Merlin rolled his eyes. "Imagine a swarm of perfect and unrelenting hatred that can reorganize matter to their whim and curse or destroy anyone and anything that gets in their way. A swarm that absolutely will not stop until Wolfric is dead.

"Alright." Eric was less contemptuous. "But Wolfric is powered by fear. It doesn't sound like they are afraid of him."

"Anger is only a bi-product, fear is still the root cause.

"They could supercharge Wolfric." It felt as though the bottom had fallen out of the pit of Eric's stomach.

"Now you understand."

"Shit."

"To put it mildly."

John scrambled up to Jared's side. "I think you should see this.", he stuttered frantically.

The group followed John up to the roof; the warehouse was one of the taller structures in the abandoned district. From there they had an excellent view of that side of town.

To the east they saw a massive plume of smoke rising from the greenbelt, now up in flames. From there a beeline of destruction and chaos marred a path to the downtown core. Several high rises were a smoldering ruin; cars, rubble, and what appeared to be bodies, floated and drifted weightlessly in the aftermath.

"We can't fight that." Eric said. He was at loss to even comprehend what he was seeing. "Do fairies have a weakness?"

"They are powerless against iron." Merlin replied. "Notice a lot of the building frames are still standing."

"Steel." Eric said. "There's iron in it. How do we use that against them?"

"I suppose you could contain them if you had enough of it, but we're talking about an awful lot. The only other alternative is to wait."

"Wait for what?"

"A fairy's lifespan is tied to magic. The more they use, the older they get until they are spent. Timmin is still fairly young though, and her swarm is new born and at the height of their power, it could take months."

"We don't have months," Red said, "more people are going to get hurt. If their law enforcement or military try to intervene it will be a slaughter. We also can't let Timmin die, she's upset, she's not evil. Plus, and I can't believe I'm saying this, Rose is in there."

"Well by the looks of it, they are almost at the downtown." Jared said, "we need a plan now."

Everyone looked to Eric.

"Oh Right," he said. "My years of experience battling monsters."

"In your mind," Merlin said, "Yes. You're the story teller. Write us an ending. What would you do?"

Eric stared out at the devastation. It reminded him of Japanese kaiju films. A light went on in his head, albeit a flickering, insane one.

"I'd want another monster. An iron monster. Red, Jacob. Which one of you is the better fighter?

"Red." Jacob said

"Me." Red replied in unison.

Jacob beheld Red in wide eyed amazement.

"What?" She said, "It's true. You just agreed."

"I know," Jacob said, "just wow. Not even a curtesy nomination?"

"It's alright, Jacob," Eric said. "I need you too buddy. We don't have a lot of time. But we do have parallel dimension. Merlin, do you have a forge in the sanctuary.

"Let me think." The wizard searched his thoughts. "It's been some time. Yes! Past the library and the pool, you can't miss it."

"We need to borrow it."

Merlin made a repeated circular motion with his hand; a doorway opened in the space in front of them.

"Don't be too long." Merlin said. "Time doesn't stand still out here."

"We'll be right back." Eric said.

△ △ △

The only exception to the expenditure of a fairy's lifeforce is during a swarm. Their power is pooled and shared throughout the collective; as well as their sensory experiences. Timmin had in fact gained some years back while her children aged only incrementally to establish a balance. The situation was unique however, with Timmin having had the most life experience, she was the guiding voice of the swarm, she was the queen.

It was the first time she felt bigger than anyone or anything. She had eyes and ears in every direction and a complete picture of everything around her in three dimensions simultaneously.

People scattered out of her path. She appreciated that, it was for their own good. The noisy horseless carriages they drove were another matter, she swept them aside like leaves. Every so often humans fired noisy projectile weapons at them. It was almost quaint, but she just didn't have the patience for any of this, she simply vaporized them.

Their path brought them steadily closer to Wolfric's glass tower. After they had exterminated all life there, she thought it would be nice to bring her children back home to meet their clan; it's what William would have wanted.

△ △ △

Wolfric watched the approaching swarm. Just when he thought he had seen it all life continued to surprise him. He was in direct communication with the control room of the news studio downstairs via his tablet.

"Ok," he said. "have the chopper do a flyby but tell them to keep their distance. We'll cut back to that as a cover shot and reduce it to picture and picture when Bryce and Colleen are on camera at the anchor desk. Send the drone cameras in for closeups, they're expendable. Get a city map and superimpose a graphic charting the path of this thing. Thanks guys."

Up on the big screen, Wolfric had the news feeds from all his rival channels; but this thing wasn't heading to the other channels, and it was sweeps week. You couldn't buy this kind of publicity.

Gale and Shifter stood next to Wolfric and did not share his optimistic appraisal of the situation. Rose was bound to a chair; a tad cliché perhaps, but Rick also knew what she was capable of. She was under the careful watch of Sheila, in full view by her desk.

"Shouldn't we get out of here?" Gale suggested.

"Gale, do you honestly think I would build this place without anticipating threats from the home country? Sheila, initiate lockdown."

"You got it." She replied.

With the push of a button metal shutters closed over the windows. Security doors sealed off the entrances and underground parking.

"Solid steel boys," Wolfric exclaimed proudly. "With a highly refined iron content. The same steel was used in the girders during construction. This tower is now the safest place in the city."

"What about your adoring public outside?" Rose chided.

"Most of the viewers are well outside the immediate area. We will mourn those we lost publicly, when the time comes, but for the most part the people don't care so long as their soaps are on this afternoon. I swear, I love this world."

"That's appalling."

"Oh, come on now. Don't give me that. How much time did you take out of your daily life to help any of them? You read a story, you feel empathy, but it doesn't really affect you personally and you don't want it to, so you can sleep better at night. Worry about your first world problems. If you're so concerned, I can let you out to share in their fate."

Rose turned away.

"How many of you did I take off the street? Give purpose to? Care for when society rejected you?"

"You murdered my mother, kidnapped me from my home and lied to me since I was four."

"Oh that was you, you're right. I'm sorry, it's hard to keep all of you straight."

"Eric will come for me."

Wolfric leapt across the room and leaned in close to Rose's face. "I'm counting on it."

"Alpha." Shifter said. "You're not going to believe this."

"What is it now?"

Shifter pointed to the helicopter feed up on the big screen.

Wolfric stood corrected; now he had seen everything. His ego exploded with gratification.

△ △ △

The swarm had slowed down when they heard the slow thunderous pounding get closer. They silenced the irritating alarm noises the tremors set off in each of the carriages around them.

And then it came. As hell-bent as she was on Wolfric's destruction, even Timmin had to take a moment to process what she was seeing.

From around the other side of the tower and just over half its size, a red armored giant stomped into view brandishing a mace and shield. That wasn't the part that surprised Timmin; the giant had taken up a position between her and Wolfric, and that simply would not do.

Timmin assumed the entire suit was iron, unless her opposer was suicidal. Her magic wouldn't directly work on it, but that didn't mean she couldn't smash it open. Full marks for originality; no doubt this was Jacob's handywork. She took no pleasure in what was about to happen to Red.

△ △ △

A few moments after they had left, Jacob and Eric returned to the rooftop

"I'm not sure what this is going to accomplish." Merlin said, flatly, "It isn't as though Red can land any significant blows, they're a swarm."

"She's a distraction." Eric replied. "We need to find a way inside that tower and shut it down. Cut the source of Wolfric's power once and for all. We have to go in."

Merlin produced a telescope to get a closer look at Red.

"How did you make her so big?" Merlin asked.

"Eat me." Eric said.

"I beg your pardon?"

"Lewis Carroll. There was a whole cake dish of them in your library. Question, where do you keep the bottle of Drink Me?"

"It should have been right next to the cake."

"I didn't see it."

"Well, I suppose we'll have to address that problem later."

Down in the main hall Jared, Jacob, Braum and Eric prepared to head out. Jacob assembled his grappling gun and sharpened his axe. Braum checked his bow. Jared kept to what he knew; if you knew the right people you could get the right things on the street. He donned his Kevlar vest and loaded his twelve-gage shotgun.

Merlin presented Eric a bundle of old linen; there was some heft to it. He brought the strange gift to the table and unraveled it.

Inside was a glimmering shirt of chainmail, a shield with a royal crest emblazoned on it, and a sword. His eyes couldn't help but be drawn to the sword.

"Is that...?"

"Excalibur." Merlin said. "The real one, from this world."

Eric backed away from the table slightly.

"Go ahead. Pick it up."

Eric hesitantly reached for the hilt and picked up the sword. It was remarkably light, one would be tempted to think it was fragile. He perched the sword on his finger just above the hilt, it balanced perfectly.

"I can't take this." Eric said. "I didn't pull this from a stone or anything. I'm not...worthy."

"No one is my boy," Merlin said, "not perfectly. But it belonged to a good man. And it should belong to another good man."

Merlin reached out to shake Eric's hand, Eric put down the sword and embraced the old man instead.

An overwhelming majority of the community gathered around Jared and pleaded with him not to go.

"Don't worry," he announced, "I fully intend on coming back. This is something I have to do. We're all at risk if we don't do this."

The murmurs from the crowd reluctantly hushed.

"John is in charge while I'm gone." Jared continued.

The hall erupted with dubious murmurs and sideways glances.

"Ashley," Jared scanned the room until they locked eyes, "You assist John." He winked almost imperceptibly, at least to John, Ashley gave her thumbs up in agreement. An amused smile crossed her face.

"Okay guys," Eric said. "Let's do this."

The four of them assembled before Merlin.

"I guess it's customary," Eric said, "to say a few words on the eve of battle..." Before Eric could finish his motivational speech, they found themselves downtown.

"Sorry, my lad." Merlin said. "Time is a bit of a factor."

"Thanks," Eric said. "I really didn't have anything."

A few blocks away Giant Red Riding Hood faced off against the swarm.

△ △ △

Red advanced and swung her mace; it crackled and sparked as it passed through the swarm. The fairies scattered to the air but regrouped behind her. A futile gesture, Red was all too aware, but Eric said to keep them busy.

Timmin was almost amused but she didn't have time for this. The swarm spiraled into a whirlwind; the tail end sucked up a car and hurled it.

Red raised her shield; the impact knocked her off balance a few steps.

The swarm vacuumed up a whole row of parked cars and shot them, one after another at Red. Each successive impact knocked her back further until she fell against a high rise. Windows shattered as the wall caved in behind her. She could hear people inside, screaming and running frantically to escape.

$$\triangle \ \triangle \ \triangle$$

Eric, Jacob, Jared, Braum and Merlin ran up alongside Red as she regained her footing.

"You alright, hon?" Braum called out.

"No problem," She replied, "I could do this all day. Just the same you should probably hurry."

"On it." Eric shouted.

They scrambled over to the front of the building; the security shutters were firmly locked down.

"Wow," Eric said, "Rick comes prepared. Iron, I'm assuming."

Merlin shot a lightning bolt from his hands, it fizzled without consequence on the surface of the shutters.

"Yes." Merlin confirmed.

"Ok," Eric said, "lets split up and work our way around the perimeter of the building, meet around back."

Eric and Jared ran to the left. Just beside the front doors was the lower entrance to the underground parking. It too was sealed off.

Jacob and Braum went to the right, the loading docks and rear employee entrance were sealed tight.

Merlin greeted both parties at the rear.

"You know," he said, "I could have verified this in less time."

"Can we blast our way in?" Jacob said. "I have been experimenting with some black powder, a gentleman from far away taught me the recipe. There's a few pounds of it in my pack."

"I'm not sure anything short of an air strike would breach those shutters." Eric said. "He would want to be able to escape somehow. Right?"

"Sewers." Jacob said, "or aqueducts or something under the ground."

"It's worth a try. Merlin can you put us down in the sewers?"

Eric's voice echoed off the dingy walls of the sewer; the floor was submerged under a few inches of what he hoped was water. A raccoon scurried along a ledge, up away from the floor. He locked eyes on Eric who recognized his furry trash companion immediately. The raccoon growled, performed what distinctly appeared to be an eye roll and left.

The tunnel shook, and pieces of cement splashed down in the toxic stream. Eric hoped Red was holding her own, it was his idea after all.

They hadn't progressed far when they were stopped by yet another iron door. The tunnel and the earth around them shook violently.

"It's going to give way!" Jared shouted.

They ran back in the direction they came. The roof of the tunnel collapsed to rubble. Eric ventured a quick look over his shoulder as he ran, his lungs choked on the dust.

A wall of light slammed down behind them and proceeded to rip up the floor. Eric fought to see through the dust and debris.

"Guys." He shouted. "I have a feeling I know what they are up to. And it's not good."

Merlin returned them to street level.

Red was down on one knee; her shield and armor were heavily damaged, and the mace handle poked up from a massive sink hole in the street.

Timmin and the swarm had surrounded the Rick Wolfe Enterprises building and formed an energy barrier around it. They rotated around the tower in unison, drilling into the ground beneath it.

"If she can't get into the building, she's bringing the whole thing down." Merlin said. "I'm afraid only William could calm her down at this point."

"What's that?" Eric said.

"William. She would cease and desist for William."

"That's it!" Eric said. "Could electricity knock them out? Disrupt them?"

"Perhaps for a moment." Merlin said, "It's just as elemental as a fairy's magic. But it would just as likely only agitate them.

"I just need a little more time!" Eric said.

He ran up to Red. She was winded.

"Red, I want you to pick up that mace and hit them with everything you have!"

"Eric, I'm causing more damage around me than I am to them. Plus, it's not as easy to move around in a body this size."

"Trust me."

Red pulled herself to her feet; She wrapped both hands around the mace handle and pulled it from the street. Asphalt tore and fell from the teeth of the mace, a water main ruptured and sprayed into the air.

"HEY!" Red taunted. "We're not done yet."

Timmin halted the drilling; obviously Red couldn't take a subtle hint. The Swarm regrouped into a concentrated mass.

Red raised her mace and charged, the swarm closed the distance to meet her.

Eric signaled to Merlin, who knew what Eric wanted him to do.

Red leapt into the air and spun around, her eyes found their target.

Merlin raised his hands to the sky and focused all his will onto the head of the mace. A bolt of lightning struck the mace head with primal force; it crackled and glowed, charged with a fiery new purpose. Red connected with the swarm; they screamed as the impact scattered them to the streets and rooftops. Red fumbled forward and collapsed, a semi-truck broke her fall.

For Timmin and the wolflings, the world went black.

"Merlin." Eric said. "We got work to do. Take me to my apartment."

"It's still being monitored by the police." Merlin said.

"Ok... then take my apartment and me somewhere safe."

△ △ △

"Tell me you got that!" Rick shouted into his tablet.

"Every minute, sir." His news director confirmed on the screen. "We just got word the army is evacuating and sealing off the downtown core with troops and heavy artillery."

"Suck it, CNN." Rick laughed.

He felt jazzed; the fear and hatred he was absorbing from the swarm had given him a contact high unlike anything he had ever felt. If he had known it could feel like this, he'd have waged war on fairies ages ago. He opened the shutter to his penthouse window.

"Are you insane?" Rose shouted. She was still struggling against her ropes.

"Sheila, tend to your sister." Rick said dismissively. "I've been offered an opportunity for personal growth."

△ △ △

Eric walked into his apartment, which was now nestled in a corner of Merlin's sanctuary. There were no walls, but all his furniture was exactly how he left it. Dr. Stephen Anderson immediately entered and curled up in his favorite chair.

Eric's drawing table, art supplies and sketches all appeared to be accounted for. Eric flopped down on his stool.

"When you connect to someone's mind, you basically know everything that person knows. Right?"

"Yes." Merlin said.

"And we're all just sums of our memories and experiences, right?"

"For the most part, I believe so, yes." The wizard put up his hands "Wait, Eric... no."

"We need him. You said it yourself. More people are going to get hurt. Red can't hold out much longer."

"You're talking about a resurrection. There's no telling what damage has been done. It's too risky."

"You said I could bend reality, write my own story. Well this story is going to have a happy ending."

"You don't know where his body is."

"Exactly," Eric said. "It's like Schrodinger's Cat. If we don't know where, he could potentially be anywhere."

Merlin was more than a little impressed by Eric's reasoning; the boy had finally grasped a larger view of reality.

Eric picked up his favorite pencil and slid it into the sharpener. When he counted to nearly three-Mississippi, he pulled it out and blew the shavings from the tip. He began to sketch; a few lines at first. He closed his eyes, and without missing a stroke the image formed even faster. It was a picture of his kitchen

Behind them, a vortex opened over his kitchen table. A loud thud echoed through the sanctuary. Merlin turned around and saw William lying on the table.

"Not bad." The wizard said. "You know, you could probably rescue..."

Rose flopped down on the sofa next to Stephen. She was still bound but also gagged. Her muffled scream lasted only a moment as she scanned the room around her.

Stephen yawned and stretched; he looked up at her for a moment before his eyes became heavy and he drifted back to sleep.

"Whaa yust haffened?" Rose mumbled through the gag.

Eric ripped the page off his pad, cast it aside and continued to sketch.

He paused for a moment, blocked.

"What now?"

"William's neck is still broken." Merlin said.

Eric began a quick sketch of William's body; his head twisted forward with a crack that sent chills through everyone's spine. Rose let out another muffled scream.

"Erich." Rose said, she was having trouble pronouncing through the gag.

"Be with you in a moment hon. Working towards a deadline."

"Oh-hay." She replied. She leaned back on the sofa and waited patiently.

"There's nothing left but to wake him up. "Merlin said.

"Will he remember anything?" Eric asked. He was worried, and it was the key to the whole plan.

"I don't know. Maybe fragments, maybe nothing."

"You'll have to transfer what you know."

"It's not that simple. There's my perception of William and there's Timmin's perception. She would know something was wrong."

"I see."

"But there might be a way. Wake him up."

Eric focused all his memory and imagination on William; on his eyes opening, him sitting up and standing. His hand drew faster than it ever had before.

"Eric!" Merlin shouted.

"Holy hit..." Mumbled Rose, though everyone understood the sentiment.

$$\triangle \ \triangle \ \triangle$$

Red, Jacob and Braum had been backed against a wall by the military; they were covered by more guns than they had ever seen, and an impressive armored vehicle with a canon that Jacob marveled over. They kept their hands up and their mouths closed for the moment.

Timmin awoke in the street the next block over. Her ears were ringing, and for such a small head she had a killer headache. Red and Merlin's blow hurt, she was mad as hell yet more than a little impressed. She found it an effort to even move. Rick Wolf Enterprises subjugated her field of vision; high up on the top floor she saw a dark speck. She strained to focus her eyes; it was an open window. A surrender perhaps? She wasn't one to look a gift suicide in the mouth. She called to her children and the swarm coalesced once more.

They ascended the tower. Wolfric, himself, greeted them at the opening. His wide-eyed grin made her blood shoot past boiling and straight into steam. She imagined what his grin would look like with the flesh peeled from his face; she mused with how she would display his skull. There were a million uses for a skull.

"Hey Timmin." Wolfric said. "I took the liberty of removing the window, so you didn't keep bouncing against the glass. I know how hard it is for flies to get their head around the concept." He chuckled.

The swarm heated up; electricity surged between Timmin and her children. One incineration, coming right up.

Wolfric's fur stood on end over tingling gooseflesh. His welcomed them with arms wide open.

"Timmin!" A distant voice registered somewhere off in her periphery.

She could almost smell Wolfric's breath.

"Timmin!" The voice repeated.

She took a casual glance down and saw Eric and Merlin. A portal was opened behind them.

"Hey sparks," Wolfric taunted. "I'm right here. Take your shot."

"Timmin," Eric called out. "someone wants to talk to you."

Rose emerged from the portal first, she led a slow hooded figure by the hand.

Timmin drifted away from the window with the swarm in tow.

"NO!" Wolfric shouted. "I'm right here. Give it to me!"

Eric guided the figure to stand before them at the base of the tower. He removed the hood.

It had to be a trick, Timmin refused to believe it.

"Ok," Eric whispered to Merlin. "We have her attention. You know what to do."

Merlin cleared his mind and reached into William's. It was a dark place, lonely and cold. He tried to recall anything of William and bring light to the void.

Timmin descended for a closer look; the resemblance was uncanny, but it could easily be glamour magic.

She left her children and went nose to nose with the apparition; she reached out to its thoughts. It recognized her.

Merlin gently reached into Timmin's consciousness; as he had hoped, she was distracted enough not to notice. He found their shared experiences, every intimate detail of their relationship, it was all there. They had been connected the entire time. It was little wonder she was so disturbed when the connection was severed. He gently stirred both their minds together.

A spark glinted in William's eyes as he saw her face. He knew that face; though it carried more sadness than that last time he had seen it. The glint watered over with tears. He stroked the back of her head.

Timmins features softened, and her glow cooled. It was him. She embraced the bridge of his snout, wept and laughed.

Timmin called the wolflings. They were long overdue in meeting Papa. A warm glow surrounded William and Timmin.

"Drop your weapons and stand down." A voice intruded on the scene over a squelching megaphone.

"Oh yeah." Eric said. "Those guys. Almost forgot."

Eric put his hands up and walked out front and center.

"No." He replied. "Everyone just stop."

The streets fell silent, truck and tank engines died, and the soldiers and police were frozen stiff.

Eric was overcome with giddiness. "I am so digging being able to do that."

"Retreat." he commanded with a grand wave of his hand.

The tanks and troops turned tail and fell back from their positions. They retreated further down their respective streets and then further still. The wind blew through the city square; the buildings seemed to channel and direct it into dust-devils of trash and debris.

"What about me?" Red broke the silence, "Everything weighs a ton this size."

"Oh right." Eric said. "Sorry. Um... Red return to normal size?" He felt he had found his groove at last.

Red contracted to her former stature; the suit of armor did not. The helmet rolled off the shoulders of the breastplate and flattened the hood of a car. Red climbed out through the neck and slid down the front of the armor to the ground. She regrouped next to Jacob who handed her back her staff.

"So now what?" Jacob Asked.

The iron shutters that barred the front entrance retracted and the automatic sliding doors opened. The silence that followed punctuated the gesture and unnerved the group.

"Huh." Eric muttered. It was a bold and very disconcerting move; after all, why would someone open a door unless they were prepared to receive guests?

Red looked around at everyone. "Are we ready for this?"

"I imagine we're as ready as we'll ever be." Eric said.

"I can't come with you." Merlin said.

"What?"

"I've meddled enough. I'll only make him stronger."

"You're one of the most power weapons we have against him."

"No, boy... I'm not." Merlin stepped forward and widened his arms to once again present the entire group to Eric. "When you needed them most in your life they rallied around you with the best they had to offer. They were here to inspire you, but it's always been your story, your fight. Put your faith in them, and most importantly have faith in yourself."

Merlin put his arms around Red and Jacob.

"You brought these two into your life, whether you knew you needed it or not, they tried to save you because you are worth saving. Red gives you her fighting spirit and Jacob gives you his ingenuity. Braum is a direct reflection of your desire to be more..." Merlin smiled and Eric. "...and we'll leave it at that."

"Thank you." Eric said.

"William and Timmin are proof no one is beyond redemption and that even the most unlikely of us can come together to make something wonderful. They both give you the gift of empathy, and if you really listen to people you will hear them."

Merlin took up a position beside Jared.

"Jared gives you the gift of leadership. He doesn't command anything; the best leaders are really servants of a higher calling."

Merlin walked over to Rose.

"Rose gives you her love," He said.

She winked at Eric and blew him a tiny kiss.

"And that's the most important thing there is" Merlin continued, "unfailing, unfaltering, no strings. It overcomes all obstacles."

Merlin stood before the group.

"So, you see, you aren't walking in there alone."

"What about you?" Eric asked. "Any parting words of wisdom?"

"Don't fight Wolfric in anger, don't let him write your story for you. And one more thing, a little gift. I'm sure you would have figured some of this out eventually, but let's just call this a crash course."

Merlin placed his index finger on Eric's forehead.

"This is going to feel... odd." He said.

"What do you mea-?" Before Eric could finish a blinding white light exploded in his consciousness. Millions of experiences and memories washed through his brain.

"What the hell?!"

"Don't try to hold on to anything," Merlin said. "your brain will blow a hemisphere. It will all be there when the time is right."

Eric braced himself against the wizard; his mind returned to as normal as it ever would be again.

"Go get'em, son." Merlin said.

CHAPTER 25:

HOMECOMING...

The front lobby was deserted and dark; none of the lights were on and the only illumination came from the outside. As they passed by the security station Eric noticed the computer screens were unlocked; there was some questionable browser history on one screen and minesweeper on another. He was amazed someone was still rocking minesweeper on a desktop.

"How many times did they tell us Rose?" Eric said. "Lock your screen when you walk away from your work station." His voice sung with mock formality.

"More than I care to remember." Rose said.

It gave Eric an idea however; 'energy is energy' echoed through his thoughts.

"Timmin," he said.

Timmin left William's shoulder and presented herself, front and centre.

"Can you get into this computer and into the network, I mean literally."

She twinkled in response.

"I'm sorry," Eric said, "can anyone translate? I promise I'll take Fairese Immersion classes when this is all over."

"She said yes." The group replied in unison.

"Wow, everyone but me huh? Jared?"

"You pick it up eventually if you hear it enough." A slightly smug grin came over his face.

"Okay. Timmin," Eric continued. "I want you to enter here and disable as much of this network as you can get access to. No matter where it leads you. Destroy everything in your path. If his programming is brainwashing people into empowering him then we need to cut that off."

Timmin and her children all twinkled and glowed, a little on the red end of the spectrum.

"What does that mean?" Eric asked

"Loosely translated, "Rose said, "they said 'gladly'. Although it's probably closer to 'hell ya' in English."

"They're kind of a raunchy people, aren't they?" Eric smiled. "Fairies."

"Oh, you have no idea." Rose said. It was a tale for another time.

Timmin gathered the swarm; static shocks buzzed between them in anticipation. Eric pointed to a USB port on one computer.

"There," he said. "That's as good a spot as any to enter."

Their individuality seemed to dissolve into a ball of pure electricity. A bolt of energy struck the USB and in a few short moments they had syphoned themselves into the computer.

"Ok, I think they can handle that from there." Eric said. "Let's go."

Eric gripped Excalibur tighter and pulled the shield in close to his body. Their footsteps echoed on the marble floor as they ventured inward.

At the end of the hall a huge set of double doors marked 'STUDIO A' opened and the red 'ON AIR' light flickered to life. Beyond the door frame was complete darkness, a cool breeze wafted out to greet them.

An old music box melody, uneven and pitchy, played out from the dark. It took Eric a few seconds to 'name that tune', it was 'Who's Afraid of The Big Bad Wolf'. A rubber ball bounced out of the dark and rolled to Eric's feet. The temperature dropped sharply; Eric was sure he could see his breath. His name whispered from somewhere beyond the door.

"Eric....Eric...Come and play with us Eric." It hushed.

"Cute, Wolfric." Eric said.

"Honestly," Wolfric's voice filled the hallway, and came at them from all sides. "Your generation is completely desensitized. Back in the fifties kids would have needed therapy after something like that."

The music stopped; the hallway lights turned back on and beyond the door the black fog lifted.

It was a forest at night. The evening air was cool and breathable with a soothing breeze. There were pockets of mist on the forest floor and shafts of pale moonlight pierced through the canopy. The forest seemed to glisten as much with its own illumination as it did with help from above.

"*Aaa-wooooooo!*" the voice seemed to come from all directions. *"Who's that I see walking in these woods? Why it's Little Red Riding Hood"*

"Really?" Eric said. He knew the song almost instantly; Sam The Sham and the Pharaohs.

"Hey there, Little Red Riding Hood, you sure are lookin' good. You're everything a big bad wolf could want...."

"I see what you did there." Eric called out.

"listen to me! Little Red Riding Hood -"

Red had never heard this song before, but she couldn't have been more insulted. *"I don't think little big girls should, go walkin' in these spooky old woods alone..."*

"Cut the crap, Wolfric!" Eric shouted.

The song faded out.

"You are such a buzzkill." Wolfric, Gale and Sheila stepped out from behind a tree; the tree turned back into Shifter.

A makeshift party banner strung between two trees fluttered in the wind; it read 'WELCOM HOME ERIK'.

"Surprise!" Wolfric cheered. "Welcome home!" He had dropped the human façade and wore his favorite three-piece suit from a rather exclusive tailor in London, his hair was perfect.

"There's 'E's in welcome." Eric said, "And my name is spelled with a 'C'."

"Gale made the sign." Rick said. "Home schooled.", he added with an aside whisper.

"What's the occasion?" Eric asked.

"I should think it's abundantly clear, it's your welcome home party."

"You know, thanks but Rose and I quit. We're going to pursue other opportunities."

"No, you're not following. We're literally back home, back in the other world, where it all started. Well, I mean, technically it was conceived of on Earth, manifested over here, but you get the idea."

"How is that possible?"

"You mean without the Tornado to Oz shooting people willy-nilly, back and forth? There are tidier ways to do it. This whole building is a doorway. More precisely it's a door jam, perpetually holding both sides open."

"Your power flows unrestricted between both worlds." Eric said.

"Genius. You get it from me, you really do. Your mom was pretty sharp too. It's not too late you know. You could still work for me. You should be working for me. I'll even forgive Rose and leave the two of you alone to run your own division, complete autonomy. Just drop this pointless quest and come home. It's over. I win."

"You're capitalizing on the fear of others."

"I'm providing people with an escape. I'm the voice on the other end of the phone or computer or TV telling them it's all going to be ok."

Wolfric walked over to Sheila who was at a table busy cutting pieces of cake and placing them on little napkins. He grabbed one and ate it.

"Merlin doesn't respect you," he continued with his mouth full, "he doesn't care about you or your friends; he marched you in here to die like a thousand pawns before you."

"You distract people away from their own truth."

It was hard for Eric to get a bead on Wolfric; there was absolutely no accountability or reason to him. He was just one distraction to the next, pure ego and sensory overload.

"You want the truth? What's easier to believe? You're on this magical adventure or you created all of this as some pathetic fantasy. You're sleeping right now. When you wake up, you'll still be alone, you'll still be working a thankless dead-end job, still in the process of writing that novel you know you'll never finish and will never sell. Every day longing for something more, every day coming up with excuses not to walk in front of a mercifully swift, oncoming train. How's that for your truth?"

Rose clung to Eric's arm.

Eric gave a slight grin, unflinching. "You talk too much." He said.

"Wow, maybe you're not my son. You're certainly no wolf; you haven't even cut your fangs yet."

"Suits me fine."

"What exactly was your plan coming in here? Was it as well conceived as the rest of your life choices?"

Rick momentarily staggered off balance. His legs trembled with an aching weakness. Sheila rushed to his side. He steadied himself on her shoulder.

"What is this?" Wolfric said, a little rattled.

"My plan. As we speak," Eric said, "Timmin is taking you off the air. You're weakened and outnumbered. I like our odds."

"Clever boy, but not all the guests have assembled yet."

A howl broke the silence, followed by another and then another. Out of the misty woods Wolfric's army emerged from every direction and held a tightly defended circle around them.

The group tightened together and prepared.

Wolfric turned to Red, "How's your grandmother? Still dead. Huh?"

Red clenched her staff tighter.

Wolfric's features dissolved away and reformed into the likenesses of both Eli and Isaac with their arms around one another.

"Hey Jacob." He said from both their mouths, "When this is all over, can we crash at your place? We're kind of between houses." They laughed through their jagged yellow teeth.

Jacob snorted and dug his hoofs in deeper.

Wolfric returned to normal and locked eyes on Jared.

"You again. I get to kill you twice, this time in front of your little girl."

Jared cocked his shotgun.

Rose turned to Jared, puzzled at first but everything soon became abundantly clear.

Jared's eyes welled.

Eric observed his friends.

"He's feeding off you!" he shouted. "Clear your minds."

"William." Wolfric said. "My sweet William. Despite all that has happened do you think you could ever do enough to wipe the slate clean?"

"Billy, ignore him," Rose said.

"I'm not judging." Wolfric continued, "far from it. But the rest of the world isn't so charitable. And this team of yours, sure you're united now, but say you defeat me. Your common enemy no longer binds you. How long until they turn on you."

"Billy, just look at me."

"And this... what is this... this fairy family of half breeds, do you think anyone is going to accept you? I'd accept you. In spite of all that's happened. I'm willing to forgive you. Your family is totally welcome here. We could start fresh."

"He's just trying to get in your head, William." Eric said. "You are the master of getting in people's heads. He's nothing, you got this."

"Your brothers miss you." Wolfric said.

Gale and Shifter looked at each other, smiled and laughed.

William locked his focus on all of them. The winds changed.

"There it is." Wolfric said. He stood tall on his own two feet. "Boys, tear these heroes apart."

William charged. "Come on Billy Boy!" Wolfric goaded.

William pounced.

"Shifter." Wolfric said.

William was inches away from Wolfric's throat when he came to an abrupt stop in mid-air. Shifter's extended arms coiled around and restrained him.

Wolfric's soldiers closed in slowly from all directions. There was really no rush, there was nowhere Eric's group could go.

"Here piggy, piggy." Gale approached Jacob with malicious glee and hunger.

The group went back to back in the center of the advancing pack.

"Stop!" Eric commanded.

The entire pack stopped. They Looked at one another then laughed and continued their approach.

"That didn't work." Rose said. Her claws unconsciously extended.

"None of you have to do this." Eric said. "Wolfric has lied to you from day one. You are all free to follow your own paths."

"I'm the hand that feeds them." Wolfric said, "you think you can make them turn on me? I'm the only one that ever cared for them."

"Maybe I can't. But you're not the only one that ever cared for them."

Eric placed a hand on Jared's shoulder.

Jared shot his gun in the air. A number of the other-worlders, unfamiliar with the technology, ran away. The rest adopted a more cautious attitude.

"I know some of you and you know me." Jared said. "I think I even recognize a glint of who you are in some of your eyes. I know what it's like to lose hope. I know what it's like to turn to anything that has the promise to make the pain go away. Life, well, life can take and take. But I promise you hope is never gone. And the things you lost can come back to you ... in surprising ways."

He looked to Rose. She smiled shyly back, her eyes watered over a little, his did too.

"Come home." He continued. "It's a lot better now, we've made some extraordinary friends. We're not alone anymore. We're not on the streets anymore. Just come home. It's not too late, there's a place for you with us, there are people who miss you. Come home."

Nearly half the pack relaxed their posture, they looked at one another. One by one they left the pack to stand by Jared.

"You've got to be joking." Wolfric hissed. "You miserable ingrates. Fine, double time and a half for every head turned in me by close of business today."

Shifter tightened his grip around William's neck.

"I'll start with this head." Shifter smirked.

"William," Eric called out. "NOW!"

William pushed his way effortlessly into Shifter's mind; the guy had no filter, no defenses. He was completely unconflicted and rather dumb. If anything, Shifter kept trying to show off his highlight reel. It was too much information, but William pushed through and then pushed it down. He suppressed it all. Shifter's grip loosened, and his eyes glassed over. He didn't fight, couldn't fight, the last twisted remnants of him even enjoyed the reversal.

William planted one last suggestion in Shifter's mind; it was the image of a tree. His body complied and transformed into a young willow. He released William and rooted himself firmly in place; his branches swayed tranquilly in the wind.

"Shifter?" Wolfric called.

The pack halted its advance, they were no longer as certain of their odds considering the loss of half their number. Double time and a half was tempting, but they couldn't spend it if they were dead.

Gale dug his feet in. He prepared to blast them all over the trees.

William leapt and landed directly in his path.

Gale smiled and growled; so much the better. He had been dying to beat that smug silence out of Bill since the day they met. Shifter was an idiot, he always needed to get up close and personal; but Gale liked to remove problems before they became problems.

"You think I'm going to even let you get close to me?" Gale said.

Gale felt a tap on his shoulder. He turned around. A furry tail had sprouted from the ground behind him. It wrapped around his chest and constricted his airways. He felt himself lift in the air. The tail tore up a path through the ground that lead back to William.

"How?" Gale strained to asked.

"Oh, that's right." Eric said. "When I regenerated William, I might have given him your powers in light of how much he hated both of you."

Gale struggled against William's grip.

"Hey man." Gale smiled. "we were just playing. It was mostly Shifter anyway. No hard feelings, huh?"

William shook his head and flashed a reassuring smile of perfect white teeth. He dug his feet into ground.

Gale became concerned.

William held Gale up front and angled slightly toward the sky. He huffed, and he puffed, and he blew Gale over the trees to who-cared-where. It felt amazing.

William enlarged himself, crouched and prepared to charge the remaining pack.

Wolfric's leftovers looked at one another, turned tail and fled through the woods.

"Well, that's disconcerting." Wolfric said. "Sheila."

But Sheila had gone. He suddenly had the full attention of Eric and his band.

"And then there was one. Right guys?" Wolfric smiled. "The power of teamwork and friendship prevails. And William, when you come back you come right the hell back. I am impressed!"

Wolfric still felt more than enough fear from the turncoats in the group. Half of them had never even been in a fight before. But the expendable front lines never had to be that skilled, just plentiful.

"Come on Eric. Believe it or not I really don't want to do this. Family shouldn't fight. You attack me, I'll get stronger and destroy you. Can't we just live in harmony?"

'Harmony' Eric thought; that was it, that was the answer. He lowered his shield and sword to his sides and listened to Wolfric. Really listened.

"He's right." Eric said, "Everyone stand down."

"There, you see?" Wolfric said. "Glad you finally see reason."

"Glad you finally see reason." Eric said, stepping on Wolfric's words.

"Now let's just put this all..." Wolfric's voice trailed off

"...put this all behind us." Eric said, right on the tail end, almost perfectly in sync.

"Cute" they said together.

"Ok that's enough."

"Is this the best you've got?"

Wolfric smiled.

"Rubber baby buggy bumpers" They said in unison.

"He thrusts his fists against the post but still insists he sees the ghost."

"I'm a scared little sissy boy." Eric let Wolfric have that one all on his own.

Eric smiled, Wolfric did not.

Wolfric approached, Eric mirrored his every move, When Wolfric circled, Eric walked in the same direction. Wolfric faked a rush for a few steps and Eric copied his gait and mannerisms.

"Well?" They both exclaimed.

"Attack me!" They shouted.

Wolfric snarled at Eric; he charged, his teeth and claws bared.

Eric charged at the same time but at the last moment slipped out of the way, grabbed Wolfric's arm and sent him into a tree.

Wolfric felt his spine crack as he collided with the trunk.

He staggered to his feet; he saw nothing but red. He huffed, and he puffed, and he'd blow Eric's head in.

A cloud of dust and stone billowed toward Eric. Eric focused his will and opened a portal in front of himself and behind Wolfric. The tempest slammed into his back but was countered by the opposing force of his breath, resulting in equilibrium. What wasn't countered was the very large tree branch that struck him in the back of the head. He dropped to his knees.

He struggled against the pain to refocus his mind and clear the stars from his field of view.

He leapt and seized Eric by the head. He attacked his mind with every ounce of will;   Eric accepted the intrusion and pulled Wolfric's consciousness inside. He travelled down Wolfric's mind, deeper and deeper, suppressing memories as he went. Wolfric fought back but it only entangled him more. He couldn't think clearly, he couldn't remember anything, there was nothing. The outside world fell away followed by any sense of self. He was scared, but only for a moment.

Eric disengaged from Wolfric who was on his knees, completely catatonic.

The studio door dissolve from view. Eric supposed it was Wolfric's influence that kept it open.

He examined his surroundings. So, this was his home; it was pretty. Come to think of it, it was Rose's home too.

"Is he dead?" Asked Rose.

"He's been put to sleep." Eric replied.

Rose stared blankly at him. "Did you just try to 'catch phrase'?"

"You know," he said, "cause he's a wolf, you know, dogs... put to sleep."

She didn't blink; literal crickets chirped off in the distance.

"It's over." Red said in a sigh of relief. "I can't believe it. It's finally over. We won."

She threw her arms around Braum and Jacob. She turned to Rose, her arms extended.

"Hard pass." Rose put up her hands. "but thanks for thinking of me."

CHAPTER 26:

HAPPILY, EVER AFTER...

Merlin, Eric and the band emerged from the portal, they were in the main hall of the community.

The people ran to greet them. The lost members reunited with friends and loved ones. Some new faces had joined their ranks as well. Much to Eric's joy, Terry was among the wolves who defected. Eric put on his best fake smile for Rose's sake.

It was unanimously agreed there was cause for celebration that night.

Jacob offered to oversee the meal for the event, but everyone insisted that, seeing as how he was one of the guests of honor, he should just enjoy himself and not lift a finger.

Rose sat between Eric and William. She sat Terry a good distance around the table for Eric's sake; Eric pretended he didn't hear him when he tried to intercede into the conversation.

'Pompous windbag. Blah, blah blah.'

After dinner the band played; Timmin choreographed the wolflings in a dazzling ballet of light and colour overhead. Rose and the proud father, William, sat back and enjoyed the show from the wall flower section. However, when Timmin spotted him she decided that just would not do. She dragged him to the dance floor, he came along more willingly this time.

Rose chuckled and helped shove him to his feet.

Jared handed her a drink.

"Is this seat taken?" He asked.

"No, go ahead." She replied.

She spied Eric across the hall talking to Merlin. It had been a hell of a week. After an interminably long pause Rose managed to speak.

"You're him, aren't you? Somehow... you're my father."

There was a hitch in Jared's breath as he tried to reclaim it.

"I'm not sure." He said. "When I lost you...her, it never felt real, I couldn't accept a universe that didn't have her in it. Every night I'd make up a story about her like I always did and tell it to myself. She wasn't gone, she was taken by a monster and someday I'd find her again. Some nights, in the trenches of some God forsaken battlefield, it was the only thing that kept me going, kept me breathing. That you would come back to me some day."

The tears streamed unabashedly down his cheeks.

Rose reached out with trembling arms; Jared eagerly accepted the offer. She fit perfectly in his arms and his chest felt whole again.

"So, tell me about this boy you're seeing." He managed.

Rose laughed until her own tears came.

"Everything ok?" Eric was suddenly there. He crouched down and placed his hand on her cheek.

Rose smiled and wiped her eyes. She took Eric by the hand.

"Eric," she said. "I'd like to introduce my father."

For a moment Eric had forgotten why he had come over. But against the past week of synchronicities the news was both a pleasant surprise and at the same time made perfect sense.

"In that case. I would like permission to dance with your daughter."

Jared fixed Eric with a dubious, but playful gaze.

"It's up to the lady." He replied.

"I think I can handle him." Rose said.

Eric prostrated himself in a formal bow. Rose grabbed his hand and towed him onto the dance floor.

They grabbed a hold of each other and found their groove; they swayed back and forth to the music. Rose rested her head on his chest.

"So," Eric said, "your dad, huh?"

Rose looked him in the eyes.

"Yeah. Is it obvious that I just ugly-cried?"

"Little bit. But under the circumstances I don't think anyone is judging."

She returned her head to his chest and move his hands down lower on her waist.

"We would have had work tomorrow. Think we're fired?" She asked.

They both laughed.

"Yeah," Eric said. "I wonder if we can draw unemployment in the other world."

Her rhythm slowed; she glanced up and studied his face.

"So, you're thinking of going back with them." She said.

"Well, apparently I have a job lined up if I want it."

"Oh."

They continued swaying, but out of step with the music.

"I mean, I didn't want to speak for you or anything." He said. "But they kind of need me over there."

"I get it." she replied softly, "A kingdom needs a king."

She dropped her gaze.

"Well," Eric said. "While we're on the subject."

The music changed. Rose couldn't place it at first, the acoustic guitar opened with a fairly uniform chord progression, but when the strings joined in the tune was unmistakable; it was 'Collide' by Howie Day.

"Oh, I love this song." She said casually.

Eric knew that.

Out of the corner of her excellent peripheral vision she detected swirling lights. She pulled away from Eric.

Timmin and the wolflings had surrounded them; they were alternating glows in time with the music.

She looked back at Eric, he was lower than he was before by a distance of one knee.

Through the lights she could see the entire hall had stopped to bear witness.

Rose couldn't breathe. The butterflies in her stomach had fluttered the air from her lungs.

Eric held up his open palm. As if on cue - because she was - Timmin landed in his hand and laid down a small, pink, ornate box. She bowed to both of them and rejoined her children.

He opened the box towards her; inside was a substantial diamond ring with a braided gold band.

"About that job," Eric continued. "I could use your help."

Rose cupped her hands over her mouth.

"Rose. Will you marry me?"

She nodded vigorously; on the verge of another ugly cry.

Eric stood up, placed the ring on her finger, choking back tears of his own.

They kissed, laughed and wept in each other's arms.

Timmin and the wolflings took to the air with bursts of fireworks. The entire hall cheered, and the celebration found renewed vigor. The band played on and they reveled into the wee hours of the morning.

Eric and Rose spent their last week in this world (at least for a little while), under Merlin's tutelage, learning the day to day realities of ruling a kingdom. Future Queen Rose got bored after the first session, and insisted Eric fill her in on the highlights later. She was much more interested in planning the wedding.

In a case of mutually defeated expectations, Red became Rose's maid of honor.

Rose asked Red out of curtesy, not expecting her to accept, and Red accepted out of curtesy, not expecting to be asked. Red was put in charge of the bachelorette; Timmin agreed to act as a sort of intermediary. As it happened two of her aunts were fairy godmothers that had some experience with royal weddings.

With Eric's help, Jacob spent his last week researching and downloading enough technical information from the internet to inspire him for the rest of his life. The concept of steam power held tremendous potential. When they got back, he planned on starting an industrial revolution.

Per Rose's suggestion and Eric's agreement, Jared and the rest of the community would come back with them to the kingdom. Eric would need a captain of the guard, the community could start a prosperous new life, and it would simply be wonderful for Rose to have her father around. Jared wasn't averse to the suggestion but thought it best to let the people decide. It might be a shock for them.

They came up with a compromise that would work for everyone; one that could also have its benefits. Inspired by Wolfric, Eric and Merlin opened a stable gateway between the two realities. One inside the warehouse and one in the courtyard of the castle. People could come and go as they pleased. Resources could be shared between both places. While the door stayed open there would be no time differential.

Feeling a little technologically deprived in their new home, Eric ran cable from the warehouse into the castle for some power. With a little spacetime manipulation and a router, he even managed to get an astonishingly good wi-fi signal; five bars a whole dimension away. He was iffy on the legalities of such a connection, but he and Rose thought it was a good way to keep tabs on things in the other world. Plus, they were both in the middle of shows they hadn't finished binge watching.

$$\triangle \ \triangle \ \triangle$$

With everyone settled and life returning to the new normal it came time for Eric's official coronation; which was to be immediately followed by the royal wedding.

The next few weeks were spent preparing the castle and main hall to receive the guests. Messengers were sent out on the fastest horses with invitations to the neighboring kingdoms.

Rose said yes to the twenty first dress, testing the patience of even Timmin's aunts; which is saying a lot considering they were part brownie. Rose picked out a lovely seafoam green off-the-shoulder gown for Red. Timmin, on the other hand, would observe the timeless fairy custom of complete nudity at a wedding. They were lovely dresses, but humans had way too many hang-ups as far as she was concerned.

For his bachelor party, Eric, along with Jacob, Braum, and William were whisked away by Merlin to a dimension where it was still Ancient Rome to watch gladiator matches; this was technically not interfering with time as it was a whole other reality.

For her bachelorette Rose, along with Red, Timmin and some of her cousins, laid siege to a nearby bandit encampment that had established itself in the absence of the king. The merciless onslaught that followed went down in legend for ages to come. However, they all agreed that what happened at the bachelorette stayed at the bachelorette.

At long last the big day had finally arrived.

In the morning, with all the guests assembled and Rose looking on with pride, Eric knelt before Merlin.

"Is your majesty willing to take the oath." Merlin asked.

"I am willing." Eric replied.

Merlin placed Excalibur's blade on Eric's shoulder.

"Will you solemnly promise and swear to govern the peoples of your kingdom, its lands and territories according to their respective laws and customs?"

Eric wished he had paid more attention during the rehearsal, that was a mouthful.

"I solemnly promise to do so." He replied.

"Will you, to the utmost of your power, cause law and justice, in mercy, to be executed in all your judgements?"

"I will."

"Will you, to the utmost of your power, uphold the code of chivalry and embody the qualities of faith, charity, justice, sagacity, prudence, temperance, resolution, truth, liberality, diligence, hope, and valor."

"All this I promise to do."

Merlin tapped the blade on both Eric shoulders.

"Then, on this day, and before all who have assembled here, I hereby knight thee, and king thee," Merlin chuckled, "rise, your majesty, King Eric The First."

Merlin placed the crown on Eric's head and, officially, presented him with Excalibur.

The audience cheered, Rose fist pumped and hollered. Eric humbly bowed to everyone, his face, slightly, beet red.

Lunch was provided at a reception immediately after the coronation. Eric spent a majority of his time welcoming dignitaries, heads of state and even other royals from neighboring kingdoms. His stomach growled as he watched the buffet grow ever smaller, unable to reach it. But it was only for one day.

Rose had been ushered away to the royal chambers for sparkling wine, hors d'oeuvres and girl talk with Red and Timmin, while hand maidens prepped her for the wedding. Rose felt she could definitely get used to this. Red invited her friends Cindy and Snowy to join them, meet Rose and fill her in on all the salacious gossip in her new social circle. Rose invited them to stand up with her to fill out the bridesmaid side, totally geeking that it would be a literal fairytale wedding.

Merlin also presided over the wedding service, there were absolutely no objections.

Eric lined up with his groomsmen, Jacob, William and Braum. He tapped his feet and fidgeted nervously.

"Stop it." Merlin said casually. Eric froze in place with a regal posture and amiable grin. "Relax, breathe."

Eric blinked once for yes; Merlin released him.

"Will everyone please stand." Merlin said.

He nodded to the organist, the triumphant notes that marked the introduction to the wedding march echoed throughout the hall.

The doors opened, and the wedding procession entered the room.

Timmin lit the way down the aisle and was also the ring bearer; she winked at William as she took up her position on the bridesmaid's side. Under his fur William blushed, he was aware of fairy wedding customs even though her glow obscured her physique. Red was next, followed by Cindy and Snowy, both in beautiful crimson gowns. The incongruity tickled Rose to no end. Red and Braum smiled at one another as she took her position next to Timmin.

Jacob was the only one in the service, as yet, unaffiliated. However, his 'plus-one' was seated down front.

As it happened an old family friend had gotten a job at a nearby pub and her parents felt more comfortable if she lived near somebody they could trust to look out for her.

He offered Porcia a spare room at his house until he could build her a place of her own; the lots next door had remained vacant for long enough. Though, as time passed neither of them felt urgently pressed to break ground. Jacob smiled and waved at her down in the audience. She blew him a kiss.

All eyes turned to the back of the hall and wave of awe washed over the guests.

Rose began her slow march down the aisle, arm in arm with Jared. Her train was freakishly long, heavy and impractical but she relished every moment of attention.

Eric's jitters were immediately replaced with calm and certainty as she arrived next to him.

"You clean up good.", he said.

"Not so bad yourself.", she replied.

The music stopped, and the audience settled down.

"Please be seated." Merlin said.

Eric and Rose each mocked a silent scream to one another.

"Who gives this bride away?" Asked Merlin.

"I do." Jared said.

Jared placed Rose's hand in Eric's and pointed at him in warning before his face relaxed into a smile. Eric smiled and nodded, the message was completely understood. Jared sat down in front next to Ashley and John.

"It is with no overt sentimentality," Merlin began, "when I say that love truly is the governing principal of the universe. As someone once wrote 'Love is patient, love is kind. It does not envy, it does not boast, it is not proud. It does not dishonor others, it is not self-seeking, it is not easily angered, it keeps no record of wrongs. Love does not delight in evil but rejoices with the truth. It always protects, always trusts, always hopes, always perseveres'. It can take faith and courage to love, certainly it can be easier to despair. But if you trust it and are open to it, love is right there, forever whispering in your ear that it sees you and hears you.

I haven't always trusted that love would find a way without my interference. My attempts to influence have resulted in some good but perhaps just as much bad. Certainly, I wasn't able to tip the scales significantly in any one way. I realize now how misguided I was. And it was without my meddling that this happy union first came together. It has been my privilege to get to know Rose and Eric, I can think of few couples so beautifully matched."

Rose squeezed Eric's hand twice and he matched the rhythm in response.

"They have both prepared their own vows, which they will now recite. First, His Majesty, the Groom."

Eric reached into the breast pocket ok his coat, rummaged around and froze. He locked eyes with Rose who responded with a head tilt and widened gaze.

He took a deep breath and held her hands.

"Rose, from the first day I saw you in training, I fell hard. You made the drudgery of a daily grind bearable and I just loved how you made me feel. I always thought I had to impress you in some way. If I talked a certain way, walked a certain way, remade myself into something I thought you wanted me to be, that you would love me. But how can you love someone for them when they aren't being themselves? When you literally took a leap of faith after me, I still couldn't believe I had anything to offer. But you helped me find the things you saw in me that I didn't see in myself. In spite of all that you are still the reason I do anything and, if you'll let me, I'd like to spend the rest of my life showing you how much I love you."

Rose squeezed his hands and her eyes welled up. Her speech was tucked into the left breast of her gown, but she too decided to wing it.

"Eric," she said. "When I first saw you, I was an unwitting pawn in an elaborate scheme to recruit you and enslave two whole realities."

Some of the werewolf guests laughed, others, who didn't understand the reference, looked at one another in confusion.

"I was afraid if you knew the truth about me I'd scare you off. But it didn't. You know the worst thing about me, and you don't even bat an eye. Even though I could easily kick your ass in a fight, I feel safe and protected around you, safe to be myself without judgement. And I'd like to let you spend the rest of your life showing me how much you love me."

The whole audience laughed.

"I love you so much", she said, "and I promise to stand by you forever."

An awe cascaded through the crowd.

"Without further ado," Merlin said, "the rings."

Timmin approached and handed the rings to Merlin; he passed one to Eric and one to Rose.

They slid the rings on each other's fingers and clasped their hands together.

"If anyone has any reason why these two should not be wed." Merlin proclaimed. "Let them speak now or forever hold their peace."

Eric swore if Terry so much as twitched he'd have him beheaded, but their union went without objection.

"Then" Merlin said. "It gives me great pleasure to present. King Eric and Queen Rose. You may kiss the bride."

Never before had they embraced and kissed quite so passionately. The audience erupted in applause. The wedding party clapped and cheered.

The royal couple lead the procession into the main hall where a lavish reception had been prepared.

Eric finally got to eat, as the head table was served first. Rose had an entire blood rare leg of lamb but observed proper table manners and used a fork and knife. She had consumed the leg with alarming efficiency and was already eyeing Eric's plate.

With the meal finished and the tables cleared it was time for the evening's festivities.

It was an open bar for everyone, however donations were graciously accepted to assist those still rebuilding after Wolfric's defeat.

The band played on and Eric and Rose had their first official dance followed by the father of the bride. A kissing game had started out all in good fun but after an hour the royal couple felt like it had run its course.

At Rose's request some bar room games had been set up in a corner. Dart boards lined one wall, which most people were familiar with; the new Queen also introduced people to billiards. Red, very comfortable with a staff in her hand took to the game quite naturally. This infuriated Rose and a good majority of the evening was spent in rematches and upped wagers.

It all came to a head near the end of the evening, after several drinks, when Rose ordered the dance floor cleared, 'by the divine power vested in her',

"What are you doing?" Red asked.

"If I'm not too much mistaken," Rose replied, "we have a dance."

Red smiled and twirled her pool cue. Rose extended her claws and transformed. She growled with ferocious glee.

Red and Rose both proved to be quite nimble in full wedding attire. After a few good hits from each of them, they had forgotten what started it all. Rose cried, hugged Red, and expressed her undying admiration and friendship for her. She bought the next round.

Eric smiled to find his bride passed out at a table with her arm around an equally unconscious Red. Braum raised his mug to Eric, they clinked glasses and laughed.

Merlin looked out over the gala and gave a satisfied nod. He turned and went outside into the night air.

Eric saw the wizard leave and followed him. He found Merlin up on the battlements gazing at the stars.

"Beautiful service," Eric said. "I never got to thank you."

"None necessary, It was my pleasure. You two will be very happy together. Don't worry, I checked."

"You're leaving, aren't you?"

"It's time. I've put it off too long. The movement of the universe is to return, the way of the universe is to yield."

"Where will you go?"

"I'm not really going anywhere, but I think I'll try to find the others I started out with. I'll check in on you from time to time. I'm leaving you the sanctuary, if you have a question the answer is probably in there somewhere. Who knows, we might run into each other in there from time to time."

Eric was certain, despite being tipsy, that it was a hug moment. He squeezed the wizard, afraid to let go.

"Take care my boy". Merlin patted Eric's back and squeezed as well.

"Take care, old man."

Merlin vanished in Eric's arms and he was left holding himself. He spent a few more timeless moments star gazing before he returned to the party. He promised Rose the last dance and then several karaoke duets. Assuming she woke up.

The next day the castle was cleaned up. Everyone was finally, officially moved in. Eric retrieved his belongings from the sanctuary; Red and Braum helped them box up Rose's apartment and bring it back to the castle. Moving day was easier with a portal.

Red and Braum moved into her cottage together, though they continually dodged the question of marriage.

Jacob and Porcia returned home, and though the house was big enough for the two of them, they thought it might not be a terrible idea build an addition, just in case.

Timmin and William decided to take the family on a vacation back on Earth but promised they would be back in a couple weeks.

'Auntie' Rose offered them a place at the castle when they returned and to take the kids off their hands whenever Timmin and William wanted some alone time. 'Uncle' Eric was not around for that discussion.

Wolfric had thinned considerably, and a layer of dust had settled on him. He had remained unmoved and unaware for weeks. The waters of his mind were a cold, dark, glassy lake; he slept dreamlessly beneath its depths.

A single drop of water rippled the surface, the sound reverberated down below; and then another drop, and then another.

Wolfric stirred, He was aware of only the sound until a light became visible somewhere from above. He looked up and followed the light to the surface.

His ears opened to the sounds around him and he felt the cool breeze rustle his fur. He opened his eyes and saw a face smiling at him.

"Alpha? Can you hear me?"

Wolfric had no frame of reference for anything she said; he just stared.

"Wolfric? It's me, Sheila. Do you remember me?"

He was frightened but couldn't look away from the other that stood before him. She cupped her hands on his cheeks and looked deep into his eyes.

"Hello?"

Wolfric efforted to copy the words he heard but only mumbled in gibberish.

"Perhaps it's a good opportunity to start over then." She said. "My real name is Morgan. Morgan Le Fay."

She was so beautiful.

"Or, if you prefer, mom."

38161197R00111

Made in the USA
Middletown, DE
11 March 2019